Revelry in the Dark

MG Ellison

SOMBERHONEY BOOKS

Copyright © 2023 by MG Ellison

All rights reserved.

No part of this book may be used or reproduced in any manner by any electronic or mechanical means without written permission from the author, except for the use of quotations in a critical article or book review.

This book is a work of fiction. Names of characters, businesses, organizations, locations, events, and incidents are either the product of the author's imagination or are used fictitiously. Any resemblance to actual events, places, or people, living or dead, is purely coincidental.

All works of literature quoted in this novel are from the public domain.

I'll have plenty of books in the future to dedicate to other people. This one right here? This one's for me.

Part One

September

By all these lovely tokens
September days are here,
With summer's best of weather,
And autumn's best of cheer.
But none of all this beauty
Which floods the earth and air
Is unto me the secret
Which makes September fair.

—— Helen Hunt Jackson, "September"

Chapter One

EVERYTHING WAS GREY - my too tight dress, the clouds heavy with rain, the long pathway ahead of me, and the stone walls of Castle Blackscar that loomed at the end of it. Even the trees and grass seemed dull, not at all the vibrant greens of late summer that they should have been. The only variation was the western tower that gave the castle its name; my brother Eli had explained that the tower had been blackened by repeated lightning strikes while the castle was still under construction. I was sure that was something they could have fixed if they had wanted to, but I had to admit it cut an imposing first impression. I wondered if my time at Westwood Conservatory would cause me to grow used to the remarkable sight.

The entrance doors were much lighter than expected despite being easily three times my height. They let me slip into the castle's grand entry hall with barely a sound except for the light creak of the hinges and a slight thunk as they slid back into their resting place. Half a dozen suits of armor stood ahead of me, lining either side of the room leading up to a central staircase covered by a wine red carpet. There were doors between each of the suits of armor, all shut tight against prying eyes.

My watch read 8:36am and I was not meant to meet with Ahra, the girl who was to be my campus tour guide and housemate, until 9:00, so I stood off to the side of the room in an attempt to be out of the way for anyone else who might be entering or exiting campus. I fidgeted with the zipper on my jacket, something I wore only because it wouldn't fit in my lone small suitcase but was glad for after discovering the unexpected chill. The small sound echoed across the vast, empty hall. Then my fingernail caught on the edge of one of the zipper's teeth and I let out a surprised curse louder than I had meant to. My head immediately shot up in fear that I would be yelled at for disturbing someone, but it was still only me and the suits of armor in the room.

The longer I stood there the more it felt like they were not empty and were, in fact, watching me from the darkness in the helmets' metal eye slots and my skin began to crawl. My watch now read 8:44, a quarter of an hour left to wait. With one last glance at the nearest suit of armor I decided that a little bit of exploring the castle might not be the worst idea.

The closed doors on the first floor were probably better left that way, so with my suitcase clunking along behind me I ascended the wide staircase that led to the second floor. The wooden handrail was smooth, but most of the polish had been worn off by people who wanted something firm to hold onto as they climbed the steps. Eli's words echoed in my head, a story he had told me when he had come home for Thanksgiving during his first semester at Westwood.

The story was about a little girl who had died here. She had been friends with the master of the castle's daughter, and one day when the two young girls were playing a game of tag they ventured too close to the stairs. The master's daughter went to tag her friend, only she accidentally pushed too hard and the girl had gone tumbling head first, breaking her neck and dying in a heap of bones at the bottom of the steps. If the upperclassmen who had told my brother this story were to be believed, then the little girl's ghost still roamed the entry hall, tugging on people's clothing if they ran too fast in an attempt to help them avoid the fate that she could not.

My brother had brought home many ghost stories from his time at Westwood and at the time I had been too scared to tell him that they gave me nightmares. It had been about a decade since I first heard those stories, and maybe half that time since any of them had haunted me in my sleep, but I was still worried about them resurfacing now that I was meant to make my home in the place where they originated.

A grand piano sat on the landing at the top of the stairs, the case of it a deep cherry wood. I ran my finger lightly across the ivory keys and was surprised to find it covered in a thick layer of dust. With the castle being home to the professors' offices, administrative services, and the conservatory library, it made sense that piano music would make too loud of a distraction, though it was a shame that the beautiful thing never got used.

The large window beyond the piano overlooked the immediate part of the campus and a breath caught in my throat as I took in the landscape for the first time. Despite my brother having attended Westwood Conservatory for the usual five years it took to complete one of their programs, I was never once able to visit the campus. My father thought I was too young to help him move in his first year and he had never needed to move out as he preferred to stay through the summer breaks. My last chance to visit would have been his graduation, but I had been sick with the flu at the time and therefore had to remain home alone.

Spread out before me was a rolling muted green view as far as I could see. The trees that dotted it were the same sad color as the ones on the outside of campus. I held onto the hope that they would turn the most brilliant shades of orange and scarlet and gold within the coming weeks as September transitioned from summer to autumn.

A large part of the castle jutted out at an odd angle to the right side of the view; I assumed that it was the library that had been built as an addition to the building several decades after the initial construction was completed. I could see a handful of large buildings in the space closest to the castle, but I knew there was even more out beyond them. Eli had described Westwood's campus as 'deceptively small from the outside' and I now understood what he meant. After several minutes of taking in the view and contemplating where to explore next, I decided the walkway to the right of the landing would be the way to go, as it might have taken me to the library if I walked far enough.

I avoided looking over the railing down to the entryway below as I walked. Instead, I kept my eyes on the paintings that lined the wall and focused on treading lightly and keeping my steps from being too loud. They seemed to be depicting various Greek myths; I recognized the moment Psyche dripped wax on her sleeping lover Eros in one and the weaving contest between Athena and Arachne in another, but for every story I recognized there were half a dozen more that were completely foreign to me.

A voice so soft I couldn't make out any of the words, only that sound was being made, drifted towards me from down the hall and I felt compelled to take a few tentative steps towards it. One of the doors near the corner of the hall was cracked ajar ever so slightly. Peering in, I saw a man sitting at a large desk that took up much of the already overcrowded room. He seemed to be muttering to himself, perhaps speaking aloud the words he wanted to write before he made them permanent on the page before him.

As he ran his hand through his salt and pepper curls, he looked up and much to my surprise and dismay made direct eye contact with me. I froze, feeling the all too familiar anxiety creep its way across my body, but before either of us could say or do anything a pair of bodies rounded the corner and collided with my own, pushing me a few steps back before their momentum died down.

"Oh my goodness, are you okay?" one of them asked. She was about my height though she had a thicker build. Her short honey brown waves framed a very concerned look on her face. There was a musical lilt to her voice and a unique pronunciation of some of the vowel sounds that made me think English was not her first language.

"I'm fine," I assured with a weak smile, untangling myself from her. "I shouldn't have been standing in the middle of the hallway anyway."

Luckily my suitcase hadn't been caught in the fray or who knows how badly we could have been hurt tripping over it. It was small, but that didn't mean it wouldn't cause damage. I wiped my hands on my thighs though there was nothing on them to wipe off - a feeble attempt at calming myself down. At this point the other girl spoke up, pushing aside her long poofy black curls to get them out of her face.

"You wouldn't happen to be Georgiana Miller, would you?" she asked, peering at me with such an intense gaze that I wouldn't have been surprised if she was trying to see into my soul.

"Uh, yes. I go by Georgie though," I stuttered out. The girl chuckled at my response while the other one took her turn to speak.

"Oh, but Georgiana is such a beautiful name!" she exclaimed. "Why would you not want to use it?" I smiled awkwardly, not expecting this pseudo-interrogation.

"It was just a few too many letters to keep track of when I was learning the alphabet. Too big of a name for too little of a girl, you know?" I let out a nervous laugh and they both nodded like they understood. "Who are you, by the way? If you already knew my name then it's only right that I should know yours."

"Right, I'm Ahra. I was put in charge of showing you and Noemi here around the campus. When you weren't waiting down by the entrance I figured you were wandering the castle. Everyone does it on their first day." I felt my cheeks redden though there wasn't really anything to feel embarrassed about. Of course this was Ahra, who else would already know my name?

Ahra held out her hand, though not very far from her body. I suspected it was because she didn't want the forearm crutches she was using to end up falling, so I stepped closer to be able to shake her hand. It was just as warm as her smile was, and I could see why she had been chosen to introduce me - and Noemi - to the school.

"I was so glad to hear that another student was coming here this term, it makes me feel less nervous about being new to Westwood myself," Noemi said.

I had not been informed about another student joining the same time as me. In fact, I had been told quite the opposite, that cases like mine were very few and far between. The only new students besides the first years were studying abroad for a semester from one of the conservatory's sister schools around the world, which must have been Noemi's situation. I flashed her a small smile and said something to the same effect as her sentiment.

With that, Ahra turned and led us back down the way she and Noemi had come, explaining how she would take us through the various wings of the castle first before touring the grounds and bringing us to Radcliffe House where we would all be living. As we passed the cracked open doorway I risked a peek inside, but the man must have been somewhere else in the room as he was no longer at his desk. I let out a silent sigh of relief that I wouldn't have to be confronted for the awkward encounter, but also couldn't help but feel the slightest pang of disappointment as something I couldn't quite place made me want to see this mysterious stranger again.

Chapter Two

AFTER A QUICK STOP at the registrar's office to get class schedules in line and an even quicker trip through the library - Ahra made it clear that she wanted to spend as little time there as possible - we made it through the Castle Blackscar portion of the tour and into the fresh air. It had been chilly when I first arrived that morning, but in the passing hours it had certainly warmed up and my jacket had suddenly become too warm for me to wear. I stopped to tie it around my waist and then had to walk double time for a moment to catch up with Noemi and Ahra before they rounded the corner of a building.

For someone who was supposed to be giving an informational tour and also had to use a mobility aid, Ahra moved much faster than expected. I was tempted several times to stop and marvel at the beautiful architecture of the various buildings we passed, but I was afraid of being left behind. Instead I made a mental note of all the places I wanted to come back to when I had time to go at my own pace.

We took a wide circle around campus, passing by several buildings for classrooms, Orin Hall where the first year students lived, and the main dining hall. While trees dotted the campus in its entirety, the northwest corner seemed to be overrun by a lush forest. The trees still sang with the last of the summer cicadas.

"Do you guys want to grab a coffee?" Ahra asked, interrupting my thoughts. "We'll be passing by the Rise & Shine and they make killer frappuccinos. My treat."

"Sure," Noemi agreed. I nodded as well, though I would have preferred a hot chocolate to a frappuccino. I had tried to get into coffee in the past few months living with my brother because he and his wife were very big fans of the drink, but I never found a flavor combination that I thought was more than just okay.

Ahra led the two of us to a small building not far from where we had been standing. The outside was made of a similar stone to the castle, but the inside looked like any modern day coffee shop with a granite countertop and a handful of tables and a couch set up for seating. Ahra, Noemi, and I all got iced coffees; Ahra's had salted caramel added to it, Noemi's had matcha, and I tried mint mocha in an attempt to mimic my favorite flavor combination, but I still thought it would have tasted better without the actual coffee.

We took our drinks from the student worker who prepared them and made our way further from the castle on the campus tour. We passed one more building, Adwell Hall where the dance classes were held, before we came to the edge of Vauxhall Lake. Looking out past the water, there was a building so beautiful it rivaled the castle in its magnificence. The front was graced with white columns and three spires reached their way into the sky; it was as if the architect had decided to make the most visually striking building possible.

"What is that?" Noemi asked, echoing the question in my mind with a voice full of awe and wonder.

"That is the Athena Areia, so named for the statue that we will see once we walk to the other side of the building. It is the home for anyone who makes it to their fifth year here at the conservatory. It houses up to 35 students, though the largest graduating class on record was only 28." As she spoke, Ahra walked closer to the building, but I felt rooted to the spot in awe for a moment longer.

"How is that possible? The first year dorm building was so huge, it seemed like it could hold ten times as many students," Noemi argued. The sister school she normally studied at must have been less harsh on its students and have a higher percentage of them be asked to return the following year.

"Westwood has a very strict standard for its students," I said, speaking before Ahra could. "Only the best of the best continue on each year. Just about two thirds of each year move on to the next one on average, and then between fourth and fifth years that percentage is cut further and only about a third make it through at most."

Anxiety rose from the pit of my stomach as I spoke. I remembered how stressed out my brother became with each passing year and the fears I'd developed over the past weeks crept back into my mind, fears about how I would never be able to make it past even one semester here. I took a deep breath and began the routine I used to calm down, focusing on and compartmentalizing everything I could feel on my body before moving on to everything I could smell like my coffee and the grass, and then continuing on with my other senses. I tried to mentally will Noemi and Ahra to continue on with the conversation and not pay any attention to me. Much to my relief, they did.

The three of us walked along the shore of the lake and by the time we made it to the statue that Ahra had mentioned, I managed to get my breathing and heart rate back under control. The statue was just as beautiful as the building that took its name and the small part of me that recovered quickly from my anxiety wondered what it would be like to live in such a place, to see the splendor of Athena as I left my magnificent home each day. The moment passed swiftly and we continued on until we made it to the closest of the smaller buildings that circled the lake, appropriately called the Lakehouses, where all second, third, and fourth year students lived.

"And this is where we'll all be living!" Ahra said, waving her hands with a little flourish. Noemi and I both laughed, the action making me feel more normal.

The building was like the Athena Areia in that it was an architectural anomaly, strange and beautiful, but that was where the similarities ended. Where the Athena Areia was white marble and grey stone, Radcliffe House was dark wood and red brick. The main building was one floor, stout and blocky, and two wide towers stuck out of it at strange places. One was very near the front of the building on the left while the other was on the back right side.

Ahra handed Noemi and I each a set of three keys and showed us which was for the front door, which was for the back tower door, and which was for our individual rooms. We then entered the building for the first time and were greeted by a modern looking living space with an open kitchen and dining area beyond. A sharply dressed young man in a wheelchair moved around the kitchen preparing food.

"Hey Vinny, I'm surprised you and River aren't making out in the living room like usual," Ahra teased as we made our way past him.

"We are not friends, Ahra, so stop acting like we are, and stop calling me by that stupid nickname. Besides, what I do with River is none of your business," he spat, clearly not wanting to put up with any of her jokes.

"It is when it's happening in the common area of the house."

Vincent flashed her a look of annoyance that bordered on threatening.

"I'm just saying, I'm pretty sure Noemi and Georgie are grateful not to walk in on that on their first day here," she answered in her playful sing-song voice.

"I guess I'll be taking my lunch to my room today," the young man muttered more to himself than any of us. Ahra waved her hand dismissively as she led us through a doorway I hadn't noticed before tucked behind the dining table.

"Don't mind him, Vincent is always a stick in the mud. They all are on that side of the house; must be a prerequisite for being one of Professor Decker's teaching assistants. Not sure what River sees in him, but he sure is easy to poke fun at."

Ahra had explained on our walk that there were ten people living in Radcliffe House, myself and Noemi included. The two of us would be taking the empty rooms in the back tower where Ahra lived with her two best friends River and Ollie. The other tower housed a tight knit group of not quite friends who were all teaching assistants for the same professor. Vincent, whom we had just met, Lourdes, Ailani, Clara, and

Damian. Ahra told us not to be surprised if we rarely saw them around as they tended to avoid other people.

The hallway snaked around the back of the house and led to a door that let us into the tower. Beyond that door were two more doors, both the same brown wood as all the others we had walked through already, and a staircase. The door closer to the stairs was plain, but the other was decorated with all sorts of dried flowers sticking out of what looked like test tubes attached to the door's wooden surface in neat lines.

"That's my bedroom," Ahra explained, noting my line of sight. "The other door is a bathroom with a toilet and two shower stalls. The second floor is where Ollie and River's rooms are, along with a linen closet. You two get the third floor bedrooms with a half bath so you won't have to come down the stairs just to pee in the middle of the night. We can go up there now so you guys can fully unpack."

Noemi practically squealed in excitement and bounded her way up the stairs, so Ahra and I had no choice but to follow. As I lugged my suitcase up the wooden steps I noticed for the first time that Noemi didn't have one with her. Before I could ask her why she turned and spoke as if she had read my mind yet again.

"I arrived here last night, too late to take a tour which is why Ahra took me around with you this morning. I'm glad I did, because I have way too many bags to be able to lug them around campus!"

On the second floor landing we ran into Ollie and River. They could not have looked more different - Ollie had dark skin and the most intense golden brown eyes with his curly hair shaved on the sides but growing out on top, whereas River had skin as pale as my own and sandy brown hair hanging pin straight in front of his mismatched blue and green eyes - and I was grateful that I wouldn't have trouble telling them apart. By the time introductions were made and we moved up to the third floor, Noemi was already working on shifting her furniture around. River ran over to help move the heavy bed frame while I made my way into my own room to drop my backpack off my aching shoulders and place my suitcase down on the ground.

The furniture was all the same shade of light brown. A simple desk and chair sat under the only window, the bed sat against one wall with an end table on one side of it, and the dresser was against the opposite wall. The bare room was the exact opposite of my childhood room, which had been stuffed with cherry wood furniture and a plethora of miscellaneous items I had grown too fond of to get rid of over the years. In the past few months, however, sentimentality had to be dropped in favor of ease of moving; first from my childhood home in Vermont to my brother's place in Oregon and then from Oregon to the Conservatory here in Pennsylvania. I was so lost in thought about how much my life had changed in the past year that I nearly jumped out of my skin when Ollie spoke.

"Would you like help moving things around?" His voice was much gentler than his intimidating demeanor portrayed, which certainly helped calm my minor spike in anxiety. "Since River is helping Noemi, I figured I'd offer you assistance."

"Oh, no thank you. I was just going to leave everything where it is. I mean, if this setup worked for the previous tenant, then it should work for me, right?" I half-joked.

"Trust me, you are like, the complete opposite of Shayna. She was very loud and always making everybody else's business her own. Now that I think about it, she had a lot in common with River," Ahra said from the doorway.

"Hey, I heard that!" River yelled from the other room.

"You were meant to!" she called back with a chuckle. "Anyway, as I was saying, you should move the furniture around however you want. This room is yours now, not Shayna's or anyone else's."

I shrugged in response. "It's all the same to me. I just don't have a strong enough opinion about it to go to the effort of moving anything around. Though if you think something would look better in a different spot, I'm open to suggestions."

"Not really, like I said it's your room," Ahra said. "I'm gonna go watch TV since Vincent has vacated downstairs. Do you want to join me, Ollie? There has to be some trashy reality show on."

"That sounds fun. If you need any help just let me know, Georgie," Ollie responded. I assured him that I would, and with that I was left alone to unpack my few belongings with River and Noemi's idle chatter as background noise.

For the next hour and a bit, I took my time unpacking clothes out of my suitcase, carefully and methodically refolding them before placing them neatly in drawers. I set my cup of pens and pencils on my desk, arranged the few books I had brought with me in a neat little stack in the sunlight next to my laptop, and put my notebooks in the desk drawer. Making the bed was always my least favorite chore growing up, but I had to admit that once my dark pink duvet cover and pillowcases were set up on the school provided bedding, the room really did look like it was ready to be lived in.

At one point Noemi came to me with an art print. It depicted a forest scene with sunlight filtering through the canopy of trees and a family of deer making their way through the undergrowth. Noemi explained that she didn't have the wall space to hang it up with her other posters and asked if I wanted to keep it in my room. I happily agreed and together we hung the picture above my bed. It did make the room look a little less bare, though from my glance across the hall it was clear that compared to Noemi's packed room, mine moved beyond minimalistic and into just plain empty. Still, I was content with what I had. My heart only ached a little bit thinking of all of the things I had donated to make my first cross-country move easier.

"Are you guys cool with having pizza for dinner in a couple of hours? River wants to try a new recipe they found online," Ahra called up the stairs. Noemi and I shouted back our approval as we surveyed our vastly different but equally finished rooms.

"Do you want to go walk around campus a bit more?" Noemi asked. "Ahra didn't show us the Galleries and I've heard they're just beautiful. Not that the entire campus isn't beautiful." I nodded in agreement and followed her down the stairs and out of Radcliffe House.

The two of us wandered along the opposite bank of Vauxhall Lake past other Lakehouses until we made it to the tennis court we had seen from the castle. At that point we turned to the southern edge of Westwood's campus and found the famed Galleries, three performance halls named Clotho, Lachesis, and Atropos after the fates of Greek mythology, which were just as amazing as the rest of campus like Noemi said they would be.

She didn't seem to mind that I stayed mostly silent, listening to her chat about how loud the cicadas sounded and how cute some of the other students we passed by were. We passed by an intricately detailed fountain and came to a wooded area just as the sun dipped low enough to be behind the tops of the trees, bathing the scene in dark orange and shadows. Noemi stopped to marvel at the setting sun while my attention was grabbed by the rustling of bushes down the path a little.

I had expected to see a rabbit or maybe even a deer bound out of the woods, but instead was surprised by the gloomy sight of two people in dark formal wear, as if they had just left a funeral service. Part of my brain tried to tell me they were ghosts, but even I knew that was a silly thing to think. It registered as strange that such people would be exiting the woods of all places until I looked past them and was just barely able to make out a few tall grey stones between the distant trees - grave markers. I had forgotten that there was a cemetery on the conservatory grounds.

The two people glanced in our direction, though I wasn't able to make out any details other than one was wearing a suit and the other a knee length dark blue dress. At that moment my attention was pulled back to Noemi, who had decided it was time for us to return for dinner. I cast a glance over my shoulder at the retreating figures, but they were nowhere to be seen. Maybe the ghost idea wasn't so far-fetched after all.

Noemi was more than excited enough for the two of us about the prospect of River's homemade pizza as it was her favorite food. She chattered on about how stereotypical it felt for that to be her favorite seeing as she was Italian, and I just chimed in with a few comments here and there to let her know I was sort of listening. My mind was more focused on the strangers I had seen emerge from the cemetery beyond the trees. It seemed to me that Westwood was full of mysterious people and I was destined to catch glimpses of them wherever I went.

Chapter Three

I HAD ARRIVED ON campus on a Saturday and classes were due to start on the following Monday, so I wasn't surprised when my academic advisor Professor Virginia Rhodes sent me an email saying that she wanted to meet with me on the Sunday that fell in between. I wore my favorite sweater, a chunky black knit piece that had belonged to my mother, hoping its familiarity would keep me from panicking. It was starting to wear thin in places but I didn't have it in me to get rid of it.

Professor Rhodes had said that this was just a casual meeting so we could get to know each other a little more, but I couldn't help feeling anxious. After all, this was the woman who my brother claimed as being the number one reason he managed to get through all five years of the history program here at Westwood, on top of which she vouched for me and convinced the Dean of Admissions to let me transfer even though I had dropped out of the program I had been enrolled in previously. The stakes felt a little too high for just a casual meeting.

Her office was on the opposite side of the entry hall and further into the west wing from the hallway where I had run into Ahra and Noemi. I was surprised to find it decorated with scenes of East Asian influence rather than the Greek I had expected. Perhaps the castle was full of art from all different cultures and the fact that the fifth year housing and the Galleries were named from Greek myths was unrelated to the fact that the first hall I had found was decorated similarly.

Professor Rhodes was a severe looking woman, her thin body all angles. Her dark skin was a sharp contrast to the off white pantsuit she wore, which was as crisp and spotless as the rest of her office. She invited me to sit down in one of the chairs across from her desk and doing so felt like when I was younger and Eli and I had to spend the evening with the neighbor who covered all of her furniture in plastic while our parents went out to dinner.

"I won't take too much of your time, Georgie, I just want to touch base and see how things stand before the semester begins. Go over your classes, expectations, that sort of thing," the professor explained. She folded her hands on the desk in front of her and it took me a moment to realize she was waiting for me to answer her.

"Oh, well, I have Anthropology with you, but of course you know that already." I was mumbling already, off to a great start. At least I managed to keep decent eye contact. "Besides that I have an online Hebrew class with Professor Schallenberg, Mathematical Concepts with Professor Bailey, and Modern British Literature with Professor Decker," I said. It wasn't until that last name came out of my own mouth that I realized that was the name Ahra had given as the Professor whom our housemates worked as teaching assistants under.

"Seems as though you have a moderate course load," Professor Rhodes said in response. I nodded in agreement even though in my eyes the four courses felt like they might be overwhelming based on what I had heard of the school. "Are there any you're particularly excited about? Nervous to be in?" I swallowed hard before answering.

"Well, I guess I'm excited for Modern British Literature, and your Anthropology course," I said, rushing my sentence. "I'm not very good at math so I'm more nervous about that than anything else."

"That's understandable, not everyone can excel in every subject as much as this school likes to pretend." There was a look in her eyes that betrayed the fact that she had many more thoughts on that than she was saying out loud. "What about your housemates, do you think you'll get along well with them?"

I squirmed in my seat as I nodded and avoided her eyes. I had no idea I would have to answer so many questions.

"I know it probably feels like I'm interrogating you, Georgie, but I promise I would just like to get to know you better. Eli spoke so highly of you, which is why I vouched for you to my superiors. I want to make sure I did that for the right reasons, and not just because you're the younger sister of one of my favorite former students."

I nodded again and squeaked out an apology, which caused Professor Rhodes to let out a sigh as she took off her glasses and pinched the bridge of her nose. My stomach sank as I realized how much I must be disappointing her, and so early on in our knowing each other. I hoped there was still a chance for me to improve my standing in her eyes.

"Everything is still so new, I have only been here for a day," I said. Both of us had to be aware that I was just making useless excuses, but I continued on anyway. "I'm sure once I've gotten through the first few weeks of classes I'll fit right in with all the students who've been here the past three years."

"That is a very tall claim. I look forward to seeing you achieve that," Professor Rhodes said. Before either of us could say anything more the corded phone on her desk rang, a clunky and ancient looking thing that I hadn't even noticed until that moment. She waved me out of the room to answer it in privacy and I all but jumped out of my chair and out the door before scurrying back to the safety of Radcliffe House.

As much as I would have loved to explore the campus more, that would have to wait until Noemi or someone else was free to walk with me. Ahra had led the dinner discussion the previous night, telling all sorts of ghost stories as a sort of rite of passage for us new students to have to hear. Some I had heard from Eli, while others were completely knew. Regardless, none of them made me feel comfortable walking around on my own with them fresh in my mind, even in the light of the sun overhead.

Chapter Four

Without River's guidance I would never have found the classroom for Modern British Literature. Luckily they were in the same class, as well as Noemi, so the three of us left together that afternoon. My morning math class had been easy to find as it was in the very first classroom upon entering Donnal Hall. On the other hand, Winsford Hall where Modern British Literature was held had seemed simple from the outside, but it became clear upon entering that it was anything but. Some hallways resulted in dead ends whereas others took unnecessary turns, confusing anyone who wasn't privy to the building's secrets. River led us around a surprise turn and across a short catwalk that connected the main building to a smaller annex I hadn't originally noticed before stopping at an unassuming door in the corner.

Half of the room was already filled up by the time we arrived, with two of the students claiming desks front and center and the other five scattering further back. The two students in the front of the room - a pale blonde and a darker skinned brunette with matching ponytails - stopped their chattering to watch the three of us walk by. I could have imagined it, but it almost seemed like River made a point to look anywhere but in their direction. Noemi chose a seat one row back and next to the windows while River sat to her right. I always felt subconscious sitting in the center of a room, so I took the seat in front of Nocmi, which resulted in me sitting directly in front of the professor's desk.

I busied myself setting up my notebook and making sure I had a pen that wouldn't run out of ink three sentences in. When I finally looked up at the professor as he was walking in, I was shocked to find myself staring at the man I had inadvertently spied on just days earlier when wandering around the castle. Things I hadn't noticed during that first encounter were now clear as crystal from this shorter distance - stubble scattered across his cheeks as if he hadn't shaved in a couple of days, a pair of simple silver studs in his ears.

I quickly turned away, not wanting him - or anyone else for that matter - to see the harsh red blush I felt coming over my face. I had no reason to be embarrassed as he probably didn't even remember the ten second encounter, but I still felt awkward about having looked in on him the way I did. I was relieved when I glanced back up to find him facing the other way to write something on the chalkboard. When he finished, he turned to address the class.

"Most of you already know me, but for the few new faces I see among us today I will go through my usual introductory spiel. My name is Adrian Decker, you may call me Professor Decker, Professor D, Decker, Professor Adrian, or anything else along those lines as long as you do it respectfully. This is Modern British Literature, so if you are not meant to be here then now is your chance to leave." He paused, but no one left the room. "Good, glad to know you can all make it to the right classroom. Without further ado, why don't we get right into things. First let's go over the syllabus so you all know what you'll be dealing with this semester, and then we're going to play a fun little game to get to know who you will be dealing with."

Someone from behind me, and I had a sneaking suspicion it was River, groaned audibly at the mention of having to do an ice breaker game. Professor Decker chuckled in response.

"Yes, I know that most of you know each other already, but that isn't the case for everybody. These are your intellectual peers, the people you will be working with for the next several months in this class, and I want you to be able to say that you know each and every other person in this room. The world of literary critique is not a solitary work, but rather a mosaic of ideas and contributions from many different people," he explained while handing out packets of paper.

He seemed to linger just a second longer in front of my desk than any of the others at the front of their rows, but before I could even react he was off to the front of the room again. I felt my face heat up, sure that the ice breaker was for my benefit as well as Noemi's, because no one else had any reason not to know each other already.

The next twenty minutes were spent reading through the policies and assignments outlined in the syllabus - the bulk of it being various novels, essays, and poems to be read, analyzed, and then discussed in class throughout the semester. In the last week of the semester there would be a collaborative research essay that had to incorporate two or more of the pieces read for class.

My throat tightened at the mention of this final assignment; I had never been one for group work and preferred to do things on my own. A few times in high school my teachers had let me do group assignments by myself but I had the feeling that would not be possible here with the way I was beginning to realize Professor Decker would run his class. I hoped that maybe I would get to work with River or Noemi for the group project, but that hope was quickly dashed as Professor Decker explained that he assigns the groups randomly by pulling names out of a hat.

"Speaking of doing things randomly, I believe that is all for the syllabus, so that means it is time for us all to learn a little something about each other."

He paused to pull out three books from his desk at the front of the room and showed them off to the class - *Lady Windermere's Fan, An Ideal Husband,* and *The Importance of Being Earnest*, all by Oscar Wilde. Though I was a fan of *The Picture of Dorian Gray*, I had never read any of Wilde's plays aside from a portion of *The Importance of Being Earnest*.

"These three plays are all brilliant examples of modern literature, but unfortunately I could not fit them into our syllabus this semester. I still want you all to know something about them, so when I pull your name from my hat you will come up to the front, introduce yourself, and then read one of the passages I have marked here. Then, we will repeat until everyone has gone. I believe there is a lot to learn about the way a person reads a character's lines, one's own personality might shine through in interesting ways."

I squirmed in my seat, not wanting to get up in front of everyone to perform a passage. I had tried to join the theater club in high school but my anxiety prevented me from returning after the teacher who was acting as the director tried to give me a main role in the production of a play he had written. I had felt fine about the situation until a few other girls involved in the production pointed out how terribly I'd do with all those eyes on me, people just waiting to see me make a mistake.

"So that whoever is chosen first doesn't feel too much pressure, I will start. As I said before, my name is Adrian Decker and I teach both English and Theater courses here at Westwood Conservatory. I have been doing so for the past eight years and plan to do so for many more. As for my passage, I will be doing Jack's short monologue from *The Importance of Being Earnest*. Clara, will you be my Lady Bracknell?" The blonde girl sitting at the front of the room nodded, leading Professor Decker to clear his throat before reciting the words, not needing to read them from the page.

"It pains me very much to have to speak frankly to you, Lady Bracknell, about your nephew, but the fact is that I do not approve at all of his moral character. I suspect him of being untruthful."

"Untruthful! My nephew Algernon? Impossible! He is an Oxonian." Clara recited from her seat, seemingly having the scene memorized as well.

"I fear there can be no possible doubt about the matter. This afternoon during my temporary absence in London on an important question of romance, he obtained admission to my house by means of the false pretense of being my brother. Under an assumed name he drank, I've just been informed by my butler, an entire pint bottle of my Perrier-Jouet, Brut,

'89; wine I was specially reserving for myself. Continuing his disgraceful deception, he succeeded in the course of the afternoon in alienating the affections of my only ward. He subsequently stayed to tea, and devoured every single muffin. And what makes his conduct all the more heartless is, that he was perfectly well aware from the first that I have no brother, that I never had a brother, and that I don't intend to have a brother, not even of any kind. I distinctly told him so myself yesterday afternoon."

Without the context of most of the play, I found myself paying attention not to the words the professor was saying though he had enthusiasm abounding, but rather to the intense look in his grey eyes that was made more clear when halfway through his piece he took off his glasses and threw them on the desk in a motion of acted passion. When he finished he seemed just slightly out of breath from the effort and I found myself wanting to clap for him. No one else in the room made a move to do so, however, so instead my hands just twitched in my lap.

River was the first student to be called to the front, and I gave them a little smile of encouragement as they met my eyes. Their monologue was from *Lady Windermere's Fan*, when the titular Lady Windermere begins to stress about waiting for a man. I had never read the play, nor *An Ideal Husband*, so I hoped that there would still be a familiar passage in *Earnest* for me to read when it came to my turn.

After a few more students went, Noemi was called up and she performed a monologue from *The Importance of Being Earnest* in which a young girl named Cecily explains to a man called Ernest how they had been engaged for several months though they had never met before that moment. She did a wonderful job of portraying the foolishness of a young girl in love, though her accent did make it hard for me to understand some of the words she was saying.

The next name called was Clara, so the girl who had helped him out earlier stood up. She and the Professor talked for a moment in hushed voices before he invited the other girl she had been chatting with to join Clara in front of the class. She introduced herself as Lourdes and the two of them said they were teacher's assistants for the professor's lower level classes. Surprise shot through me as it registered that they must have been two of the housemates I had not yet met; their names hadn't clicked with me until they mentioned being teaching assistants.

The two of them then performed a scene from *Earnest*. Lourdes read for the same character that Noemi had before, Cecily, while Clara read for Gwendolyn. The scene was mainly a dialogue between the two characters, though Professor Decker had to chime in a couple of times to provide lines for less important characters. Once they were done Lourdes looked as though she was just going to sit down so the Professor could move on, but Clara grabbed her arm and made her give a little bow, as if the two of them had given a real performance instead of just reading a passage in front of the class. Lourdes looked annoyed by this, but went along with it anyway.

As other students kept getting called to the front I found myself growing more and more anxious. My breath caught in my throat as the professor pulled the penultimate name from the hat and read from the small slip of the paper - Charlie. Not me. I would be going last and what I said and did would be the freshest in everyone's minds as they left class, which was exactly what I dreaded happening. After Charlie's reading from *An Ideal Husband*, Professor Decker waved for me to take my place in front of everyone. Once I was up there Noemi flashed me a warm and encouraging smile while River gave me a double thumbs up. I swallowed hard to try and remedy my suddenly dry throat.

"Um, hello everyone. My name is Georgie Miller and I just transferred to this school from another university back in Vermont. I am in the literature discipline and I, uh, don't really have anything interesting to say about myself," I explained. This earned some snickers that were easily disguised as coughing from people at the back of the room. I realized that no matter what I did this would be at best uncomfortable for just me and at worst uncomfortable for everyone in the room, so I decided my best course of action would be to just get my reading done quickly.

All of the passages from *The Importance of Being Earnest* had already been chosen and read by my classmates, so my options were between *An Ideal Husband* or *Lady Windermere's Fan*. My hands shook as I picked up *An Ideal Husband* purely because it was the closer of the two.

My voice wavered as I read Mabel's lines where she complained about the numerous proposals she had received from someone named Tommy. I looked up from the page briefly after the first sentence to see those same grey eyes of Professor Decker who had taken a spot among the students' seats, but instead of showing confusion or disappointment like I expected, they seemed to be encouraging me to go on. I held on to that encouragement and worked my way through the monologue. By the end of it my blood was rushing through my ears so loudly that I almost didn't catch the professor thanking me for finishing out the student introductions and asking me to sit down so he could conclude the class.

I stared at my desk for the last few minutes while Professor Decker spoke, not wanting to see if anyone's attention was on me. As soon as he said that we could go I moved to put all of my things back in my bag, pausing when I heard my name.

"Georgiana? Sorry, Georgie? Noemi? May I please speak to

the two of you for a moment? I want to talk to you guys about a few things," Professor Decker called. My cheeks warmed a bit at him correcting himself on my name, as most teachers I had known in the past didn't bother with that. I nodded and walked over to his desk.

"Actually, I have a class in about fifteen minutes and I would prefer not to be late, could I email you to schedule a meeting later this week?" Noemi asked. Professor Decker assented and she left the room with River. The two of us stood there, myself awkwardly and the professor in a relaxed manner, as the other students filed out of the room. Lourdes and Clara were the last to leave. In the doorway Clara turned and looked as if she had something to say, but instead she just gave me an odd look and was gone. At this point Decker walked over to lean back against his desk.

"Don't worry Georgie, you're not in trouble. I just wanted to get to know you a little bit. I've had most of these students in class before and even the ones I haven't personally taught I've gotten to know through department events and the like. Besides, it's not often we get a transfer student, so you're somewhat of an anomaly around here," he explained with an amused lilt to his words. "So, how are you doing? Is this your first class of the semester?"

I shook my head and waited for my tongue to catch up to my brain before answering; my fear was that this would turn out exactly how talking to Professor Rhodes had gone. "I had Introduction to Mathematical Concepts this morning, but besides that this is my first." Professor Decker gave a knowing nod.

"That's with Professor Bailey, isn't it? I heard she took over that course when Professor Michaels announced that she was going on sabbatical. Did you enjoy it?" I don't know what it was, maybe his encouraging look from before was still making its way through my system, but something about Professor Decker made it seem more like I was talking to a friend than my superior and it made me want to be honest with him where normally I would back away from the questions with a simple 'yes' or 'I'm fine'.

"Truthfully? I hated it," I said. Professor Decker raised his eyebrows in surprise at my candor. "Professor Bailey seems like a kind person, but she skipped right over the syllabus and class introductions and dove straight into the material and honestly, I'm not much of a math person." He gave me a knowing smirk.

"I have known Alison Bailey for the better part of a decade and believe me when I say she is one of the toughest teachers out there. I've heard students say that with the way she runs her classes, it's like she expects everyone to have taught themselves the material beforehand so she could just give it a light review before plowing ahead. Honestly you'd be better off taking the course with Professor Michaels when she comes back from sabbatical. She takes a much more beginner friendly approach."

I considered his words for a moment before answering, keeping my eyes anywhere but on him. "I'm only taking the minimum amount of credits required for the semester as it is, so dropping a class would put me below that."

"Why don't I add you to one of my theater courses? I had a student drop my first level stage combat class unexpectedly, so I have the space. It's worth the same amount of credits as the math course and nothing you'd previous experience for," he offered. At that point I realized I had been nervously playing with the hem of my skirt. I quickly dropped it and smoothed down the edge.

"I don't really know how the whole dropping and adding a class works here. I'm sure I'll be fine, I could just tough it out in math." I said, trying to sound convincing despite my earlier comments, but Professor Decker waved his hand dismissively.

"Oh, nonsense. You shouldn't stay in a class when you're struggling. A little bit of a challenge is nice, certainly, but this seems to be more than that. Don't you worry about switching classes. I'll take care of that for you - all you have to do is make sure you show up to Stage Combat on Friday," he insisted. His earnest and caring tone made me give in almost instantly with a quick nod and a quiet thank you. "Great! Well, I don't want to keep you too long, so I will let you go now and see you in class."

As I made my way out of the classroom, I turned back around for a second to give a better farewell, but Professor Decker wasn't looking in my direction. Instead he seemed to be staring out the window, his eyebrows furrowed in a pensive manner. Unable to help myself, I stared at him for a second before quickly leaving before he could notice.

It took the better part of half an hour to figure out how to exit the maze that was Winsford Hall, but eventually I made my way into the fresh evening air. I looked up at the wall of windows but the glare from the sun made it so I couldn't see if Professor Decker was standing in any of them looking out. I briefly wondered if he could see me leaving from his perspective, but the thought was pushed from my mind as it started to drizzle and I rushed to get someplace dry before it became a full on downpour.

Chapter Five

When I got back to Radcliffe House, Lourdes and Clara were fighting in the living room. I felt rooted to the spot where I stood in the entryway, keys still in my hand, confused and unsure of what was going on. They had seemed perfectly fine in class together, but now they shoved each other around with almost too much enthusiasm.

They must not have noticed me standing there as Lourdes threw her elbow into Clara, sending the blonde stumbling into me. I barely managed to bring my hands up in time to catch her and keep us both standing. Immediately she pulled away and scowled at me.

"What are you doing interrupting our scene?" she spat.

"Your... scene?" I stood there dumbfounded.

"We're practicing some moves for the stage combat course

we're taking this semester," Lourdes explained. Suddenly everything clicked and I felt incredibly stupid. Of course they weren't actually fighting.

"Oh, right," was all I could think to say. A weird silence lingered between us, and I struggled to find something to say. "I'm in that class too," I added as Clara moved back into place beside Lourdes. She shot me a confused look.

"When you introduced yourself, you didn't say you were in the theater discipline."

"That's because I'm not. Professor Decker just offered me a spot in the class and I said yes."

"That's what he wanted to talk to you about after class? He wanted to offer you that spot in Stage Combat?" Clara asked, one eyebrow quirking up in disbelief.

"No, he was just asking about my classes and how I was feeling being here at the conservatory so far. I told him about my math class this morning and how I was worried about struggling through it this semester, and he convinced me to drop it and join his class instead to make up for the credits." I was aware that I was rambling at this point, but there seemed to be some sort of disconnect between my brain and my mouth that kept me from stopping until I had over explained myself.

"Uh huh." Clara rolled her eyes but Lourdes spoke up instead.

"I wondered what he would do about that open spot, Adrian's never had a class that didn't fill up completely. He probably wants to learn more about you, seeing as you're the first person to transfer to the school in over a decade. You must be pretty special," she said with a smile.

"Yeah, I guess so." I hesitated, shifting back and forth on my feet as I was unsure where to go. I didn't want to walk through the middle of the room and get in the way of their practicing, but the way the couches were pushed out of the way made it impossible for me to skirt around them by hugging the walls. Clara must have noticed my indecisiveness as she gave me a look that told me I should get a move on already.

"You can watch if you want, just get out of the way," she said with a roll of her eyes. I jumped a bit before making my way over to the sofa that faced where they stood before I even considered if that was what I wanted to do or if I was just following her instructions. It felt strange watching them pretend to fight, but I figured it might help ease my nerves about transferring into the stage combat class if I knew more about what I was getting myself into.

Chapter Six

THE AIR IN THE castle felt lighter than it had the day I arrived at Westwood Conservatory.

Perhaps it had something to do with getting through my first day of classes, or that the artwork in the hall I wandered down depicted more relaxing scenes than others I had seen. One portrait showed a beautiful woman in profile, her dark skin and hair in contrast with the gold and turquoise of her headdress as silver tears ran down her face. A half circle of moons portraying the whole of the lunar cycle spread across the top part of the canvas. Such detail was painted into her features that when I ran my finger lightly over the top of the canvas I half expected it to come away wet with her tears.

"She's beautiful, isn't she?" came a voice from just to my left. I jumped, knocking my elbow into the man beside me.

"Professor Decker!" I exclaimed, bringing my hands to my mouth. "I am so sorry, I didn't know you were there." He chuckled in response as a bright smile lit up his face.

"It's alright Georgie, it's my fault for being too quiet when walking over here. I was just headed back to my office after a meeting when I saw you and figured I'd say hello," he explained. I let a small smile cross my face, and I hoped the professor couldn't tell how incredibly awkward I felt at that moment. I was never fond of impromptu meetings. "So what are you doing here? Just come to admire the art?"

"I'm waiting for a friend to finish up class and then we're going to get lunch together," I explained. "I'm just here to kill time." Professor Decker nodded knowingly.

"Well, what better place to kill time than in our own Castle Blackscar?" he asked rhetorically. "I often find myself wandering the halls to look at all the wonderful art we have collected here." His gaze turned back to the portrait I had been looking at.

"Do you know who this painting portrays?" I asked.

Professor Decker nodded, keeping his eyes on the work of art. "Her name is Mama Quilla, she's the Inca goddess of the moon, among other things," he explained.

"Are all of the art pieces in the castle meant to depict different gods and goddesses?" I looked down the hall at some of the other pieces that lined the hall, but out of the corner of my eye

I saw Professor Decker shrug.

"More or less, they show moments from various myths and stories from around the world. It just so happens that most of those stories involve gods. Each set of hallways is themed after a different culture." He paused for a moment before asking, "Do you want to see my favorite piece of art in the whole castle?" Turning to face him, I was met by a look of such excitement that I found it impossible to say no.

He led me down the hall and up a set of stairs, around a few corners until we arrived at a part of the castle I had never been to before. Professor Decker stepped aside to let me get a better view of the art he had wanted to show me, a massive work of beaded embroidery that hung on the wall of a dead end.

The piece was visceral, to say the least. Half of the surface was taken up by a snake-like sea serpent, the green of its scales glittering as the light caught the beads. Foaming water poured out of its snarling mouth. Cowering in the corner was the figure of a naked woman, chained to a rock. The embroidery was so detailed that I could read the terror in her face as the serpent reared its head at her. In the top left corner, tiny as if it were way off in the distance, flew a white winged horse. I stood there in silence, stunned by the gruesome detail until Professor Decker spoke.

"Do you know this story?" he asked. I shook my head. "The maiden is the princess Andromeda. Her mother claimed that the princess was more beautiful than all of the gods, and of course the gods did not take kindly to that. As punishment, Poseidon sent the sea monster Cetus to ravage the lands that Andromeda's parents ruled over, saying that the only way to stop the monster would be to sacrifice the young girl to it. Fearing for their kingdom, the king and queen were ready to do so, until Perseus flew by on the back of Pegasus after slaying Medusa. He fell in love with the girl on sight and knew he would do anything to save her, so he attacked Cetus. Some versions of the story say he was able to cut off the beast's head, others say he was swallowed whole and had to fight his way out of the creature's stomach. Either way, Andromeda was saved and became Perseus's wife."

Professor Decker turned to me, an expectant look on his face. I realized he was waiting for me to say something after hearing the story of the princess and the sea monster. I took a moment to try and think of something that would impress him before responding.

"Why didn't he just use Medusa's head to turn Cetus to stone?" I asked. I may not have known about Andromeda before that day, but at the very least I recognized the name Medusa from the Greek mythology unit of middle school history class. A wide, toothy grin broke out across Professor Decker's face as he let out a laugh that echoed through the narrow hallway.

"A very good question, Georgie. I suppose that would have made things a little easier. Are you a fan of mythology?" I shrugged noncommittally.

"My brother was in the history discipline when he went to school here, so I know a few stories, but his main focus was on Jewish folklore," I explained. "Though there is so much fascinating artwork here that I'd love to look into more."

"I didn't know your brother went to school here, what's his name?" the professor questioned, and I explained that it was Elijah but that he went by Eli.

"Your brother is Eli Miller? Well, that makes a lot of sense! I had your brother in a few of my classes and he nearly became one of my teaching assistants, though he went on to work with Professor Rhodes instead. Next time you talk to him you tell him I said hello, alright?" I agreed, and as my phone chimed in that moment I almost expected it to be my brother. Instead it was Ahra, letting me know she was finished with her class. I sent back a quick response and considered my words to Professor Decker carefully.

"Um, Professor, if you wouldn't mind, could you show me the way out of the castle? I've never been to this floor before and I'm afraid I'll get lost," I said with a shy and awkward smile. He chuckled and accepted, leading me back through the twisting hallways and staircases until we were finally out in broad daylight. Ahra stood a few yards away and waved when she saw me exit the castle.

"Georgie, come on! My friend Minnie's gone to save us a seat!" she called. I turned to thank Professor Decker for showing me the artwork and for escorting me out of the castle, but he just waved his hand.

"Oh, it was nothing. If you ever need anything, or if you just want to discuss mythology or literature or anything else remember I'm just an email away." I thanked him once again before jogging to catch up with Ahra, who was already making her way towards the café.

Chapter Seven

Luckily for Noemi and me, Professor Rhodes's anthropology course was not held in the labyrinthine horror that was Winsford Hall, but rather the much more simply laid out Corbyn Hall. We arrived to class on Wednesday with plenty of time to spare and were actually some of the first people there; only three people had arrived ahead of us. A girl with tan skin and bright pink hair sat at the back of the room, while closer to the front were two people locked in conversation - an imposing looking young man with a scowl so severe it looked like it was permanently etched into his face and a dark skinned young woman wearing a hijab that was surprisingly the exact same shade of green as the skirt I wore that day. I looked down at it, suddenly self conscious of my outfit choice. I felt that the young woman's long cream colored dress was much more fashionable than my boring black button down tucked into a green skirt.

Noemi and I chose seats closer to the door and farther from the other students' window seats and chatted idly about how the first few days of classes were going while the other students and eventually Professor Rhodes herself trickled into the classroom. She wasted no time getting to the point.

"Welcome, everybody, to Anthropology 101. I see that everyone here already knows who I am so there is no need for me to go on my introduction spiel. As this is an anthropology course I like to do student introductions relating to the topic at hand, but first we have a syllabus to go over." She handed out a stack of papers that had a similar list of policies as the Modern British Literature syllabus did, condemning things like unexcused late work and plagiarism.

The workload for the course seemed comparable to that class as well, though instead of novels to read we had several documentaries to watch. I almost preferred that because at least you knew how much time it would take to consume the media before you could pen your response, whereas with a novel there was no telling how long it would take to read it. There was much less group work in this class, for which I was grateful. I doodled little flowers on the syllabus as Professor Rhodes talked, daisies, poppies, and more blooming in the margins.

"With that out of the way it is now time for you to introduce yourselves to each other. I'm sorry that I don't have a clever game for you the way some other professors do, but I don't think many of you would mind that.

"Anthropology is defined as the study of human societies and cultures and their development, so I would like each of you to come up here, tell us your name and maybe a little bit about yourself, and then let us know one piece of culture that you think is intrinsically tied to your idea of self. I will let you decide what culture means - it could be an activity, or a piece of media, or a tradition you have, anything at all that helps us see who and what you are.

"For the sake of easing into things I will first say that I am Professor Rhodes, you all know me as a professor of history here at Westwood Conservatory, and my piece of culture that defines who I am is the existence of second hand bookshops where you can see what passages were underlined and which pages were dog eared by previous owners and get a sense of who they were though you might never meet them."

At this point she looked around the room, silence settling over everything for a moment until her eyes landed on me.

"Georgie, why don't you come up and start us off?" she said, stepping to the side and gesturing for me to take her place before the class. I stood up and almost immediately had to sit back down because my knees were shaking so badly from being put on the spot. Somehow I managed to make it to the front of the room and eke out an introduction.

"Hi, I'm Georgie Miller and I, uh, just transferred here from a college in Vermont. I am part of the literature discipline and I guess for the piece of culture thing I, um…" My brain buzzed with several ideas for what to say, none of them feeling correct. The five seconds it took for me to choose something felt like a lifetime. "I would say gardening is a big part of who I am."

"You would say that?" Professor Rhodes asked, keeping her arms crossed as she leaned forward in her chair. I stared at her like a deer frozen in the headlights of an oncoming semi truck. "You would say that gardening is a big part of who you are, or you do say that?" It took me a moment to be able to clear my throat, but after what felt like half an eternity I finally responded in a voice that was way too quiet for anyone other than Professor Rhodes and the students sitting in the front row to hear.

"I- I do say that." Professor Rhodes gave a quick nod, and whether it was of approval or pity I could not tell. I rushed back to my seat, narrowly avoiding tripping over the pink and purple backpack of the girl whose seat was in front of mine, and kept my head down for the rest of the class just watching everyone else introduce themselves through a veil of my hair.

The imposing young man who was already in the classroom before Noemi and I arrived was called after me. He introduced himself as Damian Little, part of both the history and linguistics disciplines, and said that the piece of culture that defines him the most is the advancement of prosthetic technologies. At the mention of this he lifted his left pant leg to reveal that his leg was made of a sleek white metal instead of flesh and blood. Part of me wondered what caused that - whether he was born without that leg or if some sort of accident took it from him - but after seeing the stern glare on his face I knew I would never have the nerve to ask him.

Several other people came and went and I realized that my brain focused more on the cultural aspects of their introductions than their names. For example, after a few minutes and several other introductions I could still remember that the girl who sat in front of me was a huge fan of tabletop role playing games and has been playing them since her father introduced her to them as a child, I could not for the life of me recall what she called herself. I always knew I was bad at names, but this felt like a new level of incompetence.

Noemi surprised me by saying that her favorite aspect of culture was learning about other peoples' food. She traveled a lot and liked to try not only the local cuisine, but also food from her home country done in the style of wherever she was.

The girl with the green hijab went last. Her name was Ailani and she said her intrinsic piece of culture was educational systems. I suddenly felt like an idiot after hearing everyone else's answers that all I had been able to come up with was gardening. Then I felt even more stupid as I watched her take her seat next to Damian and realized they must have been the last two residents of Radcliffe House, their names finally clicking in my brain. Ahra was not kidding when she explained that Professor Decker's teaching assistants were rare to find at home; I hadn't seen either of them in the days since I moved in.

"Alright, it seems we have quite a bit of time left in this class, so I think I'd like to just ask a couple of questions to see where everyone stands in terms of knowledge. It won't matter if you get them right or wrong, just trying your best will earn you some participation points," Professor Rhodes said, clasping her hands in front of her as she stood up once more.

She went down the rows, thankfully starting on the window side of the room, and asked each student one or two questions related to anthropology. Most of the questions seemed easy enough, while others were about professionals or specific anthropological concepts that I had no hope of answering if she had asked me. Soon enough my turn came around.

"Georgie, can you define for me the concept of the nature versus nurture argument?" I sat there for a moment thinking. I knew I had heard that term before but could not for the life of me remember what it meant. Flashbacks from high school biology class began popping up in my mind, but that had been six years prior and no specific information was coming through.

"Nature versus nurture is, um, well, it's a concept in biology and uh," I stuttered out, mentally berating myself for acting like this. I had told myself that this was a fresh start, that I could put everything behind me and start new at Westwood, but evidently my anxiety hadn't gotten the memo.

"Why don't you start off by defining the two words and see if that sparks anything?" Professor Rhodes suggested. Before I could answer her a comment from the other side of the room startled me enough to make me drop my pen onto the floor.

"Hearing her stutter through nonsense is actual torture, just move on like you did with all the other students who weren't smart enough to answer their questions!" The snide remark came from Damian. I stared in disbelief, feeling the sting of his words as a pain in my chest. At this, Professor Rhodes grew stern and spoke in a serious voice barely containing her irritation.

"Mr. Little, you would do well to remember that you are in my class right now. Professor Decker may give you free rein to do as you please but I am not him and you do not get to tell me how I run my class." Her voice was evenly held and not particularly loud, yet there was an edge to it that scared me more than Damian's brutish demeanor had despite not being directed at me. Without being able to help myself I burst into tears from the stress of it all, everyone turning to look in my direction at this new commotion.

Not thinking about possible consequences, I grabbed my bag from the floor and my notebook from the desk and ran out of the room. This time I did actually trip over the bag belonging to the girl in front of me but I managed to catch myself from falling just in time. I didn't look back as I left the classroom, nor when I left the building. I picked a random direction and just went with it, moving forward until the ache in my chest from running and crying at the same time made it impossible for me to breathe.

At that point I stopped and all but collapsed onto a nearby bench. It took me a moment but eventually the tears cleared up enough that I was able to see someone walking up the path towards me, and not just any someone, but Ollie. Relief flooded through me as I took in his familiar and friendly face.

"Georgie? Oh my god, what's wrong?" he asked, rushing over to me. I took a moment to wipe the tears off my face before answering.

"I, uh, had a tough time in class. I had to get out of there." I wiped at my face, hoping that he wouldn't be able to see the extent of my crying. I knew I was pushing at my skin too hard and that my cheeks would be redder for it, but I couldn't bring myself to care. Ollie gave me a knowing look and offered to take me somewhere to calm down, which I gladly accepted.

We walked for about fifteen minutes in silence until we arrived at a large greenhouse. By this time my broken breathing had quieted down into the occasional hiccup, but shame still burned on my face. Ollie opened up a side door and led me into the building, the sweet smell starting to calm me down. I turned to face my friend.

"How did you know this would help me?" He shrugged, not meeting my eyes as he rocked slightly on his feet.

"I didn't really, this is just where I go when things start feeling like too much. I just hoped that feeling of safety that I get from being surrounded by nature would transfer over to you," he explained. I couldn't help but smile.

"Well, it certainly does make me feel safe to be here. Thank you." I walked down the path, admiring the myriad of greenery before me. Already I was starting to feel much better just from the company of a caring friend and some beautiful plants. Looking around the room I recognized a lot of plants from my childhood but even more that I hadn't seen before except maybe in books or photos. I made a mental note to come back here whenever I could. "I love gardening. I used to help my mother with her flowers and vegetables when I was a little girl."

"Gardening is one of my favorite things, too. Do you not help your mother with it anymore?" Ollie asked. I shook my head and swallowed hard to keep the tears from starting back up.

"No, she uh, died. When I was seven. I tried to get my father and brother into gardening after that, but neither of them were as interested in it as I was so our garden just kind of fell to being unkempt," I explained.

Ollie apologized immediately for bringing it up but I assured him it was fine. He switched the topic of conversation, telling me about his favorite plants in the greenhouse. I took a deep breath, still somewhat shaky from my crying session, and let the plants around me calm my nerves so I could focus for once on something other than how badly I was messing everything up.

Chapter Eight

"Spatula," River said with the conviction of a soap opera surgeon.

"Spatula," I repeated, handing over the utensil. They decided that tonight would be the night they tried out a new risotto recipe they found online, something special in honor of us all surviving our first few days of classes for the year. At first they had been hesitant, worried that Noemi would judge the result now that it was known how much of a foodie she was, but she assured them that she would love to try their cooking.

A whole special night had been planned - after eating dinner, Noemi wanted to show off the new piece she had been practicing on her violin, and then the five of us would pile onto the couches to watch movies together. We had a variety of them picked out, from a Regency romance to a sci-fi adventure to a Korean horror flick Ahra had been dying to check out. We all knew that we'd be staying up much too late to watch them all, but it seemed like I wasn't the only one who had had a bad time in class that day if Ahra and River's complaints had been anything to go off of, so something nice was needed on all of our parts.

As River stirred the ingredients in the pan, I took a moment to check my phone and was surprised to find a notification for an email. I clicked open the app, not expecting to see a message from Professor Decker so late in the evening.

> Hello Georgie, sorry for the late hour but I wanted to let you know that you've officially been switched out of your math class and into Stage Combat. I look forward to seeing you in class tomorrow, and I'm hoping that you'll enjoy it as much as you seemed to enjoy Modern Brit Lit. Let me know if you have any questions, I'm always just an email away.
>
> -Prof. Adrian Decker

I reread the email again as relief flooded over me from realizing I wouldn't have to look at the quadratic formula for at least another semester. I typed out a quick, generic thanks but hesitated sending it off because it felt too formulaic and unemotional to me and I didn't want to give off that vibe to him. I added a line about how I love literature but didn't know much about stage combat or theater in general, so while I hoped so too I could not say for sure how much I'd enjoy the topic, though with him as the professor there was a good chance I'd like the class.

Clicking send, I returned my attention to River and their risotto. They assured me it was almost ready and sent me off to join the others at the table. As I settled into my seat between Noemi and Ollie, who were attempting to prove to Ahra that pineapples really do grow from the ground and not from a tree, my phone dinged again letting me know that Professor Decker had already gotten back to me.

> You may not know anything about stage combat yet, but I assure you by the end of the semester you'll want to join the theater discipline. I teach several other courses as well, and would love to see you in them.
> Who's your favorite author? You seem like the kind of person who'd be interested in the classics, so if I had to guess I'd place you as a fan of the Regency era, or maybe the later Gothic novels. It might be a little cliché, but *Frankenstein* is my

favorite novel. If you've somehow never read it, I'd love for you to borrow my copy. Just let me know.

-Prof. Adrian Decker

I hadn't realized I had started smiling until River made a comment about it.

"Who are you texting, Georgie? Meet a cute boy already? Is he asking to take you on a date?" they teased. Ahra rolled her eyes and cut in before I could answer.

"You know, for someone who's gay and nonbinary, you sure are shoving Georgie into a heteronormative box. She could be setting up a date with a girl, or a nonbinary person," she said.

"Oh please, this school is not that large and I know every nonbinary person who's out on campus, even the three first years who just started here. They're all either in a relationship, not looking for one, or Georgie is so not their type," River stated matter-of-factly.

"I'm not setting up a date with anyone," I said, suddenly self conscious and all too aware of the heat rushing to my face. "That's not really something I'm into. Professor Decker just emailed me letting me know he had switched me into his anthropology course, that's all."

"You were smiling like that because you got added to a new

class?" Noemi asked. There was no judgment, only genuine confusion.

"No, I guess I was smiling at the fact that he was able to guess my favorite book genre even though he barely knows me. I've never had a professor who actually cared to get to know me at all," I explained.

"That's... interesting," Ahra replied, clearly not knowing how to keep this conversation going.

"It's probably just because you're new to the school, we don't get transfers like that," River said with a little bit of snark in their voice.

"So I've heard," I replied, my good mood a bit soured. Of course that was the only reason Professor Decker cared - I was a change to the regular pattern of the school, and the fact that I was a whole person beyond that was of little consequence.

"River, this food looks amazing!" Ollie said, forcing a little too much enthusiasm. Still, their interjection seemed to break the weird tension that had settled and the five of us were able to get back into the happy mood of friends having a lovely night together, though my mind kept flickering back to the thought that people were only interested in me because I was an anomaly here.

Chapter Nine

My toes felt cramped in my sneakers. I bounced up and down on them a few times to try and alleviate the feeling while I waited for class to start, the motion knocking out some of the nervous energy that was worming its way through my system.

"Alright everyone, we're not going to get into anything too intensive today, just some stretching while we talk about expectations for the class," Professor Decker said, finally ready to start class.

Stage Combat was not held in a regular classroom, but rather one of the larger, more open rooms in Adwell Hall. It was strange seeing the professor wearing a pair of sweatpants and a T-shirt rather than slacks and a button down, but somehow he still managed to look scholarly and dignified. In comparison, I felt uncomfortable in my yoga pants and crewneck;

I never felt ready to leave the house in this kind of clothing, preferring to wear jeans and a nice shirt at the very least. Still, I knew that I'd be able to move better in less restrictive clothing.

I was surprised to see Vincent in this class thinking that his wheelchair would be too restrictive for this sort of physical activity, then even more surprised to see him get out of the wheelchair and lower himself onto the floor like the rest of us. I turned away, face flushed with embarrassment for judging him when I knew nothing about his situation. Luckily I was in the back of the room far from Vincent or anyone else for that matter. Besides the two of us, Clara, and Lourdes, there were six other students.

As Professor Decker led us through various stretches he also explained what the class would be like. Most of the course grade would be based on participating in class with a final performance at the end of the semester worth twenty percent of our grade.

Even though that was months away I already felt my heart pounding at the thought of it. I willed myself to calm down and reminded myself that I had nothing to worry about. River and I had talked that morning about my class because they were in the theater discipline. When I expressed my worry about performing they told me to just pretend that I was playing a character who didn't have anxiety. It sounded silly, but I repeated that sentiment to myself over and over again throughout my day, and it almost seemed to be working. Obviously I still had spikes of worry and anxiety, but I was able to push the thoughts aside to deal with at a later time.

After stretching, Professor Decker had us close our eyes and go through a series of motions to test our sense of self in our spatial awareness - stretching out our arms before touching our noses among other things. I felt silly, but figured that everyone else probably felt similarly as well.

"Now I'm going to pair you up. We're not going to do any actual fighting motions just yet, but you will have to work with each other quite closely in this course and I'd like to get you used to that sooner rather than later. Let's have Mara with Vincent, Todd with Eugene, Akasha with Lourdes, Irene with Parker, and Clara with Georgie."

My mind flashed back to the rough manner in which Clara had acted during her stage fighting with Lourdes that day I walked in on the two of them, but rather than worry about the potential of her actually hurting me I made myself think that it was a good thing to work with someone that had more experience than I did.

"Can't I work with Lourdes?" Clara complained, not even sparing a glance in my direction.

"I'd like those of you who I know have experience with stage combat to partner up with other people. That way we can all share our knowledge, okay?" Professor Decker responded, giving Clara a pointed look.

What the professor had us do felt strange; Clara and I stood with the toes of our shoes touching each other and then crossed our arms to hold each others' hands - right hand in right hand and left hand in left hand forming an X between us. I hoped mine weren't too sweaty from nerves. Hers were smooth and solid. We both slowly leaned backwards, having to trust that the other would stand strong to hold each other up. On the first attempt I freaked out and let myself fall back, letting out an undignified squeak as I went down. With an eye roll Clara hauled me back up and did not let me fall again.

"So, um, you've got experience with this sort of stuff?" I asked, my breath coming out in a huff. Professor Decker wanted us to try and hold the position for as long as we could and though my legs were burning from the angle they were held at, I didn't want to be the first to admit defeat. Rather than just stare at Clara awkwardly, I figured a bit of conversation would be nice.

"I've been doing various theater programs since I was six years old," Clara responded. There was nothing in her voice that indicated she was trying to show off how much better she was than those of us without the experience, just the stoic nature of someone stating a fact.

"That's... amazing," I said, wondering what it would be like to watch someone with that much experience perform. "Why are you taking this class then? Isn't it a beginner level?" I panicked for a second thinking that somehow despite Professor Decker's description I had gotten myself into a class way above my skill level. Distracted by my thoughts my hand started to slip out of Clara's, but she yanked me forward and held on tighter, almost too tight, in order to keep me from falling.

"I've been taking other theater courses here the past three years. This is just the first time this specific one has fit into my schedule." A determined look settled onto her face and I realized she probably didn't want to talk anymore.

By the end of class I was a hot and sweaty mess despite not having to do much in the way of actual exercise. I felt my clothes sticking to me and in my rush to get back to Radcliffe House to shower I failed to notice my phone had slipped out of my pocket. I only realized when I was halfway down the hall; luckily I hadn't made it out of the building yet.

My phone had fallen right outside of the classroom and to my relief the soft carpet of the hallway kept the screen from breaking. As I turned to put it into the side pocket of my backpack I caught a glimpse of four people still in the classroom - Professor Decker, Clara, Lourdes, and Vincent. It made sense that the professor would want to spend time with his teaching assistants.

Much to my surprise, Clara suddenly let out a laugh, smiling wide and leaning on Lourdes's shoulder for a moment. It felt strange seeing her look so happy when every encounter I'd had with her made her seem like her default emotions were anger and stoicism. I must have just caught her at off times.

I left the building, the image of the four of them together stuck in my mind. I wondered what it would be like to have that sort of close knit group, not only with peers but someone older and wiser who could help you because they had already been through all of the struggles you were having.

My mind started to transpose a memory of my father making me laugh over the image of Decker making Clara laugh and I had to fight back tears almost instantaneously. I tried not to think about my father too often because it always resulted in me crying, but I couldn't help myself as I remembered how easily he had always been able to make me laugh.

Chapter Ten

AHRA'S EYES FLICKED BACK and forth from the cards in her hand to the rest of us sitting around the table as she considered her next move. "Three fours," she finally said, placing her cards face down onto the stack in the middle of the table.

"That is complete bullshit Ahra, Ollie put down two fours last round," River asserted with a pointed look.

Ahra said nothing; she merely smirked and flipped over the three cards she had placed down - the four of hearts, four of diamonds, and four of spades.

"But that means-" River started, glancing incredulously in Ollie's direction. Ollie avoided River's eyes but had a devious grin on his face, which Noemi laughed at until she snorted. River just grumbled something about a 'lying best friend' and being 'tricked into picking up the whole deck' while the rest of us joked at their expense.

"Oh come on River, it's just a game," Noemi said. She tried to console them with a gentle touch on their shoulder, but they jerked away.

"Yeah, well, it's a game that I'm sick of losing," they snapped. "Seriously guys, you've all won at least one round each, even though Noemi had never even heard of it before tonight, and I've just come out on the bottom every time!"

"Okay, well, I think that's enough of that for now," Ahra said in a tone of voice that reminded me of when my brother gently reprimanded his children.

"What are we going to do now? It's still pouring outside," Noemi pointed out.

I turned to look out the window just in time for a bolt of lightning to flash outside, illuminating the sky enough that for just a split second I could make out in perfect detail the old oak tree that grew beside Radcliffe House. I couldn't help but flinch, Ollie doing the same beside me. In that second I thought that I could almost make out the shape of a person standing beside the tree, but even in the daylight I had thought the trunk looked strangely human shaped so I chalked it up to my imagination and a trick of the unreliable light. All the same, I felt a shiver of anxiety run through me as I tried to shake off the thought of being watched.

"Well, the cable is still out. Do we have any other card games to play?" Ollie asked, placing the useless television remote onto the coffee table. Upon hearing that suggestion, River stopped their trek to the kitchen for an after dinner snack and whipped their head around.

"Oh hell no, no more card games!" they pleaded. A silence lulled between the five of us for a few minutes while we contemplated what to do. It was only 8:30 on a Saturday, far too early for any of us to go to bed yet. At the same time, there wasn't much of a reason to stay up seeing as the rain had kept us inside all day and we'd basically exhausted all of our entertainment options.

"Why don't we cut Georgie's hair?" Ahra asked suddenly. My eyes immediately shot over to look at her, expecting her to follow up with a 'just kidding' or something along those lines. Instead, the look on her face let me know that her suggestion was made with 100% sincerity.

"Oh my goodness, yes! Georgie, you would look so cute with shorter hair! Maybe a little past your shoulders?" Noemi added. She reached over and stopped her hand just short of touching my hair, but when I didn't make any move to stop her she began to try running her fingers through my textured curls. They weren't the tight ringlets that Ahra had or the coily corkscrews that Ollie kept such good care of, but my hair still grew out thick and the curls liked to bunch together enough that more than one comb had been broken by my stubborn locks throughout the years.

"I was thinking a bob like yours would look nice," Ahra explained. "Obviously it would be longer if she straightened her hair, but I think it would frame her face nicely if her curly length was the same as your wavy length."

"I'll go get my scissors!" River said around a granola bar that was hanging halfway out of their mouth, already bounding up the stairs before I could respond.

"Wait a minute, it's my hair. Don't I get a say in what happens to it?" I countered. Ahra and Noemi both looked at me pleadingly, as if they were children trying to convince their parents to buy them ice cream before dinner. I turned to see if Ollie would back me up, but he was busying himself with reheating leftover lasagna that we had made the night before and didn't even seem to register the conversation going on.

"It is your hair, and if you say no then obviously we're not going to do this, but I really do think you'll look adorable with your hair this short," Ahra implored. "And what better time for a new look than the start of the school year?" Noemi nodded along enthusiastically. I looked at her and tried to imagine myself with my hair that short while twirling the ends of it with my fingers, but it just seemed strange in my mind. All my life my hair length had been kept around the bottom of my shoulder blades. Now, however, it was even longer than that and came to rest at the bottom of my rib cage. I nervously tucked a bit of it behind my ear as I thought about their suggestion.

"Come on Georgie, not to sound rude, but you have a serious issue with dead ends. When was the last time you got a haircut?" River asked, making their way back into the living room with a pair of fancy looking silver scissors and two different combs in one hand and a towel in the other.

"Honestly, it's been a couple of years," I admitted. "I used to cut it every year right before my birthday, but I stopped doing that after I graduated high school, so just about four years?"

"Oh you definitely have to let us do this then," River exclaimed in an overly dramatic voice. "Four years is so long to go without even so much as a maintenance trim!" I thought it over for a minute while the three of them continued to try and convince me. Eventually I conceded to their points. At Ollie's request, Ahra led us all into her room so we wouldn't be cutting any hair where the loose ends might end up in someone's food. He then sat down at the dining room table to eat his lasagna in peace.

"What are those flags for?" Noemi asked while River set me up on a chair with the towel over my shoulders to catch any stray clippings.

"That one is the flag of South Korea, where my mom is from," Ahra explained, pointing to one with the red and blue circle and black lines. The other had three vertical stripes -

green on the left, yellow in the middle, and red on the right - with a green star on the yellow stripe. "And that one is the flag of Senegal, where my dad is from. I've had them ever since I was a little girl because I wanted to feel connected to my heritage."

"Oh that's so sweet!" Noemi said. The two of them sat on Ahra's bed and began to trade snippets of stories from all of the places they had been. Even if I hadn't been distracted by the craziness that was letting River cut my hair, I couldn't have contributed much to the conversation; I had never left the country and before moving to live with my brother, I had never even left the east coast.

"Alright Georgie, I'm gonna tie your hair into two pigtails to cut the majority of it and then it's just a matter of making sure it's even," River explained. "Are you ready?" I nodded though I was unsure if that was the truth. River did exactly as they said they would and put my hair into two low pigtails with the actual hair ties resting just below my shoulders. "Do you want to cut the first one off?" they asked, catching me completely off guard. "When I cut my super long hair short the hairdresser let me do the first snip. I found it to be super helpful with the adjustment process because it was like taking the activity into my own hands."

"Uh, sure." Everything was happening so quickly that I probably would have said yes to anything they suggested.

River handed me the scissors and recommended I cut below

the hair tie so I wouldn't accidentally take off too much. With the scissors in one hand and a clump of hair in the other I took a deep breath to try and calm my nerves regarding the situation. Before I could overthink and stop myself I took the scissors to my hair and cut off a large, lopsided chunk. My immediate reaction was to gasp and drop it unceremoniously into the trash can, making my friends laugh. River took the scissors out of my hand and told me they were proud of me with a pat on the top of my head before continuing with cutting my hair.

"So when is your birthday, Georgie?" Ollie asked from the doorway after swallowing a mouthful of lasagna. "You mentioned before that you usually cut your hair around that time."

I looked over at him out of the corner of my eye, careful not to move too much so that River wouldn't chastise me for making their job harder. "It's the end of this month. September thirtieth." Noemi instantly let out an excited squeal.

"Mine is the first of October! We have to celebrate together!" she exclaimed.

"Those are coming up so soon, we totally have to do something special for you guys," Ahra agreed. I was tempted to hide my face because I was certain it was turning a particularly interesting shade of red at the moment, but River was still working on making my hair even and I didn't want to mess them up.

"We could have a little party down by the amphitheater, it's not like anyone goes near it anymore since the theater department stopped putting on shows out there," River suggested. Ahra loved the idea, and she and River spent the rest of the time my hair was being cut discussing their ideas for the 'little party' with Ollie and Noemi throwing in their thoughts every now and then. I stayed quiet, having never planned a party before.

"It has to be at midnight so we can celebrate from Georgie's birthday into mine," Noemi said, and with that the plans were solidified. Luckily my birthday landed on a Friday so we wouldn't have to worry about having classes the next day.

"Alright, what do you think?" River asked as they shoved a hand mirror in front of my face. I took it from them in order to get a better look at my reflection.

At first I was tempted to think I hated it, but I knew that was just because it was different and I wasn't used to it yet. If I had seen this haircut on someone else I would have thought it was cute, so I tried to convince myself that the same was true of it on me. After a good long moment of looking at myself and hearing my friends compliment me, I turned to River and thanked them.

"All in a day's work," they said, a satisfied smirk on their face as they cleaned up the hair that had missed the trash can. Noemi and Ahra cooed over my new look, and Noemi even took a seat after me to let River trim her grown-out bangs. The night rolled on with a buzz of excitement in the air as the party planning continued, the storm that kept us locked inside forgotten completely.

Chapter Eleven

Despite Ahra's groaning and grumbling, I felt a surge of excitement course through me when we stepped foot in the library. Libraries had always felt safe to me, though Ahra clearly did not feel the same. The only reason she agreed to come with me was because it was too humid to stay in Radcliffe House any longer. The library had central air, so I had reserved a private room for the two of us to do work in.

As I sat down to get started on my Hebrew assignment for the week I moved to pull my hair out of my face, forgetting that it was short enough that it wouldn't stay tucked behind my ears for long. It had been almost a week since my haircut and I still hadn't completely grown used to it. I made a mental note about asking Noemi if I could borrow a few of her hair clips when I next saw her before settling into my work.

"Did you hear River and Vincent's fight last night?" Ahra said, breaking the silence only a few minutes in.

"No, I didn't," I responded plainly, still focusing on the poems I had to translate.

"It was the same as always, one of them getting jealous of the other one hanging out with other people and then arguing that they weren't even a couple anyway. This time around it was River hanging out with Ambrose, this third year that they had a little fling with last year while they were really on the outs with Vincent, and boy did Vinny not like that at all."

"Uh huh."

"I wish the two of them would just admit to each other and themselves that they don't want their relationship to just be a casual one anymore. They're both so stubborn, and River still isn't over the fact that Deck—"

"Ahra, please, can I just get through this poem? I've got like, twelve of them due by midnight and I can't focus on them with you talking so much," I interrupted, exasperated.

"Sorry," she mumbled, half annoyed and half embarrassed.

"How about this? I'll set a timer on my phone for like half an hour for us to do work, and when it's up we can take a break to chat. Does that sound good?" She nodded.

I managed to get through two poems before the timer went off, startling both of us as we had been focusing so intently on our work. I looked over at Ahra, who was working on a practice exam for her anatomy class.

"Alright, so what is this about Vincent and River and their relationship problems?" I asked.

Ahra shrugged. "It's not really more than what I told you. River was hanging out with their ex, I suspect it was to make Vincent jealous but you know they'd never admit to that. I can't believe you didn't hear their argument, they were in the kitchen yelling as loud as if they were on opposite sides of campus."

"Maybe the sound just didn't carry up to my room," I suggested. "The floors and ceilings are pretty thick."

"Yeah, that's fair. Hey, when's your next meeting with Professor Rhodes? Didn't you say she emailed you again about setting one up at a time different than when you usually meet?"

I sighed before answering. "It's set for next Tuesday, so four days from now. I really don't get why we have to keep meeting every week like this, I feel like I never have anything new to say to her, and she always asks too many questions."

"I hate professors like that, like can't I just come to you when I need help with something? Luckily my advisor isn't like that, we only meet up two or three times each semester," Ahra responded.

"Yeah." We both sat in silence, unsure of what to say next. "How about we do another thirty minutes of work? Is that alright with you?"

Ahra let out an over dramatic sigh. "I guess," she said with a smirk to let me know she was just playing around.

We went on like that for a few hours, setting aside blocks of time to work and chatting in between. I managed to get my poems translated while Ahra continued studying for her anatomy test.

"Ah shit, Ollie and River asked about dinner like, two hours ago. Looks like we're on our own for food tonight," Ahra said, checking her phone as we packed up our stuff.

"The café is closed by now, isn't it? Why don't we just go to the Scullery for dinner? I don't really feel like cooking anything," I said. I had only been to the main dining hall on campus once before when I spent too long at the greenhouse and didn't have the time to cook like I had planned to do that day.

"Only first years go to the Scullery," she protested, but ultimately agreed to go.

It was still hot and muggy outside, but with the sun slowly setting the air was definitely cooling down fast. I shivered as a particularly cool breeze worked its way through my light jacket. A strange shape lurked in the corner of my eye, only a glimpse of it visible through my hair that fell into my face yet again. When I turned to get a better look, nothing seemed to be there anymore.

"What are you looking at?" Ahra asked, following my line of

sight and not seeing anything either.

"Nothing, I just thought I saw something weird, but it must have been my imagination," I answered. We resumed our walk.

"Maybe it was a ghost." Her voice was serious, but when I looked at her she was smiling.

"You don't honestly believe in ghosts, do you?"

"Not really, but on a campus like this with such history you can't help but admit that it definitely feels like something is there sometimes," she admitted. "My roommate from first year, Laura, became obsessed with the stories after we had our own little encounter. That's the only reason why I know practically every ghost story there is," Ahra said. I turned to face her.

"What do you mean, your own encounter? You saw a ghost?" I questioned incredulously.

"Well, no, but the two of us have no explanation for what happened except for it being a ghost." She paused and I had to gesture for her to continue speaking. "Basically we both went to sleep the same as usual, but in the middle of the night we woke up pretty much at the same time for no reason whatsoever. Our window, which we had closed because it was December, was wide open, and when she moved to close it Laura saw two new polaroids taped to her photo wall, one of each of us sleeping from that night. Neither of us were hurt, but it was so creepy."

"Are you sure it wasn't one of your friends just playing a prank on you?" I suggested. "I mean, why would a ghost do any of that?" Ahra shook her head.

"We kept our door locked at night and we were the only two with keys, except for the head of housing who I doubt would have done it. Besides, if it was a friend then they would have owned up to it, right? Well, everyone we told was just as confused and weirded out by it as we were."

"I see." A sudden breeze came by and I rubbed my arms to get rid of the goosebumps that had sprouted out. Whether they were from the breeze or the thought of ghosts I couldn't say.

By then the Scullery was in sight and without saying anything, the two of us walked a little bit faster to get there a little bit sooner. Though neither of us could say with conviction that we believed in ghosts, I don't think either of us would want to be caught outside in the dark should they prove to be real, either.

Chapter Twelve

THE FIRST DAY OF autumn came on a warm breeze that felt more like early July than late September, but I still couldn't help the buzz of excitement that always came with the advent of my favorite season. I tried to slow myself down when packing up my things after Modern British Literature ended, but part of me was too eager to rush out of the classroom. Ollie, River, Ahra, Noemi, and I had made plans to have a picnic on the lakeside for lunch and I was eager to try the apple pie River and Noemi had baked especially for it - the two of them had gone to pick the apples fresh over the weekend.

My hands fumbled as if they had too much energy than they knew how to handle, and I ended up launching my copy of *Mrs. Dalloway* a foot or so away from me in an attempt to get it into my bag. I leaned out of my chair to grab it but before I could another hand picked it up and held it out to me. I looked up to see Professor Decker, a playful smile on his face like he was trying not to laugh.

"If you don't like the book, Georgie, you can bring that up in class," he joked. I let out a chuckle and nervously played with the lock of hair that had become untucked from behind my ear.

"I actually really like it," I said. "I'm just a little anxious to get out of here"

"Oh? Any special plans?" he asked.

"My friends and I are going to have a picnic to celebrate the start of autumn."

"Sounds like a good time. I had hoped that you would come with me to my office for a moment as I have something I want to ask you, but if it's not a good time we can schedule something later." Something in his eyes made it seem like he really wanted to meet now, and I didn't want to disappoint him.

I looked over at Noemi and River, who were waiting for me by the classroom door. River had a strange look on their face, something a little sour, but the two of them still assured me that I could go and meet up when the meeting was done.

I watched my feet self-consciously as we travelled; I hadn't been walked anywhere by a teacher since my freshman year of high school when my nose had started to bleed in the middle of Spanish class and I had no idea where the nurse's office was. Professor Decker made a few comments as we walked over to Castle Blackscar, but for the most part we walked in silence enjoying the clear weather. My mind flashed back to my first day on campus when I found myself looking up through the cracked open door and making eye contact with him. I wondered briefly if he remembered that encounter but then quickly shook my head of the thought.

When we made it finally there I was surprised to see all of his teaching assistants already assembled there. Clara and Lourdes must have known that this meeting was going to happen and headed over quickly as I hadn't seen them on our walk over. It was my first time seeing the five of them - Clara, Lourdes, Ailani, Damian, and Vincent - all together. Despite living in the same house as them, they tended to make themselves scarce, always either out studying or running errands for the professor when they weren't locked up in their tower.

"Thank you all for meeting at such short notice. If you would all please come in, I have a proposition I'd like to make," Professor Decker explained as he unlocked his office door. Everyone else filed into the room before me, all sporting confused looks that I'm sure matched my own. At first I lingered in the doorway, unsure if I belonged, but I had to step fully into the office when Professor Decker asked if I could shut the door behind me.

The office was definitely not meant to hold seven people at once, especially when one used a wheelchair. Because of the crowding, I found myself practically on top of Damian, though I did my best to push further into the bookshelf on my other side than into him. His usual angry scowl was ever so slightly softened by a look of curiosity.

Professor Decker sat behind his desk and waited in silence for everyone else to settle into the space that was left for us in his office. Considering all of the walls except for the far one were covered in overflowing bookshelves and his large desk took up most of the floor, it took a little maneuvering until we were all comfortable.

Ailani and Lourdes stood closest to Professor Decker and were almost right on top of his desk on the left side with Clara taking a similar position on the right, Vincent and Damian took opposite corners, and I was left to stand in front of the door. There were two chairs that I assumed were meant for students to sit in during meetings, but not only were there too many of us for them to be of much use, but they were also covered in piles of books that would not fit onto the cramped shelves.

"So, as I'm sure most of you are aware by now, Ms. Lucas is going to be studying abroad next semester, so her place as my teaching assistant for Travel Literature will need to be filled. I know several of you have been vying for that position as it is one of my most popular early year courses, and believe me, I have spent a good, long while thinking over who I would like to take Ailani's place," Professor Decker began. He looked like he was going to say more, but before another word could leave his mouth he was interrupted by another voice.

"What is she doing here, then?" Clara said, her voice bursting out loudly. "You're not actually thinking of taking her on as a TA, are you? She may be some special case transferring here, but she's still only been here for a month," she asserted. Professor Decker took the interruption in stride and responded calmly.

"Actually, Ms. Williams, that is exactly what I've been thinking. Ms. Miller may have only been at Westwood for a short period of time, but I think she is every bit as intelligent and capable as the five of you, and I guarantee that had she been here from the very beginning, she would have been in the same pool of candidates that I chose the five of you from."

"Are you kidding me, Adrian? You know I've wanted to TA for that class since day one! You're just going to give it to some random nobody who you barely know?" Damian roared. I flinched at the sudden increase in volume and hostility.

"Oh, give it a rest, Damian," Vincent groaned.

"Mr. Little, you seem to have forgotten your place with me. Make sure it doesn't happen again. I am still your professor and your superior," Professor Decker responded. His voice had an edge to it like he was barely able to contain the annoyance and anger he was feeling towards Damian.

Damian huffed, clearly upset, but said no more. At first it seemed as though he would stand there quietly for the rest of the meeting, a big change in his demeanor, but after a moment he turned and stormed out of the room. I had to practically dive out of the way to keep out of his path and I was sure the door was going to come off its hinges from the force he used to throw it open. Luckily that wasn't the case. Clara put a hand on Professor Decker's desk to draw his attention back to her.

"I understand why you would want to give this opportunity to someone who might not have the chance at something like this again, but really Adrian, I think you should give this to one of us who have been working with you for a while now. You know that one of us could handle two courses. There has to be another professor willing to give her a teaching assistant position if she's really up to the task." Clara's voice had a surprisingly similar tone to Professor Decker's - on the surface it was calm and level, but there was an edge to it that showed just how upset by this situation she really was.

"Ms. Williams, I will not have you stand here and question my decisions like this. I value your opinion, which is why you have the position you have with me, but telling me what I can and cannot do is crossing a line. You and Mr. Little are acting more like spoiled children and not the respectable academics you should be." Clara let out a dissatisfied 'hmph' but stepped back from the desk and kept her mouth shut.

"Professor, if you'd like I could take Georgie to get coffee or something and we could discuss what would be expected of her as your teaching assistant. Then she could make a more informed decision about whether or not this is something she wishes to pursue," Ailani said. She and Lourdes shared a quick glance.

"That sounds like a lovely idea, Ms. Lucas, but I believe Ms. Miller has plans," Professor Decker said. "Perhaps she would like for you to walk her to her next destination, however." Both he and Ailani looked at me and I quickly nodded, unsure of how to respond to this unexpected turn of events.

"I'm sorry about Damian and Clara," Ailani said once we were no longer within earshot of Professor Decker's office.

I waved my hand in a gesture that was supposed to be easy going, but felt more stiff. I immediately dropped my arm back to my side. "You have nothing to apologize for. This was probably a big shock to them, you all seem like such a tight knit group that adding me to the mix would be strange."

"I promise they're not that bad all the time," Ailani assured. "Well, Damian can get angry pretty easily, but he has a sweet side. And Clara just doesn't like being one-upped by anybody, so it was nothing personal towards you."

As we walked together Ailani told me about her experience

being Professor Decker's teaching assistant for the last few years, how she was invited to work with him during her second semester at Westwood and the duties she's had in the position, though she seemed distracted as she spoke. Something was on her mind but I didn't have the nerve to ask her what it was.

"It's not that big of a deal as people make it out to be. Decker is well respected in his fields of study, which is why working with him is so sought after compared to working with other professors. Putting his name on your resume looks great, and if you have a personal letter of recommendation from him you're guaranteed to get into any English or theater program of your choosing, or it'll land you a job through one of the countless connections he has."

The conversation trailed off, so I asked a question that had been on my mind since the meeting. "I understand Clara being upset at an outsider like me being invited into your group, but why was Damian so mad? He seemed upset specifically because of this course being the one in question."

"Damian came to Westwood specifically for Decker. He's been idolizing the man ever since his father went to school here with him. Travel Literature was the course where Decker and Damian's father first met, so it's a point of pride, I guess. Damian and I also took the course our first semester here.It's where we got to know the professor. We get along well enough now, but part of me still thinks he holds a grudge against me for getting this class when he wanted it so badly." I nodded; I may not have known Damian for very long but based on what I did know, that seemed like the sort of grudge he would hold.

"So, do you think I should take the position? Wouldn't it be better to just let Damian have it? Then I wouldn't put myself further onto his bad side." Ailani gave me a lingering look like she was sizing me up against something in her head.

"I can't make that decision for you, Georgie. Give yourself some time to really think over the choice, and feel free to ask me any more questions you have." I nodded and thanked her for her company.

I paused as I approached the edge of Vauxhall Lake, watching my friends on the shore, eating and drinking and laughing along with each other. Then I turned to see Ailani already heading back to Castle Blackscar and Professor Decker.

Chapter Thirteen

I arrived at Professor Rhodes's office for our meeting while she was still out. The sign on the door said that she would be in a meeting until 3:00, which gave me about five minutes plus however long it took her to walk back to her office. I decided that time would be well spent indulging in my newest favorite pastime, wandering the halls to look at the art.

Whereas Professor Decker's office was in a hallway containing art inspired by Greek mythology, this one felt distinctly Asian. I couldn't tell if the art was narrowed down to a specific country, I assumed it was, but I made a mental note to ask Professor Decker about it later figuring that he would know. Most of them were nature scenes depicting mountains, oceans, and cherry blossom trees, but at one place I came across a pair of stunning portraits that sat on either side of a stairwell.

On the left panel stood a tall woman in a purple outfit, golden crown, and traditional Japanese makeup. She was attended by three servants: a monstrous red cyclops with a head that seemed much too large for its body and a single horn, a withered old crone with a tongue extending out of her mouth like that of a lizard, and a little bearded girl carrying the severed head of a man on a golden stand. The right panel portrayed a woman creeping down a set of wooden stairs. She wore a many layered yellow kimono with blue trim and a red pair of pants. A wicked look was held in her yellow eyes that peeked over her fan as a host of bats spiraled around her.

Though there was nothing immediately connecting the two pieces other than the style and where they were placed in the hallway, something about seeing the two of them together stuck with me. I made a mental note to look into them further when I had a chance.

Glancing at my watch, I cursed inwardly and walked as quickly as I could have without running back to Professor Rhodes's office. I had lost track of time, but luckily I arrived just as she was unlocking her door. I hoped she couldn't see how labored my breathing had become when I returned her smile.

I was barely seated in the now familiar green chair in her office before she started in on the questions while she unpacked her bag.

"So Georgie, how has everything been going? Anything new to talk about?"

I was going to give my usual mumbled reply that no, there was nothing new going on, but then I remembered what had happened earlier in the week. "Actually, Professor Decker has offered me a position on his team of teaching assistants."

At this Professor Rhodes paused while moving some notebooks around on her desk and looked up at me, one eyebrow quirked questioningly. Her eyes told me that she wanted to hear more about this.

"One of his teaching assistants, Ailani Lucas, is going abroad next semester and Professor Decker asked if I would want to take over being the teaching assistant for Travel Literature while she's gone," I explained. She nodded knowingly.

"I take it from the way you're talking about it that you haven't yet accepted the offer." Professor Rhodes moved her bag to the floor and finally sat in her chair, giving me her undivided attention. I chafed under her strong gaze.

"Professor Decker and Ailani both encouraged me to think about it for a little while, but I think I'm going to accept. After all, it's not every day this sort of opportunity comes along."

"And what about next year when Ms. Lucas comes back? Will you be expected to step down from the position?" the professor asked. A silence filled the room as I contemplated her question, something I hadn't thought of before.

"I'm not sure," I answered quietly. "It didn't seem like that was the case, but Professor Decker hasn't said anything of the contrary either." Another thing to add to my mental list of things to ask him about.

Professor Rhodes cleared her throat. "Well, on another topic, I received an email from your brother this morning."

My head shot up from looking at my lap. "What did he want?"

"He's concerned about you, Georgie. He says you don't answer his texts half the time, and when you do respond you push away his questions and don't tell him much about what is going on in your life."

"And what did you tell him?" I asked with a grimace. It couldn't have been anything good.

"That you act the same way in meetings, keeping to yourself when asked even the most simple of questions." There was no judgment in her voice, but I felt my cheeks flush in shame. "Then I asked if he'd be interested in sitting in on one of our meetings. Virtually, of course. I wouldn't ask him to come all the way out here unless it was absolutely necessary."

"No!" I called out instinctively. "No, that's... that's okay, he doesn't have to go out of his way to do that. I know he's busy."

"He cares about you, Georgie. I know that he's more than willing to make time for you," she assured. I shook my head.

"He shouldn't have to. I can take care of myself."

"Very well, I'll let him know that we don't all need to meet right away."

"Thank you," I said, breathing a sigh of relief.

We chatted idly for a few moments longer, but once it was clear that we had nothing more to discuss I wished Professor Rhodes a good rest of her day and was on my way. Too late I thought of asking if I could start having these meetings with Professor Decker instead. Ollie had told me that he changed academic advisors three times before finding someone he was comfortable meeting with, so I didn't see why I couldn't do the same. That would be the third thing added to my list of things to ask him. Hopefully he wouldn't grow annoyed by my questions.

Chapter Fourteen

My birthday arrived with the changing color of the leaves, but despite the beauty of the day it didn't feel like anything special. Even the promise of a celebration later that day didn't excite me, though I hoped as the day went on my anticipation would grow. Truth be told, it stopped feeling like my birthday was any different from a regular day after my mother died. She had always been the one organizing the parties and baking the cakes, so after her death the day became less 'let's take a day to celebrate you' and more 'here's your present now go play with it' from my dad.

Ollie had surprised the whole of Radcliffe House, or at least those of us who were friends, by making breakfast for us all, waffles with fresh fruit and several different types of syrup. My stack had a candle sticking out of it for me to blow out, but besides that one moment of cliche birthday celebration the day went on feeling like any other. After breakfast I spent some time in the greenhouse looking after the flowers and then went to Stage Combat class.

Once class was over, Professor Decker surprised me by wishing me a happy birthday and giving me a copy of *Paradise Lost* by John Milton, explaining that he had received it as a birthday present when he was my age and thought he might pass it on for me to enjoy. All of his teaching assistants received gifts from him for their birthday each year, and though I hadn't officially accepted the position it seemed like I was being pulled into their ranks regardless.

Before leaving I remembered to ask him the questions I had on my mind. He did in fact know more about the art in each hallway and informed me that the one I was enquiring about was filled with only Japanese art, even knowing specifically the paintings I had seen by the stairwell. The two women were kame hime and osakabe hime. The answer to the question raised by Professor Rhodes was simply that we - himself, Ailani, and myself - would discuss it together when the time came. I kept my third question to myself.

I had a few hours to kill before the birthday celebration with my friends, so I sat on the couch and flipped through the book Professor Decker had given me, surprised to find that it was annotated. Certain passages were highlighted while others were underlined; there were notes in the margins of most pages ranging from insightful little quips to full anecdotes of moments from Professor Decker's life that the lines reminded him of. At least I assumed they were the professor's notes; for all I knew they could be from the person who had given this book to him all those years earlier. Something about the notes made me believe they were from him, however, like maybe they were put there just for me to read, though I knew the probability of that was slim to none. Still, I enjoyed exploring this secret insight into the previous owner's mind until the sun began to set and it was time to go.

River had a bag that looked suspiciously heavy and Ahra brought her backpack, but the rest of us didn't bring much out of our normal day to day items as we trekked through the woods on the northwestern side of campus towards the mystery location. Noemi had her purse and its usual contents, Ollie had his camera stored in its protective case, and I had my cell phone and a tube of chapstick in my pocket. I didn't know what we would be getting into tonight, so I didn't think to bring anything else.

We arrived at the old amphitheater in the woods around 10pm. The moon hung bright in the sky and provided decent lighting in the area, but Ahra pulled out half a dozen battery operated lanterns and hung them from a couple of nearby trees to brighten up the area. The amphitheater was a dirty gray color; most likely it had started out a creamy marble but after years of use and then further years of disuse it had been left as we found it. Several trees had grown from the edges of the foundation and one had even burst its way through the middle of the amphitheater itself. The reclamation of the space by nature made the scene more grand than it otherwise would have been.

"Are you guys sure we're allowed to be here?" I asked, nervously playing with the hem of my shirt. I was worried that a member of Westwood's safety team would find us here and we'd all get in trouble.

"Well, it's not off limits if that's what you're asking. We're not exactly encouraged to hang out here, but we won't get in trouble for it," Ahra assured. She busied herself setting up a speaker at the base of a tree out of which came unfamiliar music. I nodded, still a little uneasy about my thoughts but trying to get into the party mood.

River brought out several bottles of alcohol, which I guessed was what made the bag they were carrying so heavy. Noemi went to grab a bottle of cider and River jokingly pulled it away from her.

"Hey there missy, you're not 21 yet, you have to wait until after midnight to drink," they quipped. Noemi rolled her eyes but had a wide grin on her face. She reached for the bottle again, but River kept it just out of her reach.

"Come on River, the legal drinking age is 18 in Italy, so I think it's fine if I have some now," she countered. River pretended to contemplate this for a minute before handing the bottle over to her.

"Fair point. Here you go, drink responsibly," they said, making all of us laugh.

Ollie then reached into the backpack Ahra had carried over and pulled out two plastic packages of lightly squished cupcakes. One had vanilla cakes and the other chocolate, but both packages had red, orange, and yellow autumnal colored icing.

"I wanted to get a real cake, but I figured this would be less messy to deal with out here," he explained.

I grabbed a vanilla cupcake with yellow icing as well as a bottle of sangria and sat on one of the stone benches that would have held the audience had the amphitheater still been open for performances. The five of us sat there eating, drinking, and laughing for a while. At one point Ahra tried to teach us some trendy dance to one of the songs that played, but River was the only one of us that came remotely close to getting it. Noemi tried her best, but Ollie and I were hopeless, which made us the laughing stock. Then River pulled out a deck of tarot cards and offered to do readings.

"Birthday girl first, Georgie!" they exclaimed, pulling me over to the bench where they had set all of their stuff up. "You're next, Noemi! Don't go anywhere!" She giggled in response.

River's set up looked quite professional to my unfamiliar eyes. A dark blue cloth was spread across the middle of the bench. It was just long enough that it missed brushing the ground by barely an inch on either side. At the center of the silver-threaded design was an interlocking sun and moon, and radiating out from that were twelve lines forming twelve spaces that held strange images. Due to the dim lighting and the way the cloth was falling over the sides of the bench I didn't realize at first what the images were, but after a moment of looking I realized they were the zodiac constellations. The star pattern was there with an illustrated version of what they represented overlaying that. Directly in front of me was my sign, the scales of Libra.

"Okay so here is how I like to do this. I will shuffle the cards and then hand you the full deck. I want you to pull any three cards from anywhere in the deck and place them down between us," River explained. "I do read with reversals, so I will read them with the orientation they have with you."

I nodded, glad that I understood what they were saying. I never got into tarot cards myself, but an acquaintance from high school knew a lot about them and told all of our friend group some basic knowledge about the reading process even if none of the rest of us bothered to learn the card meanings.

Our three other friends gathered around us to watch as River pulled the large deck of cards from a dark blue pouch that had a matching sun and moon design to the cloth. They spent a few minutes shuffling overhand before switching and doing a riffle shuffle seven times. I could not help but be amazed; my fingers were never coordinated to attempt that shuffle with a regular deck of cards let alone one that was bigger and had more cards. There always seemed to be a few sneaky cards that liked to get away from the bunch. After they were done shuffling they handed me the deck and told me to pick out the cards that called out to me without looking at what was on them.

I held the cards close to my chest and even closed my eyes for a bit of dramatic effect, running my thumb down the side of the stack a couple of times. After a moment I pulled three cards out at random and placed them down in front of me, handing River back the rest. They put them back in the pouch they came from before turning back to the ones I had chosen. Pointing to them each in turn, from the one on my left to the one in the middle to the one on my right, they explained what each card meant.

"This one represents your past and the things that might be holding you back from true growth, this one represents your present and the opportunities or challenges that are currently presented to you, and this one represents your future or things you need to keep in mind as you move forward. Are you ready to see the cards?" they asked, looking me dead in the eyes. I nodded and they turned the first card over.

The card representing my past showed a figure in a cloak facing away from the viewer and standing at a river. There were two upright goblets to the figure's right and three overturned ones to their left, showing spilled wine and water.

"This is the five of cups. In its upright position it represents disappointment, loss, grief, and pity. It shows that you have clearly been through more than your fair share of upsetting and life changing events and because of that you feel stuck as to where you can go from there. You don't want to move on from them because you're afraid that doing so will mean forgetting about what they mean to you, but the cards are trying to tell you that acceptance and finding peace with your grief are the path to healing."

I was stunned into silence, not expecting the results of this to be so hard hitting, especially not something so accurate to the truth. My mind flashed through several prominent memories - my father bringing me to the hospital when I was seven and seeing my brother's unconscious body being led to the surgery room, later being told that my mother had passed from the same accident that hurt my brother, my father's much more recent passing from heart disease not even a year earlier. Neither River nor the others seemed to notice my stunned discomfort and I wasn't about to bring it up, so the reading carried on.

The second card showed an old man sitting on a throne. He had a crown on his head and in one hand he held a staff while in the other he held a golden orb. The title at the bottom of the card read "The Emperor".

"This card represents authority, control, structure, and masculine energy. There is something going on in your life right now that wants to provide these things for you, to give you that support you might be lacking. If it was reversed I would read it as the cards warning you against giving into that, but since it is upright I'd say the opportunity is something you should look into but stay cautious about."

River flipped over the last card right away. It showed three figures - one standing upright holding a set of scales and two on their knees seemingly begging him for something. There were six golden discs with stars on them floating above the figures. This was the only card to be facing River rather than myself.

"Okay, so the six of pentacles reversed for your future. Not going to lie, that's kind of a tough one. It represents gifts with strings attached, selfishness, and domination. I'd read this as a warning to look closely at any opportunities that may seem too good to be true, because if they feel that way then they probably are too good to be true," River explained. "Do you have any questions or anything you want me to clarify?" they asked. I shook my head and without a word moved out of the way for Noemi to take my place.

I tried to pay attention to her reading, if only because I found River's explanations to be interesting, but thoughts of my family just kept swimming through my head. Noemi seemed much more pleased with her results than I had been with mine, a cheerful smile gracing her face as she moved off the bench and let Ahra take a seat. Before River could even begin to shuffle the cards again a shrill alarm went off from inside Ollie's pocket, making us all jump a little. He rushed to pull his phone out of his pocket and turn the sound off before turning sheepishly to the rest of us.

"It's midnight now, so, happy birthday, Noemi," he said. We all laughed and sang happy birthday to Noemi. Our collective voices were significantly more slurred than they had been only hours before when the song had been sung for me.

"Thanks, you guys." Noemi said with a big smile. "I'm going to find some place to use the bathroom. I don't think Orin Hall is too far from here, and there's bound to be a first year who will let me in." I offered to go with her so she wouldn't be stumbling alone in the dark, but she turned on the flashlight on her phone and said she'd be fine before making her way off into the trees towards the rest of campus.

Ten minutes passed with the rest of us still fooling around with River's tarot cards, drinking more alcohol, and eating cupcakes. Then fifteen minutes passed, then twenty. When the time on my phone read thirty five minutes past midnight I stood up and announced I was going to see what was up with Noemi. The rest of our friends agreed that she should have been back already and we decided to all walk in slightly different areas in the direction she left, thinking she might have just gotten confused by the monotony of trees.

The longer I walked in the woods the more I began to think that was the case. Once we were out of sight of the lanterns, there was nothing to distinguish what was ahead from what was behind. There was still enough daylight when we had walked over that I hadn't realized just how creepy the woods would be at night. I kept my phone light facing straight ahead of me in my left hand, my right touching each tree as I passed by, partially to keep myself heading in a straight line and partially because I didn't trust my inebriated self to be able to catch myself if I tripped over a root or something.

I walked for what felt like hours but was only about twenty minutes according to the time on my screen when I stepped on a spongy item too strangely textured to be a lump of dirt. Thinking it to be the remains of a dead animal I gagged a little before steeling myself and cautiously turning my phone to shine the light on it.

What was revealed before me was not a dead squirrel or possum, but rather a human arm. There was a smudged footprint of dirt on the forearm where I had accidentally stepped on it and my eyes followed the path it made leading back to a body. The shoulder was bent at an unusual angle, as were both of the legs. I fought back another gag as I convinced myself to look at the face. With my vision swimming from both the alcohol and the horror of the situation it took me a minute to accept the truth of what I was seeing - the face that seemed to be smashed up and covered in blood and dirt belonged to Noemi.

I let out a scream from deep inside my gut, letting it tear up my throat as the sound escaped into the night around me. Then the terror took over and I slapped my hands over my mouth, worried that whatever had done this to Noemi might now be coming for me. Still, terror rooted me to the spot and I was forced to stare at the awful scene in front of me as burning bile rose in my throat. I turned so as to not vomit on the body of my potentially dead friend and came face to face with Ollie and River.

"What is it? What's wrong?" River asked. With a shaking finger I pointed behind me, unable to put any words to the situation. Ahra was not far behind them and pulled my trembling body to her own as River and Ollie stepped closer to Noemi.

"Oh my god," Ollie said before his words were taken over by retching sounds.

Rubbing her one hand down my back while cradling my head against her shoulder with the other, Ahra whispered simple calming phrases in an attempt to quiet my sobbing. I steeled myself in an attempt to avoid a panic attack and focused all of my attention on her voice, noting the slight tremble to it as she undoubtedly tried to keep herself from crying as well. I couldn't tell which of us was shaking harder as we stood in the night cradling each other.

Part Two

October

October is the treasurer of the year,
And all the months pay bounty to her store;
The fields and orchards still their tribute bear,
And fill her brimming coffers more and more.
But she, with youthful lavishness,
Spends all her wealth in gaudy dress,
And decks herself in garments bold
Of scarlet, purple, red, and gold.

—— Paul Laurence Dunbar, "October"

Chapter Fifteen

I VAGUELY REGISTERED THE weight of a shock blanket being settled over my shoulders as I stood with my friends at the edge of the trees. The cold air made my skin feel as numb as my emotions after my body was drained of the adrenaline and panic of finding Noemi.

Another police officer approached us, calling out for me and requesting that I repeat my statement to him. The sound of Ahra telling him off buzzed in my ears over the rushing of blood as I stared at the trampled grass in front of us. Just moments prior, Noemi had been carted off on a stretcher and loaded into the ambulance that would bring her to the hospital, leaving campus by way of the service road that provided the only access to the grounds for a vehicle. The relief I had felt when the paramedic announced that Noemi was still alive for now, that she had a pulse however weak, was quickly doused when they insisted on getting her out of there as quickly as possible because she was in critical condition.

The lights of the ambulance had been blinding against the backdrop of the black night sky. River absentmindedly mentioned it being the devil's hour, around 3:00 in the morning. Bitterly, I thought that there couldn't be a more perfect time for something like this to be happening.

"Excuse me, could I please talk to the four of you for a moment?" a voice I hadn't heard before asked. I turned towards this new voice and was met with the visage of a man who looked to be in his forties wearing a grey suit that made him stand out amidst the police and paramedics.

"We've already told our story a dozen times, we're not repeating ourselves again," Ahra insisted, stepping forward. The man held his hands up as if in surrender.

"I'm not here to ask you your story, Miss Ndiaye. My name is James Hansen, and I am an assistant to the President of Westwood Conservatory," he said, wiping the sweat off his forehead and balding hairline with a handkerchief. "I would just like to speak with you so we all come to the same understanding about how things will be going forward regarding this... situation."

"Situation? You mean our friend nearly getting murdered?" River half shouted. Whereas Ollie and I had almost shut down from the overwhelming nature of things, River and Ahra seemed to channel their emotions directly into anger. The man took a step back before answering.

"What happened to Miss Caruso is heartbreaking, truly, and I wish her a speedy recovery, but as a member of the conservatory's administration there are some things that need to be discussed involving how you go about speaking of this event to any other people who may ask you about it. For the time being, we would appreciate it if the story you told was that Noemi was attacked by a wild animal, like a bear or bobcat. That seems to be what the case is at this point in time."

"I don't know what you were looking at, Mr. Hansen, but we all saw Noemi's body lying there on the ground," Ahra responded. "An animal attack wouldn't result in her looking like that. Her limbs were bent at all the wrong angles, and there were cuts all across her body like someone slashed at her with a knife. She had to have been attacked by a person. What if there's a crazy killer hiding somewhere on campus getting ready to attack more people? Everyone deserves to know about it," she insisted.

"With all due respect, Miss Ndiaye, we simply don't know what happened here tonight. Until we find out the specifics, the conservatory administration believes it would be best to keep any frightening rumors at bay. Our Public Safety department will be launching an investigation immediately and will make an announcement to the whole of the school once we are sure of the truth." All throughout his statements he looked squarely at the four of us, but during the end of his last sentence he refused to meet any of our eyes.

"Why aren't you letting the police handle the investigation?" I questioned. Even my voice sounded dull, like it too was exhausted by what had happened. Mr. Hansen cleared his throat and pulled at his tie as if to loosen it.

"Westwood Conservatory values its privacy, Miss Miller. When the four of you accepted your spots in this school you all signed agreements stating you'd follow the instructions of school administrators should anything outside of normal circumstances occur. Well, I am a school administrator, this is an occurrence outside of normal circumstances, and your instructions are to remain quiet about whatever theories you have about the situation and instead only share the officially approved story until we conclude our investigation. If you'll excuse me, I have other matters to attend to regarding what has happened tonight."

Without another word, James Hansen turned and began walking back in the direction of campus proper, leaving Ahra, Ollie, River, and I amidst the police and paramedics who remained. The lights from their cars and drowned out all of the stars above.

Chapter Sixteen

One week had passed since the ill-fated birthday celebration. One week of excused absences from classes for the four of us who were there, one week of no updates about Noemi for the sake of her family's privacy, one week of staring at the ceiling as the events of the night replayed themselves over and over in my head. They were there when I fell asleep and they were there when I woke. I tried reading books and watching movies, going for walks and working on assignments, but nothing could chase the image of what I thought was Noemi's corpse from my brain.

I struggled to keep my eyes open. If they closed I would fall asleep and things were always worse when I was asleep. As I felt my eyelashes flutter closed on my sob swollen cheeks I forced myself to get out of bed. The cool wooden floor against my bare feet served as a sort of wake up call and I felt more awake than I had in days despite it being well past sunset.

A notification blinked on my phone - Ahra had asked me to come down for dinner hours ago and I never noticed. Even if I had seen the message, I probably wouldn't have gone down. I scrolled through my other notifications - a few texts from various friends, a couple of emails from Professor Decker and Professor Rhodes, a missed call from my brother Eli. He had probably heard about what had happened from Professor Rhodes. It was late here, but he was three time zones behind on the other side of the country so I figured it wouldn't be too bad if I called him back. He picked up on the third ring.

"Georgie? Shouldn't you be sleeping?" was his greeting.

"I should, but... I want to go home, Eli," I admitted, my voice breaking on the word home. I rocked back and forth on my feet as I spoke. "I just keep thinking about how it could have been any one of us getting hurt in the woods that night, and I'm just so scared."

"You're safe now, Georgie. They said it was some wild animal, and it can't get you while you're in your room."

"That's not what I mean."

Eli sighed. "I mean, I guess you could visit me out here for a little bit, but then you'd fall behind on your classes and you know you can't drop out of another school this year. It's best just to wait for the holidays and then you'll be here for a month," he responded. "If you need me, I could probably swing a few days off work and come see you." His voice was soft and comforting, but I knew he didn't understand how I was feeling. How could he?

"No Eli, I want to go *home* home. Back to Vermont. With dad." He let out another sigh, one that was equal parts pity and frustration.

"You know that's not possible, and thinking about it won't change that. Dad is gone. It's just you and me now."

"I know," I replied, my voice quieter than I meant. "I keep dreaming about it."

"Dreaming about it? What do you mean?"

"I mean I go to bed and I close my eyes and I see it all playing out again - the fall, the ambulance, the doctors reassuring me that he'd be fine and then him not being fine. It's not just that though. It's seeing Noemi's body just lying there in the woods and then watching the paramedics take her away, it's seeing her hooked up to all of those machines the way I imagine she is at the hospital. It's also you. And mom." More words rushed to the forefront of my mind, but I knew he wouldn't want to hear them. He didn't need someone else to bring up one of the worst things that's ever happened to him.

"I see." There was a long pause. "Have you tried talking to someone? A professional, I mean?" he asked. I thought about lying to him, saying that I've talked to one every day, but where would that get me?

"Once. I talked to her the day after it happened." Noemi's birthday. "She said I could come by her office whenever I wanted, but I haven't been able to work up the nerve. I'm going to go soon, though. I promise."

"You should go. I know the stuff people say about therapy, but it really does help. Now get to bed, sleep deprivation isn't going to help anybody." He sounded tired.

"You're the one who called me first," I countered. "I was just returning the call."

"I called four hours ago, Georgie. Now it's late enough that I should be getting to bed. If you want to talk more, give me a call after four my time tomorrow. I'll be done working then and we can figure out a time for me to visit."

I assured him that him coming here was unnecessary, and that if I needed him I'd call, so we said our goodbyes and he hung up. I continued to stand there with my feet pressed into the cold wood floor, hoping it would keep me from getting lost in my mind again. As distanced and clinical as the conversation had felt, just hearing Eli's voice did bring me some comfort. With it gone, there was nothing to keep the bad thoughts away.

Chapter Seventeen

AFTER DAYS OF HOLING myself up inside, Radcliffe House was beginning to feel more like a prison than a home. I needed a change of pace and a walk felt like the easiest option. River always preached the importance of looking good so that you could feel good and while I wasn't totally convinced of the correlation, I had to admit that I couldn't go out in the pajamas that I'd practically been living in for three days straight.

I took my time getting ready, washing my hair and using my favorite shower gel that smelled like oranges. It was the kind of shower I reserved for the mornings where I needed the most waking up, but it worked just as well in the afternoon. I put on a comfortable pair of jeans and my mother's black sweater. The bright sun and lack of clouds in the sky meant it was a little too warm out for it, but I needed the comforting familiarity.

I hesitated for a moment before leaving, wondering if maybe I should bring some of my classwork in case I decided to sit for a while and needed something to occupy my time. In the end I just grabbed my copy of Stevie Smith's poems that we were reading in Modern British Literature because it was small enough to fit in my purse.

There was a collection of picnic tables near the Galleries that I had done work at before, so I made my way to them. If by the time I got there I decided I didn't want to do work outside or there wasn't a free table, I'd continue on to the café for an early dinner.

To my surprise only one of the picnic tables was in use. There sat Ailani and Lourdes, papers scattered all across the table surface with corners held down by books and cups and phones to keep them from flying away in the wind. As I debated whether or not I should stop and say hi, the decision was taken from me as Lourdes looked up. A smile crossed her face and she excitedly waved me over.

"Georgie! What a pleasant surprise!" she called out as I approached. Ailani looked up from what she was writing just long enough to give me a little wave.

"Hi," I said awkwardly. I stood off a bit to the side, unsure of what to do until Lourdes invited me to sit down with them, scooting a bit down the bench and clearing a spot for me.

"I feel like I haven't seen you in so long, how are you doing?"

she asked.

"I'm... fine," I answered. I really did not want to talk about myself. "I've just kind of had a lot going on."

Lourdes nodded knowingly. "We heard about Noemi. How awful! Any news on how she's recovering?"

"Not really. Her family asked for privacy after coming to collect her things, so we haven't heard anything new," I explained. I hoped neither of them could tell that I was starting to feel nauseous just from thinking about everything. I let my awkwardness linger in the air for just a moment before asking what the two of them were up to.

"I'm just finishing up my paper for Anthropology, and then I've got some stuff to do for my internship at the law firm," Ailani answered.

"Are you writing the entire paper by hand?" I asked, amazed. She nodded.

"I write all my papers by hand before typing them up. It feels more authentic to me, like I can get all of my ideas out better by writing them out," she explained.

"I couldn't imagine doing all that, my hand would cramp so bad," I said. Ailani broke her focused facade with a smile while Lourdes let out a chuckle.

"I have so much planning to do for the Trans Day of Remembrance event. I'm trying to organize speakers to come, but apparently everyone and their secretary is terrible at fully responding to emails. I'm glad I got started on this early," Lourdes said in a half joking tone.

"Oh, that does sound like a lot of work," I replied. I couldn't imagine dealing with the stress of putting together such an event.

The conversation lulled, so I pulled out my book of poetry and tried to read. I was able to focus for a little bit but eventually my mind wandered to its usual horrible topics of thought. If Noemi had never been attacked, she and I would probably have been discussing Stevie Smith's poetry together.

I made the excuse of having plans to eat dinner with friends at the café and packed up what little stuff I had brought with me.

"Make sure you all walk back together if you're heading back after dark," Ailani warned. "It could be dangerous for someone like you to walk home by yourself."

"Wh- what do you mean?" I stuttered. Did she know something about what happened to Noemi that night, about what had attacked her? Ahra was still convinced that it wasn't an animal, and her theories played into my nightmares.

"You haven't heard about the recent string of sexual harassment on campus? Like, three or four girls have come forward talking about a guy following them around at night trying to get them to go home with him. Luckily they were all smart enough to get away from him as quickly as possible, but there hasn't been word about the guy being caught," Lourdes explained.

She leaned in conspiratorially before continuing in a softer voice. "Some people think he hasn't been caught because he's really a ghost." She then leaned back and let out a light laugh, as if that statement was meant to make me feel better about the situation instead of more freaked out.

I swallowed hard. "Do you think the police are going to catch him soon?" I asked. I had the sinking feeling that sexual harassment would be a new theme to my nightmares.

Ailani snorted. "As if the police would be allowed on campus to look for him. The school only lets them in when something truly bad happens, and even then they prefer to keep things internal. Adds to the mystery of the school to the outside world, you know?" This made sense considering what that one man, Mr. Hansen, had said when he visited us the night that Noemi had been attacked.

I assured the two of them that I would not walk by myself after dark and hurried my way to the café. I ordered a salad but found myself barely able to pick at it, my stomach churning at the new thoughts my mind had come up with, inspired by Lourdes and Ailani's warning, to torture me.

Chapter Eighteen

I HAD BEEN AWAKE for nearly an hour, unable to will myself into moving, but the soft knock on my bedroom door pulled me from my dark thoughts.

"Georgie? Are you awake? Is it okay if I open the door?" Ahra called. I gave a noncommittal grunt and heard the door slowly creak open. Moments later a gentle weight rested on the end of my bed. "Come on, you should get up. River and Ollie made us all pancakes and it would be a shame if yours went to waste," she said, her voice clearly trying to entice me into doing what I didn't want to do. Reluctantly, I sat up.

"What kind are they?" I asked. A smile broke out on her face.

"Come and find out," she teased. I rolled my eyes but was grateful at her attempt to get me out of bed. I picked the nearest sweater and pulled it on over my pajama shirt to fight off the cold morning air, then followed an eager Ahra down the stairs. Once we reached the first floor I was greeted by the delicious smell of chocolate and cinnamon and the warm sound of my friends laughing. It had been too long since I had heard that.

"Georgie, there you are!" River called out to me. "Come see Ollie's terrible attempt at pancake art."

In the kitchen, Ollie had his eyebrows furrowed and his tongue stuck out a bit through his teeth as he hunched over the electric griddle. On the hot surface was one large circle of pancake batter with a strange assortment of ingredients arranged strangely but neatly in it. Banana slices formed a crescent smile with blueberries as eyes and strawberry pieces as a severe blush. A heavy sprinkling of chocolate chips covered the top portion of the pancake and slightly down the sides, making me assume it was meant to be hair. Despite feeling as sour as I had been for days, the strange creature Ollie was making out of our breakfast was enough to get me to chuckle.

"Is that supposed to be a clown?" Ahra asked, voicing a thought I also had. Ollie flashed her a confused frown.

"What? No, it's Georgie," he said in complete earnestness. The rest of us could not hold in our reactions and we all laughed harder than before. River wiped tears from their eyes and told us that they had asked the same question before Ahra and I came downstairs.

"It looks wonderful, Ollie," I assured. He and River finished making the pancakes while Ahra and I set the table with plates, forks, knives, and anything we could find that we might have wanted to add to our food.

We had made it through most of breakfast talking about mostly nothing before Ahra changed the subject drastically.

"So Georgie, are you ready to go back to class tomorrow?" she asked. I paused, my fork halfway to my mouth, and put it down before answering.

"I actually haven't decided if I was going to stay at school or not," I said, letting them in on the one issue I had been trying to keep from even myself. "I'm not sure if I can handle it. I had to drop out of my last university back in February because my father passed away," I admitted, staring down at my half eaten pancake portrait. Ahra immediately looked like she regretted asking anything at all. This was why I had a tendency to keep things to myself; I couldn't stand the sadness, the well wishes, the pity that everyone wanted to push my way.

"Georgie, I'm so sorry," River said. I waved them off.

"It's okay. I mean, it's not okay, but it's fine. I'm fine. Sometimes I just don't handle things well," I said.

"You seem to be doing about as well as any of us are," Ollie chimed in.

"I mean, yeah. I am definitely doing better than I was, but still. The main reason I haven't brought up leaving is because

I know my brother would be so disappointed in me."

"I'm sure he'd understand," Ahra said.

"He'd try to. He just doesn't feel things as much as I do."

"Well, we understand you, Georgie. We know what you went through because we've gone through it, too. You stay here, and we can be your support system," River pointed out.

I contemplated for a minute but couldn't find fault with their argument. Agreeing to stay at Westwood with my friends did seem to lift a bit of the burden weighing on me, even if I wasn't totally convinced that I was making the right decision.

"Now she can help with the investigation," Ollie said.

"What investigation?" I asked.

Ahra sighed. "Well, I wasn't going to bring this up to you until you were feeling better," she paused to shoot a look at Ollie, "but we want to figure out what really happened to Noemi."

"What do you mean? That guy from administration told us that they're sure it was an attack from a wild animal. Even though they promised to look into it further they said the results wouldn't turn out any different." I had been trying to convince myself that I could believe that, but deep down I knew there was doubt. I looked at all three of my friends; all of them had a look of sad skepticism on their faces.

"You don't genuinely believe that, do you? I mean, one of us would have heard something," River said.

I tried to argue that we were drunk and far away, but that wasn't their only reasoning behind this.

"Okay, but you saw her body. The way she was left... no animal would have done that." A look crossed their face and they put down their fork, clearly not able to eat while thinking of what happened to Noemi. I mirrored the action.

To this I had no response, thinking back to what Ailani and Lourdes had told me about girls being followed around on campus by some strange man. Maybe the man had found Noemi and was able to take advantage of her in her drunken state. I brought this up and the three of them all agreed that it was a possibility.

"The higher ups like to keep things hushed up. If word got around that a student was attacked by someone on campus then the media would spread it around and ruin the school's image. They said that their private investigation didn't turn up anything supporting that idea, but we don't trust them to ever tell us the truth about it," Ahra added.

"You guys really think you'll be able to figure it out on your own, whether it was this strange guy or someone else?" I asked.

"We should at least try to figure something out," River exclaimed. "She was our friend, don't you want to know what really happened to her?"

"Of course I do, but I just don't think getting into this investigation would help me get over everything that's happened,"

I countered.

"That's fine, Georgie. You don't have to help. We just need you here with us," Ahra insisted.

"Okay." I gave my friends a weak smile, hoping that they couldn't see past it at how freaked out I really felt.

Chapter Nineteen

Somehow in the midst of all the craziness that was going on, River had convinced me to audition for the school's production of *Pygmalion* with them. All of the fourth year students in the theater discipline were required to take part in the production as a member of either the cast or crew, but the auditions were open to all students. Even though River wasn't particularly fond of the man, Professor Decker was directing the show and River knew that telling me this would help convince me to come along, even if they had a sour look on their face while they explained.

When we arrived at Clotho, the smallest of the Galleries and the place where auditions were taking place, I was surprised to see Professor Rhodes standing alongside Professor Decker on the stage. Neither of them seemed to notice me, but seeing the two of them made my self consciousness sink in that much deeper.

As we entered the room someone standing off to the side of the doorway handed me a slip of paper with the number 14 on it; River received one from someone on the opposite side and had the number 6. All in all there seemed to be maybe forty people present for the auditions. My stomach churned with anxiety but I remembered River's words about pretending I was playing a character who didn't have that problem. For some reason that trick actually managed to calm me down a bit. Once all of us were settled into the auditorium seats, the professors made their announcements to us.

"Welcome, everyone, to the auditions for this year's fourth year performance. As you are all aware, we will be putting on the classic *Pygmalion* by George Bernard Shaw and are looking for just the right people to play our Eliza, Higgins, and all the rest. Professor Young would normally be my co-director, but as they left this semester to have their baby, the lovely Professor Rhodes has volunteered to help me out," Decker stated. Even when he wasn't playing a part the professor was enchanting; everyone in the room was listening intently to what he was saying. He was a natural on the stage.

Professor Rhodes then stepped forward to explain how the auditions would run. "Each of you has been handed a piece of paper with a number on it. When your number comes up you will join the two of us on stage and read from the scene we have printed out. You may read as either Eliza or Higgins while one of us will read for the other character," she said, gesturing to herself and Professor Decker. "You may leave once your audition is over or you may stay and watch the others who come after you."

Once the auditions actually started, things seemed to rush by in a whirlwind. River read as Eliza once their turn came up which seemed to surprise several people - despite being non-binary they tended to present themself in a more masculine way, so people must have assumed they would read as Higgins. I was grateful they had chosen Eliza, as I was unfamiliar with the play and seeing how they and the others who went before me portrayed her gave me an inkling on how I should perform the lines. I kept repeating to myself over and over that Eliza did not have anxiety and therefore I could not show mine on stage.

Vincent auditioned just before me and did a wonderful job. Truly I was a bit scared to follow up such a great read, but I forced myself to push that feeling down. The professors talked in quiet voices for a minute after Vincent's audition and the longer I waited for number 14 to be called the harder it was for me to hold onto the calm facade I had built. I reached over to grab River's hand for moral support but right at that moment Vincent rolled by in his wheelchair and River gave me a rushed apology before following him out of the auditorium. I didn't have time to worry about being left alone because it was then that I was called to the stage.

The moment I stepped onto the stage it was as if my body had gone on autopilot; I remember both of the professors being pleasantly surprised to see me auditioning before gesturing for me to start the scene. It was as if the people there to audition weren't even there and I was talking to myself in my bedroom, that's how easily the words flowed out of my mouth. Once I thanked the professors for their time and stepped off the stage, however, my anxiety flooded back in the form of nausea in the pit of my stomach and my knees turning to jelly. I walked out of the room as fast as my legs could carry me hoping some fresh air would do me good, only to interrupt an argument held in hushed tones between Vincent and River.

When the two of them noticed me standing there they stopped their conversation, though it was clear from the way they glared that the issue between them had not been resolved. Vincent went off down the hall towards the bathrooms while River picked up their bag and began to storm out of the building. I rushed over to catch up and put my hand on their shoulder, but they just shrugged me off. I didn't want to push too hard so I stopped trying to follow them and gave them space to cool off. I couldn't tell what possessed me to stay and wait for Vincent, but it felt wrong to just leave him there after witnessing what I did.

"What do you want?" he asked brusquely.

"Get dinner with me," I offered, surprising myself as much as I surprised him. He cocked an eyebrow but didn't say anything. I rushed to keep speaking in order to fill the silence. "I don't know much about what's going on between you and River—"

"You could say that again," he grumbled.

"—but it's clear that neither of you are having a good time right now. River made it very clear that they would like to be left alone right now, but that doesn't mean you want the same thing."

"Thanks, Georgie, but even if I was looking for a rebound, you are not my type," Vincent countered.

"That's not what I meant. I just want to be there as a friend."

"Are we friends?"

"I don't see why we can't be. If I take the teaching assistant position with Professor Decker then we'd be working together more, and I think being friends would make that a much more pleasant experience."

Vincent contemplated my words for a minute before responding. "Alright, fine. Meet me at the café in two hours, friend." There was a hint of sarcasm to his voice, but something in his countenance made me think he was actually grateful that someone had reached out to him like this.

I wasn't sure why I did what I did, but I couldn't back out

or I'd risk Vincent thinking I was rude. Part of me worried that River would be mad at me for doing this, but another part genuinely wanted to befriend Vincent. I pushed my worries aside for the moment and resolved to figure my issues out later. My anxiety had tired me out and I only had a little bit of time to rest before meeting with Vincent for dinner.

Chapter Twenty

THE CAFÉ WAS MUCH less crowded than I expected it to be, but then again, I had only ever been here during the lunch rush between classes and not around dinner time. Vincent was already waiting for me at a table near the entrance.

"Have you been here long?" I asked, avoiding eye contact by looking at the menu even though I knew I'd probably get one of the same few dishes I always ordered when I ate here.

Vincent shook his head. "No, I just got here maybe five minutes ago. I appreciate you not showing up late. It's good to know that not everyone has terrible time management skills." I knew he was talking about River but I didn't want to bad mouth my friend, so I simply nodded and took a long sip from my water.

The waitress, a student I recognized from my anthropology

class but couldn't remember the name of, wasted no time in taking our orders. Vincent ordered some type of pasta dish while I had my favorite chicken parmesan. Not many places I went to made the chicken as crispy as I liked, so finding out they made it just to my liking here was a pleasant surprise.

"So…" I said, fishing through my brain for something to say. "Are you in the theater discipline? I hadn't expected to see you at the auditions today." Only after the question was asked did I remember he was in stage combat, though he hadn't shown up to several of our recent classes. I wondered if it was because of his health; he did seem more tired than usual when I looked at him now.

"Theater and history, though if I had gone to a regular university I probably would have studied mathematics. I have too many interests to settle for just one thing," he explained. "And you? I could have sworn you were just literature, but you are in stage combat so perhaps you're in both like Lourdes and Clara?"

"No, I'm just in the literature discipline. River convinced me to audition with them, and I joined stage combat because I needed a class to replace the math one I was dropping. Not all of us are geniuses in every subject," I said with a smile. I was relieved that Vincent returned the gesture with one of his own instead of thinking I was making fun of him.

Dinner with Vincent was a lot less awkward than I expected.

It seemed like he was almost grateful for someone new to talk to. I guess with a relationship that's always on and off and a collection of friends that he really only hung out with because they worked together with Professor Decker, he must have been wanting something to do that didn't have all those strings attached. Thinking about the other teaching assistants, I steeled my nerves and decided to ask more about them. If I was going to potentially join their ranks, I didn't want to be caught off guard by anything.

"So about Clara and Damian getting upset over Professor Decker offering me the TA position for his Travel Literature class…" I started. Vincent didn't even wait for me to finish a sentence before rolling his eyes and launching into an answer.

"I promise you they're not always that annoying, but definitely more often than anyone would like. When Decker called them spoiled children the other week he refused to acknowledge that he's the reason they act like that - he's the one that spoils them. He gives them every little thing they ask for, or more like whine for, and if he didn't do that then they wouldn't get upset when he tells them no every once in a while. Honestly your best bet is to stay away from both of them as much as possible.

"Damian is a whiny man baby who uses fear and aggression to bully people into giving him his way, and let's face it, you seem to be exactly the type of person who would easily fall for his attempts. Clara on the other hand is a devious little shrew with a sour grapes complex. If she doesn't get what she wants she'll try and ruin it for everyone else. Of course they're both extremely smart, and they have their moments of being decent people, but there are a lot of extremely smart students here at Westwood who have much better manners than they do. I really don't see why Decker bothered to work with them in the beginning."

I was speechless. Clearly Vincent had been bottling up his complaints for a long while. It made sense - when they were on good terms he and River probably didn't want to talk with too much negativity, while anyone else he interacted with daily would either already understand the complaints or get angry at hearing them. Luckily I was given a moment away from the conversation when the waitress came back to ask about dessert. Vincent ordered a personal-sized chocolate lava cake and convinced me to do the same.

"What about Ailani and Lourdes? How do they fit into this whole dynamic?" I asked. "Not that I'll work too much with AIilani after this semester, seeing as I'll be taking over her spot if I accept the position," I added. It felt strange getting information on them this way, but Vincent seemed more than willing to give that information up.

"Ailani is an absolute sweetheart, and she often has to act as a mediator between the rest of the group. Honestly, she does not deserve the grief. Lourdes on the other hand is quite reserved, kind of like yourself. She has always been in Clara's shadow, and I guess standing back has been easier than standing up for herself. I've tried to convince her to not let Clara get in her way, but it's her life and if she doesn't listen to me then that's her decision. I'm glad Ailani and Lourdes have each other, everyone needs someone in this world."

"They're dating?" I asked incredulously. I hadn't picked up on that at all, though thinking back I hadn't interacted with the two of them at the same time very often.

Vincent nodded. "They've been together since the end of our first year here."

The conversation lulled while we ate our cakes, and when we were done I decided to push my luck a little further. I took a long sip of my drink to calm my nerves before asking another question.

"So what's up with you and River? And why does Ahra tell me you're always so rude? I mean, you were rude to her that first time we ran into you, but you've never been anything but reasonable to me," I tried to make it seem like the first question wasn't a big deal by softening the blow with a second less private one, but I could tell that it came off as me prying. Luckily Vincent didn't get upset and instead actually answered the questions, albeit with a sigh.

"Ahra is like a thorn in my side. Because of my... situation with River, she likes to think that we are friends when we definitely are not. She annoys me in the way a sibling would, and I've had many foster siblings throughout the years so I know how annoying they can be. I'm kind to you because you have been kind to me."

He paused for a moment, as if letting his brain catch up with his mouth. I didn't speak for fear of interrupting.

"As for River, we hook up sometimes, nothing more and nothing less," he stated, the slightest edge of anger in the words. "They've made it very clear that that is all our relationship is, especially as of late. They haven't said it out loud, but actions speak louder than words as the saying goes."

"But... you want it to be more," I said cautiously, aware that I was poking the hornet's nest.

He sighed heavily before responding. "Yes, I do. I know any sensible man would give up and find someone who can commit, but there's something about River that I can't leave," he admitted. I couldn't imagine why he was letting me in on all of this when we hardly knew each other, unless he really was that lonely.

"I think River is more into you than you think. At least from what I've seen, they are more dedicated to your relationship than they let on. Some people just aren't good at speaking up about what they want," I suggested. Vincent pursed his lips.

"And what about you, Georgie? Any relationship troubles

you want to get out in the open?" he asked, allowing himself a bit of a sardonic smirk.

I felt my eyes widen as I shook my head. "Oh, no. That sort of stuff, sex and dates and all that, it's just not for me. It took me a while to realize that I wasn't a late bloomer or whatever you want to call it. I'm just not into people like that." I paused, waiting for the look of confusion or the 'you just haven't met the right person' speech that I was so used to hearing whenever I told anyone about my sexuality, or more accurately, lack thereof. Instead Vincent just nodded knowingly.

"You seem like the lucky one here. What I would give to not be this lovesick loser anymore."

Our conversation faded out, which was good timing as the waitress came by to tell us they would be closing the café soon. I mentioned heading back to Radcliffe House together, but Vincent said that he was meeting up with Lourdes to do some late night studying instead. I wished him a good night and decided to take the short way around the lake back to the house, my mind on the warning to not walk home alone as I watched as one by one the stars twinkled to life above my head.

Chapter Twenty-One

Anthropology was cancelled on Wednesday due to a personal issue Professor Rhodes was dealing with. She sent out the email while I was already headed out the door to walk over to Corbyn Hall, so rather than waste the time I had spent getting ready I decided to check on the plants in the greenhouse. The day was as bright as it could have been, though a bit overcast, yet I couldn't help feeling worried as I walked alone.

My mind was still focused on the warning Lourdes and Ailani had given me; no matter how bright it was or how public the space I still found myself feeling overly aware of my surroundings and anyone who might have been a threat. I knew the feeling would probably subside, that I was only so fixated on it because it was fresh in my mind, but for now it was what drove my anxiety. At least it kept the images of

Noemi's body, broken and bloody on the ground, at bay for a little while.

The greenhouse was a literal breath of fresh air - with the concentrated smell of sweet flowers it was a world away from the blank chill of the air outside. All of the plants looked freshly taken care of. I wondered who else came here besides myself and Ollie; I had never seen anyone in the few times I was here. I silently thanked the strangers anyway.

With nothing else to do, I sat on the bench at the end of the greenhouse and closed my eyes, allowing myself to breathe the scent of the plants in deeply. I hadn't realized how stressed I had become until the weight of it all began to melt off of my shoulders.

The fact that Noemi's family refused to tell us how she was doing, Professor Rhodes and my brother's concern over the fact that I wasn't spilling each and every one of my thoughts to them, Decker's still unanswered offer to become his teaching assistant, and more - none of those things mattered for the few moments I let myself relax. It was an unfamiliar but welcome feeling to not have my constant companion anxiety churning in my stomach.

Someone had cut a few fresh bouquets of some of the flowers that were in bloom and left them by the door with a sign telling people to please take one. I did this with a smile, hoping that when I left my greenhouse sanctuary this little trimming of it would help keep me grounded.

Chapter Twenty-Two

"Georgie, can I talk to you after you're done stretching?" Professor Decker's voice snapped me out of my inattentive daze. Today's stage combat class had been rough and I had lost myself in the cool down stretch as I soothed my aching muscles. Vincent, Clara, and Lourdes lingered longer than the other students as they always did after class, but the professor waved them on so it was just the two of us in the room.

"What's up?" I asked, doing my best to act nonchalant in an attempt to distract myself from the way sweat made my clothes cling to my body. Professor Decker pushed his hair out of his face and took a drink from his bottle of water before answering. He definitely didn't push himself as hard as the students in this class, but it still amazed me how he could come out of it still looking so clean and put together.

"I just wanted to check in with you. Things have been so busy that we haven't really gotten to chat after what had happened to Noemi. I know that can't have been easy to go through," he said. He placed a heavy hand on my shoulder and gave it a comforting squeeze.

"I... I'm doing as well as I can," I answered.

It was the best I could come up with, but even that felt like a lie. Sure the nightmares had lessened marginally over the past couple of weeks and my anxiety was almost back to its usual levels - that is to say, not great but manageable - but it was almost as if Noemi's lack of presence was more noticeable than her being there would have been. I always paused by her now empty room whenever I walked by and sometimes found myself staring at the empty seat where she used to sit in Modern British Literature. I had forgotten about the poster she had given to me on the day we moved in so her family didn't take it when they retrieved her belongings; having it loom over my bed felt too much like a ghost in my room so I had to take it down and face it towards the wall. Whenever I did anything with Ahra, River, or Ollie I would wonder if she'd have tagged along with us.

"Well, at this point that's all anyone can ask of you," Professor Decker conceded with a sad sigh. He dropped his hand and his gaze at the same time and seemed to look down at our shoes for a long moment.

"I've decided that I want to take on the teaching assistant position," I blurted out, unable to handle the silence that had fallen between us. I didn't like seeing him sad and wanted to cheer him up with my news.

"Are you sure? I don't want you to make any decisions you aren't ready to commit to," he said. He cocked his head to the side, obviously surprised at my bringing up the topic, but there was also an excitement to his voice.

"I'm sure." I nodded along with my words. "If you think I'm suited for the position, then I trust you. I'm up to the challenge." I pushed down any shakiness that threatened to enter my voice and forced myself to believe what I was saying.

"That's wonderful, I'm so glad to have you joining my team," the professor beamed. "I really do think we'll be able to work well together."

I smiled, his encouragement making me feel much more sure of myself. As we both packed up our things to finally leave the stage combat classroom, he chatted about how excited he was to be working closely with me and promised that he would let the other teaching assistants know the wonderful news. I worried for a moment about how Clara and Damian might act, but pushed that thought away and reminded myself that Professor Decker would keep them under control.

Chapter Twenty-Three

The student worker behind the reference desk at the library glared at me as I slid the books I was returning over to them. "We charge late fees here, you know," they said in a monotonous, almost bored voice. "Just because the school owns the library doesn't mean it doesn't work like a normal one."

"I am so sorry, I didn't know they were late," I said, fumbling with the zipper on my bag in an attempt to pull my wallet out. "How much is the fee?"

They typed a few keystrokes into the computer before answering. "Four books, all three days late, fifteen cents a day per book, that comes out to one dollar and eighty cents. Don't bother with the change, I can just have it charged to your tuition account."

"Oh. Thank you." I let my bag drop back to my side and stood there awkwardly waiting for something, I'm not quite sure what, to happen. The student worker eyed me strangely from behind their computer and the student waiting behind me cleared their throat, so I shuffled off into the stacks without another word.

I breathed in deeply as I took careful, measured steps through the aisles. A smile subconsciously graced my lips as I took in the scent of old books, my second favorite smell after freshly cut grass. A book on the bottom shelf caught my eye; a deep emerald green surrounded by browns and greys. I crouched to get a better look at it, pulling it off the shelf and balancing it on my knee as I flipped through the old, yellowed pages.

"So then she—Georgie?" a voice from behind me said. Startled by the unexpected sound of my name I teetered on my toes for a second before managing to rise shakily to a standing position, the green book gripped in my right hand.

Ailani and Damian stood before me, both looking like they had no idea what to say in this unexpected encounter. That made three of us.

"Um, hi." Each second of silence felt like an hour. "Did Professor Decker tell you—" I started, deciding to face the elephant in the room head on.

"He did," Damian interrupted. His voice was hard, making

clear his displeasure, but not outright angry. Decker may have convinced him to get over his initial outrage over the topic of me becoming a teaching assistant, but that didn't mean he couldn't hold a grudge.

"Congrats, Georgie. Welcome to the club," Ailani joked, though the humor didn't reach her eyes. The cream colored hijab she wore only made the dark bags under her eyes more prominent. I could only imagine how much work she already had to do each day, and now I had added the extra task of showing me the ropes as the teaching assistant for Travel Literature.

"Thanks. I look forward to working with you more closely," I said, but focused on Ailani instead of looking over at Damian.

"You better take this seriously," he then said, forcing me to glance up and make eye contact with him. He wasn't too tall, probably just under six feet, but with his wide shoulders and straight posture I couldn't help but cower under his gaze.

"Wh- what?"

"I know you're some special case getting in here on special recommendation from one of the professors, but that doesn't mean you can just do whatever you want. Decker may have a soft spot for you but if you slip up even the slightest bit I promise he'll have no problem dropping you for someone he knows he can trust."

With that Damian pushed past me to continue down the aisle of bookshelves. Ailani put a hand on my arm and quietly apologized before moving on to follow him. I stayed where I was, struggling to deal with the emotions that surged up within me.

Everything Damian had said hit on the biggest insecurity I had - that I didn't belong at Westwood Conservatory. Sure I had wonderful grades from my old university and professors there had spoken highly of me, plus I had to do the same application and essay that all prospective literature discipline students had to go through, but part of me always felt like the only reason I had gotten accepted was because of Eli and Professor Rhodes. It couldn't be denied that without them I wouldn't have been able to apply here at all, but I tried to tell myself that it was my own merit that made them accept me. Some days that was easier to believe than others.

I hadn't realized I was still holding the green book in my hand until my fingers began to cramp; it was that uncomfortable sensation that pulled me from my spiral. I placed the book at the end of the row to show that someone had at least looked at it.

Standing in place, I went through one of my usual routines to calm down. I felt rusty moving from step to step - it had been a while since I had used this one, not since the night of my and Noemi's birthday celebration. I shook the thought from my head and started over, pushing aside the fact that anyone around would see me and think me strange.

Rocking slightly from my toes to my heels and back again, I closed my eyes and focused on the feeling of my lungs expanding and compressing as I slowly breathed in and out as deeply as I could. I stretched out my hands as they rested by my sides, holding my fingers spread until they started to ache before letting them drop and tapping a random rhythm against my thighs.

I don't know how much time had passed, but eventually my heart rate and thoughts were back under my control. Then, as if the whole scenario had never happened, I pushed my anxieties to the back of my mind and moved on to the next aisle to browse the books and see what caught my eye.

Chapter Twenty-Four

A KNOCK ON MY door pulled my full attention from the book I had been reading in bed.

"Yes?" I called, trying to read a few more sentences, a handful of lines, before I had to put it down. It was *The Woman in White* by Wilkie Collins and I had come across it quite by accident, finding it misplaced on a shelf of biographies where it stood out like a sore thumb. I was hooked from the first page and wanted nothing more than to continue reading.

"Can I come in?" River's voice asked, only slightly muffled by the door. I called out in agreement and continued to read as much as I could in the few moments before they stood before me.

"What's up?" I sat up from my half slouching, half lying down position and brushed the non-existent dirt off my pants.

"Do you want to go for a walk before class? I just... I need to get out of this house," they explained.

I looked over at my book for half a second before agreeing to go. I had no idea how long we'd be out, so I made sure to bring everything I would need for Modern British Literature with me.

At first it seemed as though we'd be walking in silence. Something was clearly on River's mind, evident in the way they were constantly running their hands through their hair and gnawing on their lower lip. I wondered if it had anything to do with the investigation they were doing with Ahra and Ollie into what had happened the night Noemi had been attacked. Part of the reason I had asked to remain on the periphery of the investigation is because I feared that it would set off my anxiety more than usual.

Suddenly River spun to face me, stopping us both in our tracks. "Has Vincent said anything about me to you?" they asked.

"What?" I was sure that the guilt I felt over not telling River I had had dinner with Vincent was written all over my face. Vincent must have told them though, otherwise when could he have said anything to me about River?

"You're a teaching assistant now, so I figured you'd seen him more often than usual," they explained. So Vincent hadn't mentioned our dinner either. It didn't make sense that we were keeping it a secret, it hadn't been anything close to a date, but it still felt like it would be strange for River to hear.

"Um, no, he hasn't said anything to me about you." How could I explain the ways Vincent had lamented about his relationship with River without letting it slip that he and I were becoming friends almost behind River's back? "Why, is something wrong?"

River shook their head but spoke as we resumed walking. "I feel like he's pulling away from me. We haven't gone on a date or anything in a while, and whenever I text him it's fifty-fifty as to whether or not he'll respond."

I thought my words over carefully before saying them out loud. "Maybe he just doesn't realize how you feel about him," I suggested. "Have you told him that you want to go on more dates?"

"No, but I feel like the enthusiasm I do show on our dates should show him pretty easily that he's what I want."

"Enthusiasm?"

"I don't think you want to hear about our sex life, Georgie," River said with a wry chuckle. My face immediately flushed and I was glad they couldn't see me as they walked ahead. I agreed that that was something I very much did not want to hear about.

"Maybe you should try telling him anyway. Some people like hearing things out loud instead of having to guess what people are thinking," I said. This was met with a sigh from River. Having heard both sides of the story from their own mouths, I was beginning to see why the two of them could have such relationship troubles while being so into each other.

By that point we had traversed most of the campus and wound up near Winsford Hall, so the two of us headed to class despite it being much earlier than we would normally arrive. Another professor was still using the classroom, so the two of us found an alcove down the hall to wait in, the window ledge in it just wide enough for the two of us to sit side by side.

"So…" River trailed off. I looked over at them. "How is it working with Professor Decker?" they asked. "I know it's only been a few days, but you were basically already there before you officially accepted the position."

"I mean, we haven't really done much. He wants Ailani and me to go over expectations and things more before I actually sit in on the class with the two of them. That's not going to happen until the end of the semester, probably."

"Oh. That makes sense."

Again I could tell that there was something on their mind, but I didn't want to pry and risk upsetting them. Instead I knocked my knee against theirs and hoped they understood that it meant I was here to listen whenever they were ready to talk. They returned the gesture with a smile. A silence settled over us while we waited for class.

Chapter Twenty-Five

"Georgie, thank you for coming to meet with me on such short notice," Professor Rhodes said as I entered her office. We originally planned not to have a meeting this week, but she had emailed me an hour before our usual meeting time asking me to come in after all.

"It's no problem," I answered curtly. I wasn't trying to be rude, but she could probably tell that I did not want to be there. On top of the usual issue of not having much to talk about, I was very nearly done reading *The Woman in White* and I couldn't help being a little upset at the interruption. As I settled into the chair I had come to know so well, Professor Rhodes fiddled with her computer.

"I am sorry to spring this on you seemingly out of the blue, and I know you didn't want your brother to sit in on any of our meetings, but he has brought some things to my attention that I feel like we should all address," she said before swiveling her monitor around to show my brother's face on the screen.

Every nerve ending in my body suddenly felt like it was on fire from the shock of confrontation. I thought we had agreed not to bring my brother into our meetings - why would she not mention this in her email this morning? Did she think I wouldn't have shown up had I known this was going to happen? In all honesty I probably would have tried to make an excuse not to meet, but a warning still would've been nice. All of these thoughts flashed through my mind in the ten seconds it took for me to respond vocally.

"Um, hi Eli," was the best that I could manage.

"Hello, Georgie. How has your day been today?" he asked as though he didn't already know the way this meeting would have made me panic.

"It's been alright. Why are you here?" I squeaked out.

"I was talking to your brother and mentioned that you had accepted Professor Decker's offer to be his teaching assistant, a fact I learned from Professor Decker himself, and Eli was surprised as you hadn't mentioned anything to him, either," Professor Rhodes explained.

"I guess I forgot." I tried my best not to meet her eyes.

"It seems you forget to tell me about a lot lately," Eli said. His voice wasn't accusatory, but I felt ashamed nonetheless.

"I'm sorry," I mumbled.

"Georgie, we're not here to make you feel bad. We just want to make sure everything is okay," Professor Rhodes assured. Seeing her and my brother next to each other, both sitting so calmly while the ambush set my anxiety off, angered me for reasons I couldn't quite explain. I held on to the anger as it was something different from the anxiety I knew so intimately.

"I'm fine," I insisted. "With classwork and everything I just have a lot going on. I promise to do better at keeping you updated."

"That... situation with your friend wasn't that long ago. It's okay if that's getting to you more than you want it to," Eli said.

"That 'situation' was her almost being killed, Eli. Of course I'm not over it, but this isn't like with dad. I can handle myself." I let out a hard sigh before trying to pull my emotions back in. Losing my cool would do nothing to get Eli and the professor to believe I was okay. My brother frowned a bit as if he wasn't sure how to respond.

"No one is saying that you can't handle yourself. We just want to make sure that you have a strong enough support system to help you." My mind started wandering back to when my mother had died and all of my teachers started being extra nice to me. The same hadn't happened when my father died, at 20 I had been too old to be babied, but all of a sudden I felt like I was being infantilized.

"I have my friends. They were there, they know what happened, and I've just been going to them when I need someone because they're closer," I snapped. I don't know what possessed me to speak the way I did; I never could have imagined talking to my brother or a professor like that before now. Something about the way they were treating me flipped a switch in my mind.

"I... I'm glad you have people you can reach out to," Eli said. It was obvious that he had more he wanted to say but held back on. I wasn't going to ask him to elaborate. "I'm sorry for surprising you like this."

"It's fine," I answered. "If that's all the two of you wanted, may I go now? Like I said, I am very busy, and I have a lot of things that I have to get done today." It was a lie, I had planned to spend the whole day reading and possibly working a bit on an essay for Modern British Literature, but they had no way of knowing that.

Professor Rhodes nodded. "Thank you for coming in. I'll see you next week."

Without another word I picked up my bag and stalked out of the room. I knew I should have held on to my emotions better, but I was tired of being treated like a child who had to be taken care of all the time. Instead of going back to my room to read as my original plan for after the meeting had been, I decided to walk around campus for a while to blow off steam, hoping the movement would help me push through my surging emotions.

Chapter Twenty-Six

I PULLED MY EARBUDS out, the combination of loud music and walking through the campus on such a brisk day managing to calm me down. I breathed in the scent of decaying leaves and slowly let out a sigh, letting the last bits of my anger out. I hadn't paid any attention to where I had been walking, only making sure I stayed away from both the woods where the old amphitheater sat abandoned and Radcliffe House. This led me past the Galleries and to the southeast corner of campus where I hadn't been before.

Eventually I found myself following along a wrought iron fence wrapped in ivy and morning glory plants. On the other side of it was a thick row of cypress trees that blocked me from seeing anything more than vague grey shapes. Just as I was going to turn around and start heading back the way

I came, the fence's gate came into view, above which was a sign that read 'Silent Gardens Cemetery'. A memory clicked in my mind of the day I had arrived at Westwood; Noemi and I had gone wandering around the campus and we had seen two people exit the cemetery, though that had been further up towards Radcliffe House.

Somehow in the time since then I had forgotten that it existed. I lingered at the entrance unsure of what to do, but eventually my curiosity got the better of me and I entered despite the whispers of ghost stories in the back of my mind. There was a statue off in the distance that looked like it could have been an angel, but something seemed off about it. My interest was piqued and I wanted to get a closer look.

The paths through the cemetery were just dirt instead of the paved walkways I was used to on the actual campus. The first headstone closest to the entrance had the name Michael Andrews on it and the dates revealed he had died just fifty years earlier. I wondered if he was the last person to be buried in this cemetery - a brief glance at the surrounding headstones made me think that much was true. I guessed that when the school acquired Castle Blackscar and all of its lands for the campus, the cemetery started to fall out of use by the general public. Still, the graves looked well tended to and there were even fresh flowers on a few of them, so someone had to have visited recently.

A loud rustling sound to my left caught my attention, and as I turned to look that way something small and brown came flying at my face. I let out a scream and stumbled backwards, barely catching my footing to avoid falling over a gravestone. After pausing for a second to catch my breath it became apparent that what had come flying at my face was in fact just a squirrel jumping out of a tree. It chittered angrily at me before running off towards the entrance I had come from. I let myself breathe for a few more moments, letting out a nervous chuckle to assure myself that everything was fine, before continuing towards the statue that marked my goal.

Upon arriving closer I could see that the statue was not green from plant coverage, but instead it was the mint of old copper. The large angel could have easily been twelve feet tall if it had been standing, but it was sitting on a throne with its wide wings outstretched at least five feet in each direction. Its hands reached out in front of it and it held a sword, the point down in the ground. As my eyes traveled up the statue's body I gasped, catching a glimpse of its face for the first time.

Black stains streaked down its face giving it the appearance of having cried some sort of inky tears. The eyes themselves were a solid black and I felt like it was watching me approach. I repeated to myself that it was only a statue, but I couldn't help the suspicion that if I took my eyes off of it for even a second that it would move on its own. I circled the angel slowly, but there was nothing of note on the other sides, though I did pause to marvel at the beautifully sculpted wings. When I reached the front again I noticed the name engraved on the stone beneath the angel's feet for the first time - Abigail Miller.

My mother's name.

This couldn't have been my mother's grave, my mother died and was buried in Vermont, but the exact spelling and lack of dates indicating when this Abigail Miller had lived and died sent my mind racing and my heart pounding. Suddenly it felt like I couldn't breathe.

I looked to the angel as if for help but it just glared down from its imposing height. I took a step back, then a second, then a third, eyes locked on the angel's own black gaze. My heel caught on something solid and I found myself stumbling backwards at an impossibly slow pace until I slammed on the ground, getting the air knocked out of my lungs. All I could see was the angel looming over me and all I could hear was the pounding of blood rushing through my ears. A dull pain radiated out from my shoulders. For half a second I imagined wings like the angel's growing out of my own back.

Moments of agony passed until my heartbeat had slowed down enough for the sounds of birds chirping and wind rustling the leaves to enter my ears. I dug my hands into the soft dirt below me and slowly pushed myself to a sitting position. The thing I had tripped over was the jagged edge of a headstone, which had torn my stockings just above my left ankle as I fell. My body hadn't registered the sting of it slicing my skin until I saw the trickle of blood. It was barely a cut, but the fresh redness of it sent my mind spiraling back to the night of my birthday and my vision blurred.

Somehow I managed to pull myself off the ground; I just started running. I kept my eyes on the ground enough to focus on not falling again, but everything else was gone to me. It wasn't until I reached the greenhouse that I even recognized where I was. I let myself in, grateful that no one else was there at that moment. The bench I liked to sit on was at the other end of the building, too far for my already tired legs to go, so instead I just threw myself on the ground in a heap and let myself cry. I was sure my mascara had to be running down my face, marking me the same way the angel guarding Abigail Miller's grave was marked.

Chapter Twenty-Seven

THE ROOM WAS ABUZZ when I made it to Stage Combat class. I had been worried that I was going to be late because I had gotten home the night before well past when I should have and forgot to plug in my phone. It had died in the night so I missed my alarm. Instead of doing warm up stretches like I expected, everyone in class was split into twos and threes chatting excitedly about something. My skin began to crawl as I felt everyone's eyes turn to me.

Lourdes broke away from where she was talking to Clara, who shot daggers at me with her glare, and Vincent, whose face made it hard to tell what he was thinking. She bounded over to me and threw her arms around me in a surprise hug, wishing me congratulations.

"Um, thank you," I responded while pulling myself out of

her embrace as politely as I possibly could. "What am I being congratulated on?"

Lourdes looked at me quizzically. "Didn't you see the email that Adrian sent out this morning?" It took my still half asleep brain a moment to realize that the Adrian in question was Professor Decker. It still felt strange to me that some people referred to professors by their first names.

"Oh, uh, no. I forgot to charge my phone last night and it died."

"The cast list for *Pygmalion* was sent out, you were cast as Eliza!" she squealed, clearly more excited than I was.

"That's... what? Why?" I asked, just as confused as everyone else.

"Yeah, that's what we were wondering," one of the other girls, Irene, spat.

"Obviously everyone thought it'd be Clara, and if by some miracle it wasn't then it'd be one of us," Akasha added. "Not some newbie who isn't even in the discipline."

My attention had been so focused on the two of them that I hadn't even noticed Clara stalking her way over until she started speaking.

"How did you convince him to give you the part, huh?" she asked, her voice low.

"I- I didn't do anything," I stammered. I looked frantically around the room, but it seemed like Professor Decker had been running late that day, too.

"Guys, leave her alone," Lourdes tried to protest. She was jostled away as Akasha, Irene, and Clara backed me into a corner, spewing more accusations.

As my anxiety rose, churning in the pit of my stomach, I tried to tell myself that I was playing a character who remained calm when confronted like this and that the other girls were just acting like mean girls in some high school coming of age movie. Their words and accusations all began to blend together. I thought about telling them I would pass on the role so one of them could have it, but my mouth wouldn't move.

"What's going on here?" Professor Decker's voice cut out across the room. Immediately Clara, Irene, and Akasha backed off.

"Nothing," Clara muttered, shooting me one more glare. Professor Decker looked around as if suspicious, but seeing as things broke up once he entered the room he couldn't do anything about what had happened. I did my best to look normal, not wanting to cause a scene.

"Okay, well in that case let's get this class started. Before we do, however, I would just like to mention that the cast list for *Pygmalion* went out this morning, though I'm all sure that you all know that already. I'll be hosting a Halloween dinner party for the cast and crew this Monday night and I'd love to see you all there. Costumes are encouraged, but not required."

With that, class began in earnest and we started learning how to handle fight scenes with three people. Thankfully I had been grouped with Lourdes and Parker, who was a small, quiet person that kept to themself much like I did. Lourdes made sure to situate us in a corner of the room furthest from where Irene, Akasha, and Clara worked. As we ran through the motions of the scene, Professor Decker worked his way around the room to critique all of the groups. When he came to our group, he pulled me away for a moment and let Lourdes and Parker work on their own.

"Georgie, are you alright?" he asked, hand on my shoulder.

"Of course I am, why wouldn't I be?" I responded, feigning ignorance.

"I'm not sure what I walked into when I came to class, but if you say it was nothing then I trust you." I gave a reassuring smile. "You'll be able to make it to the dinner party this weekend, right? It wouldn't make sense for the star of the show not to be there."

I nodded, not wanting to let the professor down. "Of course, though I'm not sure I have a costume." His comment about being the star of the show hit me like a punch to the gut; my eyes drifted over to Clara to see if she was paying attention, but luckily she seemed to be enthralled in her practicing. I wasn't sure if I wanted the role, if I could handle being front and center on stage like that, but the excitement in Professor

Decker's eyes kept me from voicing those concerns, at least in this moment. I could always think about it and bring my worries up later.

"Why don't you borrow something from the theater's costume department? Vincent can take you to where we store everything," Professor Decker suggested.

Not knowing how to respond to that, I just smiled and nodded again. With a smile of his own, the professor moved on to the next group and I returned to my partners. My anxiety had me believe that everyone was staring at me while my back was turned, but I convinced myself I was being foolish. Even so, I kept myself from turning around just so I wouldn't accidentally meet eyes with anyone who was upset with me for getting a role I hadn't asked for.

Chapter Twenty-Eight

"I'm amazed at how well this fits, it was like it was made for you!" River exclaimed as they laced up the back of the gown I had borrowed from the theater department's costume stock.

It was a deep blue Victorian-esque dress that probably wasn't entirely historically accurate, but that didn't bother me. Ahra pulled my hair back into an updo that seemed impossible given how short it was, but with her determination and more bobby pins than I could count, she made it work. If anyone asked what my costume was, I would tell them that I was the heroine of a Gothic novel.

River was dressed as some comic book character I'd never heard of in a skin tight green piece wrapped in fake foliage. To top off the look they even sprayed their hair red with temporary dye. They were matching with Vincent who was dressed as some other character I had never heard of, but I was glad to hear that the two were on better terms now.

"Are we all heading over together? Me, you, Vincent, and Lourdes?" I thought about adding Clara to the list as I knew with reasonable assurance that she would be attending the party, but figured she was the least likely to want to join us.

River shook their head. "He's probably over there already. Even if he wasn't so strict about arriving to everything early, him and all of Decker's other teaching assistants probably got there super early to help set up, even the ones who aren't part of the production." There was a venom to their voice that I couldn't quite place.

I suddenly felt self conscious. "Should I have gone over there early? I mean, I am one of his teaching assistants now..."

"I'm sure it's fine," River replied tersely, shutting down that conversation. I nodded quickly, trying to tell myself that it really was fine, and fidgeted with my sleeves as I waited for them to fix up their hair in the mirror. In the end it looked the same as it always did aside from the color, but I didn't say anything about that.

Professor Decker lived in a large house just off of campus that nestled itself into the woods just far enough that you couldn't see it from the road, only when walking up the driveway. It was close enough that walking from campus was no problem, but with the amount of fabric I was wearing I could feel myself starting to sweat even in the late evening air. I was glad that I decided to wear comfortable shoes instead of the heels Ahra had pushed for; Ollie had stepped up and talked some sense into her.

Stepping into the house had a totally different feeling than walking into Decker's office, though it was obvious that the two places belonged to the same man. This space was much neater and everything looked freshly wiped down, but there were still bookshelves full of tomes and trinkets along one wall and matching dark wood furniture giving the space a classic yet cozy feel. A staircase lined the left side of the room and as my eyes followed it up I couldn't help but stare in awe at the brilliant chandelier that hung down from the high ceilings.

"Miss Miller, Mx. Mercer, welcome to the party," came a voice to our right.

"Professor Rhodes, I was not expecting to see you here," I said, turning to face her. The professor was not in costume, wearing instead one of her usual suits, this one a tan color. She gave me a small smile.

"I figured as this is an event for the play, it made sense for the assistant director to make an appearance. I can't stay for dinner, however. I just popped by for a moment," she explained.

"Well, I'm glad I was able to say hi while you're here," I responded, surprised to find that I meant it. I had gotten over my anger at what happened during our last meeting, though

I was still under the belief that she shouldn't have ambushed me with my brother like that. I knew the two of them were just checking in with me, though I wished sometimes that they would back off a bit. She gave me a pleasant smile before moving on to greet a few other students.

River and I moved further into the house and I was surprised at how many people were there. Aside from the fourth years who had been cast in roles or as understudies, there were people from every year and various disciplines who had signed on as members of the crew. Some people I had seen around campus while others I'm not sure I had ever run into, and the costumes were not helping with my struggle to recognize people.

I turned to say something to River, only to find that they had spotted Vincent and ran off to his side without saying anything to me. I gave a short wave in their direction before heading the opposite way; the space had become much too crowded for my liking. A few students lingered on the second floor landing space, so I made my way up there to clearer air.

More bookshelves sat in the upper floor's hallways, though these were much less organized than their counterparts on the ground floor. Professor Decker must not have thought many of the students would wander up this way. I stopped to look at what books were up here, letting their comforting smell distract me from everything else going on. The chatter of the other party-goers became background noise as I ran my fingers along multicolored spines, surprised to find that there was very little dust on them.

"Why Georgie, I hadn't expected to find you here, though I should have guessed that you'd be wherever the books were." I nearly jumped out of my skin, turning to find Professor Decker standing behind me, a playful grin gracing his lips. He wore a fine looking suit that matched his usual demeanor but seemed to be from a much older time period. He had on a vest as well as an overcoat and a black hat with a curled brim.

"I'm sorry, professor, I didn't mean to intrude on your space," I apologized. He waved his hands dismissively.

"I don't mind, Georgie. I wouldn't have invited curious students into my home if I wasn't okay with them looking at all of my fine books." I gave a relieved laugh and returned his smile. "I see you took my advice to borrow a costume from the theater department, is there any specific character you're dressed up as tonight?" he asked, eying my gown.

I shook my head. "I figured I would go with a generic Gothic heroine," I replied.

"Ah, a Jane Eyre or a Catherine Linton, I see. It seems we've gone for similar costumes this year. I just threw together this late Victorian ensemble at the last minute."

"It's a very nice suit, professor," I complimented.

"Oh please, you don't have to do with all that 'professor'

business, especially while we're not in class. If you want, you can call me Adrian," he insisted.

"Alright, Adrian," I tried out the name. It felt so strange on my tongue, but given that his other teaching assistants almost always called him by his first name, perhaps he was expecting me to do the same.

"Perhaps tonight I'll go by the name Maxim. It seems fitting for the outfit, doesn't it?" I nodded, turning away so he wouldn't see me blush. "Well then, Mrs. de Winter, shall we make our way to dinner?" Professor Decker offered me his arm and, playing along with the charade of us being characters from *Rebecca*, I took it. It seemed as though everyone's eyes were on us as we descended the stairs.

A collection of banquet tables had been set up on the massive back patio, providing more than enough seating for everyone attending. It was an unseasonably warm night, but I wasn't going to complain about that when the stars shined so beautifully above us. Once everyone was seated, hired caterers began to bring out the most amazing looking dishes and wine that couldn't have been cheap. I began to feel like I was truly a rich woman in a Gothic novel attending a dinner party with all of her upper class friends, though the motley assortment of costumes did mar the image a bit.

Professor Decker naturally sat at the head of one table with myself on his left and Lourdes on his right. The rest of the seats were filled by Vincent and River on the same side as Lourdes, two students whom I did not recognize on the same side as me, and Clara taking up the opposite end as the professor.

As the main course of roasted turkey was put out, Professor Decker - Adrian, I had to remind myself to think of him as Adrian - excused himself for a moment. The turkey reminded me of a Thanksgiving meal and all of a sudden it felt strange to me that my father wasn't sitting in the empty chair next to me prompting everyone to list what they were grateful for like he did every time the holiday came around. I quickly shook the thought from my head as the person on my other side, Jason, I thought their name was, refilled my glass along with theirs. I did not want to focus not on the fact that this upcoming Thanksgiving would be the first without my father around.

Though everyone else buzzed with excitement and chatted about anything and everything, Clara sat quietly throughout the event, only answering a few questions when they were asked to her directly, and even then she gave much more detailed and enthusiastic responses to Professor Decker than she did anyone else. When I asked what her plans were for after graduation she waved the question off and deflected it to Lourdes, for the two apparently had similar goals, without even a glance in my direction.

Lourdes was more than happy to have the attention for a moment and I remembered Vincent's words about her living in Clara's shadow. With a wide sweep of her arm as she talked, Lourdes nearly knocked over her glass of wine before Vincent caught it with a laugh. Out of the corner of my eye I thought I saw a brief scowl cross River's face, but it was gone in a moment and I chalked it up to the alcohol messing with my perception. I decided to switch to water for the rest of the night - after I finished my already full glass of wine, of course.

Conversations switched topics and the evening passed by in a haze of alcohol and emotions. Vincent and River went to grab slices from the large cake on the display table, and Lourdes went to the bathroom, and Clara had to take a phone call. Everyone was moving so fast it was hard to keep track of who was at the table at any given moment. At one point Vincent made a sore joke at River's expense, the enchantment of the night seeming to wear off of them. Professor Decker pulled him aside to talk privately. Lourdes returned from the bathroom, tripping over the step down onto the patio and stumbling into Professor Decker, who caught her with swift and strong arms.

Then Jason arrived from the dessert table with a cupcake for me and I was distracted from the commotion. The other person at the table, Noah or Nolan or something like that, cracked a joke that had all of us at the table laughing, to my surprise Clara included. As I hunched over, holding my too full stomach, I realized how stiff my back had become from sitting still for so long. I turned in my seat to try and stretch it out, catching sight of two people standing close in the dimmed light of the foyer. They seemed familiar, but my alcohol-addled brain couldn't quite place them, so I figured they were only familiar due to being at the same party.

For a second one of them had their hand cupped around the other's face in an intimate and tender gesture, but I blinked and the moment passed. When I looked again they weren't even there anymore. Suddenly everyone was at the table once more. Professor Decker - Adrian - squeezed my shoulder reassuringly as he moved past to get to his seat and I flashed him a wide grin, grateful to have been cast in the play so that I could be here.

I caught Clara's eyes as I looked back to find my water amidst the table full of dishes, her eyes narrowed in annoyance. She drained what was left of her glass of wine and immediately poured herself another one. Professor Decker seemed to notice the tension, and so as he sat down he asked Clara to tell everyone about the internship she had been invited to partake in the next semester.

"I'm sure they all have things they would be much more interested in hearing about, especially Georgie. She probably just wants to hear more about Travel Literature. If only Ailani was here, right? Unless she's already told her everything about it, in which case why doesn't she just teach it by herself now since she's so perfect," she fussed, crossing her arms and turning away from the table. Professor Decker shot her a sharp glare. I did my best to avert my gaze to keep from provoking her more, but continued to watch the scene unfold from the corner of my eye as my heart beat faster in my chest.

"There is no need for that tone of voice. Your bad mood is ruining this for everyone else," he responded with a stern voice. Clara threw down her fork and knife.

"Well if all I'm doing is ruining everyone's night then I might as well leave!" she shouted. Before anyone could say or do anything she suddenly pushed her chair back from the table and stormed away, stomping inside and upstairs like a child throwing a tantrum. Professor Decker shot an apology to the rest of us before hurrying after her.

Those of us who remained tried our best to salvage what was left of the night, but things felt off after that moment; it was as if the absence of Clara and Professor Decker was an overbearing presence in itself at the table. Even the other tables seemed to notice that something was wrong. I mentally chastised myself, sure that I had done something to piss Clara off. About half an hour later I decided it was late enough that I should be making my way home and Lourdes insisted on escorting me, reiterating the sentiment that no one should be walking about by themselves this late at night. I turned to ask River and Vincent if they wanted to come with us, but they seemed lost in a hushed conversation and I didn't want to disturb them.

My head swam as we walked and I was sure that Lourdes felt similarly; the two of us clung to each other with each step in order to keep the other from falling over. The idea was so absurd that I couldn't help but laugh which in turn set her off, and the two of us giggled our way back to Radcliffe House.

"This was so much fun, Georgie, we definitely have to get together for another big group dinner again," Lourdes insisted. She finished the statement with a hiccup.

"I would love to," I responded. Then I remembered why the night had come to such an abrupt end. "Though maybe if Clara's there it's not the best idea," I amended. Lourdes scoffed, the rude sound feeling out of place for such a normally sweet person.

"Oh, let the queen bee pout for a night. She's just so used to being the favorite that she can't stand the thought of someone else having Adrian's attention for more than a minute. Even the rest of us are basically just competition to her, and we're supposed to be her friends," she said. I couldn't see her face in the dark but from the tone of voice I assumed she was rolling her eyes in annoyance.

"Does his attention really mean that much to her? I mean, she's already one of his teaching assistants, so it's clear that Professor Decker holds her in such high regard," I questioned.

The silent night enveloped us for a long moment.

"Clara's home life isn't the best," Lourdes answered in a quiet voice. "She told me when we were first years that her parents are super controlling. Her dad's a politician and her mother is one of the top surgeons in Philadelphia, so they've got high expectations for her and it can be really stressful. I can understand why someone would crack from the kind of pressure she's under. Not that I'm trying to make excuses for her."

I bit my lip as I tried to come up with the right response. "I didn't know that about her, I figured she was a bitch because sometimes people are just like that." It felt wrong to call her names after learning why she acted the way she did, but it was true. The rare moments that Clara was nice and happy and got along with people were few and far between, often forgotten among the times her anger and attitude got in the way.

"She was drunk when she told me. I ran into her crying one night during the Winter Festival. She had just gotten off the phone with her mom and, well, you can probably guess how that went. But you can't let her know that I told you. She made me swear myself to secrecy after explaining all of that to me and I don't want to upset her."

"Why would I bring up something that would make her hate me more?" I questioned. Then my mind latched onto something else Lourdes had mentioned. "What's the Winter

Festival?"

"It's an event that the school holds in the middle of December right before finals. A bunch of the clubs on campus set up booths with games and things that are all winter themed. The fourth year play happens the same weekend, so we'll miss part of it when we do *Pygmalion*," Lourdes explained, her voice souring at the last comment.

"That sounds like so much fun!" I exclaimed, bringing the mood back up. Lourdes giggled at my enthusiasm. At that moment I stumbled, almost bringing the two of us to the ground. In response I laughed so hard I snorted, which only made us laugh even harder at ourselves.

By this time we had arrived back at Radcliffe House and Lourdes seemed to be doing the brunt of the work getting us to the door. I began to dig through my purse for my key, pulling River's out instead.

"Oh crap, I forgot to give this back to them," I said.

Lourdes shrugged as she unlocked the front door for us. "It's alright, Vincent can let them in. Even if they did start arguing, he wouldn't leave them out there all night."

"Yeah, but Vincent doesn't have a key to our tower and the door locks when it closes. I'll just leave my shoe wedged in there so they can get in," I said, coming up with a solution to my own problem.

Wishing Lourdes a goodnight, I tiptoed my way up to the

back of the house and to the tower there, being sure to keep the door from closing all the way. Once I reached the top of the stairs I paused to catch my breath; that many stairs when I couldn't see or walk straight had certainly been a challenge. I turned for a moment to face the door to what had been Noemi's room. With the night so quiet and the door shut I could almost pretend she was in there sleeping.

Almost.

Even inebriated I couldn't forget what had happened to her and I suddenly felt upset with myself for enjoying such a wonderful night when we still hadn't heard back from her family. It almost seemed disrespectful to Noemi. If she hadn't been attacked, maybe Adrian would have seen how brilliant and talented and amazing she was and given her both the teaching assistant position and the lead in the play. She would have deserved it more than I did.

I bit my lip to keep a sob from breaking out of my throat and quickly turned to my own room. I didn't even bother to change into my pajamas. Instead I did my best to pull at the lacings of my dress so I could strip it from my slightly sweaty body and drop it unceremoniously to the floor, leaving me in just my undergarments. Then I locked my door and slipped under the covers to fall into a dreamless sleep.

Part Three

November

No sun - no moon!
No morn - no noon -
No dawn - no dusk - no proper time of day.
No warmth, no cheerfulness, no healthful ease,
No comfortable feel in any member -
No shade, no shine, no butterflies, no bees,
No fruits, no flowers, no leaves, no birds! -
November!

-Thomas Hood, "November"

Chapter Twenty-Nine

AN EAR SPLITTING SCREAM right outside my door pulled me from my slumber the next morning before the sun had even fully risen above campus. I rushed to stand up, nearly falling over as my feet tangled in my comforter, before throwing open my door. My eyes noticed River first, disheveled and still half in their costume from the night before, but then they focused on something shiny sticking out of the door between us at about chest height - a knife, pinning a piece of paper to the door. I stumbled back a step as Ahra and Ollie joined River.

"What is it? What's wrong?" Ollie asked, his voice as gentle as ever. I almost didn't hear him over the sound of the blood starting to rush through my ears.

River pointed at the knife as they answered, my shoe gripped tight in their hand. "I came up here to thank Georgie for leaving the door propped open for me, but then I saw the threat."

Threat? I took another step back, my knees folding against the edge of my bed. I dimly registered that I wasn't clothed, the morning air chilling my skin, but my heart was pounding too distractingly hard inside my chest for me to think about getting dressed.

Ahra pulled the paper down off the door and I flinched at the sound of it tearing around where the knife had punctured it. "Oh my god," she murmured before passing the note to Ollie. Her eyes lingered on me for just a second too long as she did so.

"We need to go to the police," he insisted. He, too, looked up at me after seeing whatever was on the paper.

"What is it?" I asked. I rose shakily to my feet.

"Georgie, I don't think—" River started. In a second I was back across the floor, taking the paper from them.

It was a grainy picture of myself and Noemi taken sometime when it was warm enough for the both of us to be wearing shorts and tank tops as we ate together at one of the picnic tables at the café. There was a giant red X crossing out Noemi's face and a circle around my own. In the space next to me on the page was a handwritten note - "it was supposed to be you" with the last word underlined twice.

I felt my breath catch in my throat and my mind go dizzy. This had to have been a message from whoever had attacked

Noemi. My mind felt far away from my body at that moment and I started to hyperventilate, my breathing coming out in harsh wheezes, but it felt like I was watching myself have the beginnings of a panic attack from a third person perspective. Someone's arms wrapped around me and I suddenly felt more grounded within myself as Ahra pulled me close to her chest. I vaguely registered the scent of lavender laundry detergent and tried to focus on it. Someone started to gently pull the note from my hand and I let them take it.

"I don't think we can go to the police. There's a note on the back saying that if the cops or any professors are notified we'll be added to their 'list', and whatever that means, it doesn't sound good," River stated.

"Well we have to do something," Ollie protested.

I let out a long, shuddering breath. Ahra squeezed me tighter and while my anxiety attack wasn't easing up I could feel it stabilizing, which was usually more than I could hope for.

"Can I have a minute?" I asked, then repeated myself a bit louder so that it wasn't muffled by Ahra's sweater. "I... I need to process this. And get dressed."

At that point everyone else seemed to realize the state of undress I was in and left, though Ahra whispered to me that I didn't have to be afraid and that they'd figure out what was going on as she let go of me. Once I was alone I picked up the note from where River had left it on my dresser. I couldn't stop staring at it.

The threat made it clear - everything was riding on me. For some unknown reason, I was the explanation for everything that had happened and I would be the reason my friends got hurt if things escalated more. When I had asked to stay on the periphery of my friends' investigation into what had happened to Noemi, I had no idea that I was at the heart of it to begin with. I felt the weight of the world weighing on my shoulders, a weight only increased by the concerned voices of my friends on the other side of my door wondering out loud about what we should do. I knew deep inside that it didn't matter what they did; everything came back to me in the end.

Chapter Thirty

AFTER FINDING THE NOTE pinned to my door with a knife, my friends assured me that whenever I left the house one of them would be there by my side. Of course that meant that when no one was available to walk with me I had to stay inside Radcliffe House, but it was a small price to pay for a little more peace of mind. Ahra had pointed out that the threat being on my door meant that the person had been able to get inside, but because I had left the tower door propped open for River, it could have been anyone. From then on we opted for a policy of keeping all doors closed and locked at all times.

Even though River offered to stay with me the entire time, I opted to stay home from my meeting with Professor Rhodes. After the stress of the morning I wanted a bit more time to relax and not deal with people. Professor Rhodes was more than understanding in our email exchange, telling me that she hoped the migraine I told her I had would ease up soon. Lying to her felt wrong, but I wasn't going to go against the threat and risk my friends' safety more than I already had just by existing.

It was around noon when I finally felt ready to leave my bedroom and venture downstairs for something to eat; even if I wasn't ready, my growling stomach definitely was. When I stepped foot in the living room I was surprised to find two people in the kitchen already - I guess I saw them so rarely in the house that I had nearly forgotten about the residents of the other tower.

Vincent and Damian sat at the dining table eating breakfast together. I lingered in the doorway as they chatted about a project they were working on together for a class. Then Vincent looked up and noticed me, startling us both for a second.

"Oh, Georgie. Hello," he said. "Don't mind us, we'll be finishing up here soon." There was an odd tone to his voice. It was flatter than usual, like there was some underlying annoyance he wasn't going to admit to out loud.

"It's alright, take your time. I'm sorry for interrupting you," I replied quietly, moving around the table to grab something from the fridge. I had planned on making myself an omelet, but something about turning my back on people, even if they were my people who I had been working with and getting to know better, made me feel wary. As I fished out a container of leftover pizza I decided to eat cold, I sensed someone behind me.

"Hey, can I talk to you for a second?" Damian asked, his voice softer than I ever imagined it could be.

I shot to my feet immediately, banging my head on the freezer door handle. I nodded, resisting the urge to rub the sore spot on my skull in an attempt to play it off. Damian gave me a strange look before putting his plate in the sink and continuing to talk to me.

"I just wanted to... apologize."

A moment passed before I realized he was waiting for me to respond. "Apologize for what?" I asked, chastising myself for sounding like an idiot.

"For snapping at you over Travel Literature. I mean, it was a pretty rude thing to do. I didn't think before I said anything."

"Oh." I resisted the urge to point out that he had snapped at me a couple of times for various reasons, and that apologizing for one time and not the others was a bit odd. "Thank you. I appreciate the apology."

"Yeah, I mean, being rude is no way to get what you want, right?"

"What you want... you mean the Travel Literature course?"

"Right, I've been thinking, and I figured maybe you and I could switch, that way the course gets a better teaching assistant and you can still work with Decker," Damian explained.

I nodded again, though I was more stuck in my thoughts than I was paying attention to him now that he had shown his cards. I should have known he had an ulterior motive and wasn't just apologizing out of the good of his heart. Still, if it would get me on his good side...

"Well, I have to get to class, but you think on this and we'll talk later, yeah?" he said as if we were good friends.

"Yeah, sure," I responded, not doing a very good job at keeping my suspicion out of my voice. With that, Damian flashed me a grin that seemed out of place on his normally scowling face and went back over to Vincent. I stared after them as they gathered their things and left, the door to the fridge still open where I had abandoned my search for cold pizza.

In that moment I didn't trust either one of them. I wasn't even sure if I trusted my friends, though I knew it would be stupid to doubt them. Everything was spiraling like a whirlpool and I felt like all of my anchors had been uprooted and washed out to sea.

Chapter Thirty-One

My hands would probably still have been shaking if not for the steaming mug of hot chocolate that Ahra had pressed between my fingers. I hadn't had another panic attack, but being home alone all day while I waited for my friends to get back had my anxiety going in a constant buzz throughout my body. None of the other Radcliffe House residents were home and from what we knew they wouldn't be for quite a while, so the four of us met downstairs at the dining room table where there was space for all of us.

The knife and note sat on the table in front of us. I positioned my mug so that I couldn't see the grainy picture of myself with the target circling my face. My eyes kept flashing over to the knife, imagining all the gruesome ways it could harm me despite it being just a normal kitchen knife like the ones the conservatory supplied to all of the Lakehouses. I was sure that if I went to our kitchen I could find one just like it, though it wouldn't have the paint residue from being jammed in my door. I absentmindedly wondered if I would be charged for repairs, or if the damage was too small to matter.

Ollie pulled his face from its resting position in his hands. "I think we should go to the police, or at least campus security. This is a real threat and with what happened to Noemi, I don't think they're kidding about hurting Georgie."

"Then they're probably not kidding about hurting you guys, too," I replied. "I don't want to put you all in danger because someone is after me."

"What I don't understand is why anyone would even be after you," Ahra interjected. "You just started here this semester, it's not like anyone could have some deep seated grudge against you."

"Maybe it has to do with my transfer?" I suggested. It was the only possibility I could think of. "My first few weeks it was all anyone could talk about - how strange and unusual it was that I was able to transfer into a later year when that sort of thing hasn't happened in years. Maybe someone is jealous." I took a sip of the hot chocolate even though it was much too hot still. The burning peppermint mocha flavor helped keep my mind in the moment in front of me.

"Yeah maybe, but whoever left the note had to be a student.

Why would someone be jealous of you for something they already have?" Ollie posited.

Before any of us could say anything more on the topic, our eyes shot to the front door where the unmistakable sound of a key turning in a lock kept our attention. Vincent wheeled his way in, a frown etching itself onto his face as he noticed River.

"Oh, so you are here. Glad to know you're not off with someone else when you had plans with me," he stated.

Sudden realization dawned on River's face and they tried to stutter through an excuse. Vincent wasn't paying attention, however, because his focus had been pulled to the assortment of items on the dining room table.

"What's all of this?" He looked at each of us in turn, but we all remained silent. His hand shot out to grab the paper and despite Ahra's attempt to get it back he was able to read it and look at the picture. "What is going on here?" he demanded.

"An investigation," I said, speaking up when no one else would. "We thought something strange was going on with what happened to Noemi, that it was more than just an animal attack, and with this threat it seems like we were right." Somehow I managed to keep my voice calm and steady despite the fact that I wanted to burst into tears all over again.

I tried to tell myself that there was no point in lying, that letting Vincent know about the investigation was not the same as going to the police or any professors about the threat and that doing so wouldn't put my friends in any more danger than they were already in.

"Is this why you've been standing me up for weeks now?" Vincent exclaimed, turning towards River who suddenly looked like a deer in headlights. "I thought it was just to hang out with Ambrose and those other guys and I thought we'd worked past that, but instead you've been keeping this dumb investigation from me?"

"I—" River started, but Vincent refused to let them get a word in.

"It's probably just some prank being played on you by an asshole who thought a bunch of people traumatized by their friend's injury would make an easy target. You honestly have been breaking plans with me and leaving me out to dry because of some stupid conspiracy you all have going on," he scoffed.

"Vincent, that's not what happened," River insisted. Vincent was having none of it. Instead he ignored River completely and turned on me.

"As someone who actually made it to be one of Decker's teaching assistants," he started, flashing a quick glance at River, "you should be smarter than this. You better hope I don't tell him about this stupid investigation of yours, I doubt he'd want to keep such an idiot on his roster."

"Please don't," I pleaded, barely more than a whisper, not even wanting to contemplate losing the good standing I had with the professor. My fingers burned where they were pressed impossibly tight against my hot mug.

River tried one more time to convince him that what he said wasn't true, but Vincent ignored them and went to his tower, pulling the door shut tightly behind him. A second later another door slammed shut, presumably Vincent's bedroom door. After a moment of us all standing there in stunned silence, Ahra spoke up.

"Well that was... unfortunate timing."

River turned on her and began yelling. "Unfortunate timing? That's what you're calling this? That was terrible for all of us! Not only does he now know about everything when we were explicitly warned not to tell anyone, but there is a very real chance he's going to tell Decker about it!"

"Did you ever stop to consider that maybe he's the one behind all of this?" Ahra asked, her voice low. The question stopped River in their tracks.

"Ahra, what are you talking about?" Ollie questioned.

"I've been thinking about it all day, and I realized something. Georgie says she left the tower door propped open for River to get in since she still had their keys. That made us think that anyone could have gotten in to make the threat, but that's not true. The front door was still locked because you assumed Vincent would be able to get River that far. That means that the most likely culprit is someone living in this house. Vincent,

Clara, Lourdes, Ailani, or Damian."

"It can't have been Vincent. I... I was with him all night," River said, though their voice betrayed that they weren't completely confident in what they were saying.

"You know that when you drink you sleep like a rock. He could have easily snuck out and done this without waking you up," she pointed out.

"Well, it could have been any of the rest of them just as easily," they countered.

"I don't like this train of thought," I whispered. Ollie seemed to be the only one who heard me. He reached out and placed his arm around my shoulders, giving me a comforting squeeze.

"So where do we go from here?" he asked the group.

"I think we should continue on as we have been, with the four of us investigating the attack on Noemi. I think I've finally gotten somewhere by getting into the school records to see what Mr. Hansen refused to tell us about that night," Ahra explained.

"I think I have to tell Professor Decker that I can't be his teaching assistant anymore. If one of them wants to hurt me or worse... I can't stay in that position," I said.

"Well, as long as you have one of us or the professor with you, or you're not alone with just one of them, or even if you are but you're in a public space in the daytime, then I think you'll be perfectly fine," she countered. "Honestly, it might be a good idea to have you stay in the group. You have an in where none of us do and can probably figure out who made this threat. Then we can take care of it faster."

I had no idea what she meant by 'take care of it' but I tried to make myself believe in her words. Letting myself decide things would only result in me being locked in my room crying until the conservatory kicked me out and sent me back to my disappointed brother, which was definitely out of the question.

I promised that I would stay safe and do my best to figure out who the culprit was, satisfying Ahra but not calming any of our nerves. The four of us stood around looking at each other, unsure of what to do for the next several moments. One by one we left the living room to go about the day with an air of anxiety and uncertainty filling the house, the knife and note being tucked away back in Ahra's room where she promised to keep them.

Chapter Thirty-Two

It was hard to believe that anything outside of the threat and investigation could possibly be happening, but life went on despite my issues.

Pygmalion rehearsals began that Wednesday night. As it was our first time meeting as the full cast in a setting like this, instead of working on any specific scenes we all sat in one large circle on the Clotho stage to read out the words. River and I made sure to take seats as far away from Vincent, Clara, and Lourdes as we could.

Despite my nerves at being cast in the lead role, I found myself grateful for it as so much of my brain had to focus on my lines, leaving my predicament to be forgotten for a few hours. Unfortunately the time passed quickly when I didn't have any worries in the forefront of my mind and before long the reading was over and Professors Decker and Rhodes were dismissing us.

The zipper on my bag was giving me trouble and I focused on closing it without any of the teeth separating. The only other thing I was aware of was the light squeaking of the stage as people crossed it.

"Hey Georgie," Lourdes said, making me jump. I glanced over at River, who seemed just as wary as I felt but was doing a much better job at hiding it.

"Hi, Lourdes. What's up?" I hoped she couldn't hear my voice wavering.

"I was just wondering if you'd like to go see this new movie with me, it's called *The Willows*. It's based on this Gothic story from the early 1900s and I know you like that sort of thing, so I figured we could go together."

Lourdes sounded as kind and friendly as she always did, but I couldn't help feeling the slightest bit suspicious. It was true that she had walked home with me the night of the dinner party and if she had wanted to harm me she could have done it then, but I wasn't ready to completely strike her name from the list of suspects.

"Um… I'm not sure. I'm very busy with classes and now the play and everything, you know?" I muttered. Lourdes nodded knowingly.

"I'll text you the possible dates and times and you can get

back to me, alright?"

"Yeah, that sounds good." I wondered how long I could let those messages sit unanswered before she confronted me about them.

"Okay, I'll see you around then." With another one of her bright smiles, Lourdes excused herself and went back to collect her things.

As River and I moved to leave the stage, I caught Professor Decker's eye. He smiled, something warm and deep and reassuring, but made no move to leave the conversation he was having with Professor Rhodes to come talk to me, for which I was grateful. Still, in that brief moment of eye contact River had managed to move further ahead of me and I had to half jog in order to catch up before leaving the building. My heart pounded hard in my chest the entire silent walk back to Radcliffe House and didn't settle down until I was in the comforting embrace of my bed that night.

I stared at the ceiling and listened to the chitter of the night birds outside my window, wondering how exactly I was going to make it through the rest of the semester without losing my sanity or my life.

Chapter Thirty-Three

THE REST OF THE week had passed by without incident and that should have calmed my anxiety, but I still found myself jumping at every sound and scanning my eyes across every room I entered to be sure no one was looking at me in a way that I found suspicious. By the time the weekend rolled around I was emotionally exhausted.

I left my room as little as possible throughout the week and aside from the couple of dinners my friends made and forced me to eat, my diet consisted mainly of the jelly beans and crackers that I kept in my desk drawer to snack on while studying. I didn't want to risk running into any of my fellow teaching assistants outside of the public eye. Even though Ahra did her best to assure me that I was safe inside the house, the chip in my bedroom door where the knife had stuck into it made that statement hard to believe.

I had no idea what time it was. My stomach hurt too much to move so I just laid face down on my bed for who knew how long until a knock at the door drew my attention.

"Georgie? You alright? You haven't come out of your room all day," Ollie's voice called. I sighed, the sound muffled by my pillows.

"I'm fine. I just- I'm fine," I replied, propping myself up. The door creaked open ever so slowly and I chastised myself for forgetting to lock it. Even though we made sure the tower door was closed at all times, I should have been more diligent about my own door. Ollie peeked his head through the opening, and once he realized I was not planning on telling him off for it, he opened the door more fully and stepped through.

"Do you want to go somewhere? Being in this house feels..." he trailed off.

"Suffocating?" I suggested, and he nodded in agreement.

"I was thinking of stopping by the greenhouse, and then getting dinner at the Scullery afterwards," he said, nearly getting interrupted by my stomach as it let out another loud howl of hunger. I grimaced in embarrassment, but Ollie just laughed, a light sound that cheered me up. "Or maybe before." This time it was my turn to nod, and off we went to find food and flowers.

It was much easier to keep the bad thoughts away with a

stomach full of pasta and I even found myself smiling as Ollie and I checked on the plants at the greenhouse, a feat I wouldn't have thought possible that day.

"So, anything on your mind? Aside from the obvious, I mean," Ollie asked, breaking the relaxing silence. I drew in a tense breath and thought for a moment before responding. Besides the threat against me, the fact that we'd resigned ourselves to never hearing back from Noemi's family, and my normal day to day struggles, there was one thing that I found my thoughts circling back to again and again.

"Have you ever been to the graveyard?" I asked. Ollie nodded. "Well... I was walking around campus a little while ago and ended up there, and there was this statue of an angel," I said, pausing to see if Ollie knew what I was talking about. It seemed that he did not. "It was a massive statue and honestly it was terrifying, but the scariest part about it was that the grave had my mother's name on it." I swallowed hard, trying to keep the anxiety at bay.

"Your mother's not buried here, is she?" Ollie asked, and I shook my head no. "Well, is it a common name?"

"Sort of? Her name was Abigail Miller," I replied. A look of recognition crossed his face which confused me.

"Georgie, do you know the story of how Westwood Conservatory came to have its campus here?"

I thought for a moment, sure Eli had explained the story

to me years ago, but found myself scrambling at half-formed memories. "No, I don't."

"Castle Blackscar was built by a man named Alfred Miller who had made his fortune in the railroad industry. He wanted something to show off his new money, and what's more showy than a castle? His wife's name was Abigail and when she died, she was buried in the cemetery along with all of the others who had died while living or working on the castle grounds. Fifteen years after her death, Alfred sold the castle and its land, cemetery included, to the people who founded Westwood Conservatory here on the premises. You must have found her grave, and it's no surprise she had been given such a grand grave marker. I can recommend a book on the history of the school and what was here before it. The library has several copies."

I nodded along to what Ollie was saying, my mind swirling with thoughts. So it truly was a coincidence that the name on the angel's grave was the same as my mother's. At the very least I could be relieved of that one stressor.

The rest of the day passed quietly as Ollie and I tended to the plants. When the sun was just beginning to set we decided to make our way back home so as to not be out too late after dark. A chill shook me to my bones as we crossed the campus back to Radcliffe House and I pulled my jacket tighter over my body to try and ward off the feeling that something terribly wrong was on the horizon.

Chapter Thirty-Four

My weekends were normally open for me to do what I pleased, but the Sunday after his dinner party Professor Decker asked if I would meet up with him for a quick chat. His email made it sound like he was sorry for being too busy to check in with me sooner. Ollie walked me to the castle, and once we were down the hall he left me to go to the library where I promised I'd meet him after talking to Professor Decker.

I knocked on the professor's door and it swung open before my knuckles could connect with the wood more than once.

"Oh, it's just you. Come in, come in," he said, though it felt more like he was speaking through me rather than to me with the way he looked back and forth between the opposite ends of the hallway while addressing me.

I entered the cramped office and sat down on the one chair

that had been cleared of books. A strange metallic sound clicked somewhere in the room; I figured it came from the typewriter the professor had moved from a shelf onto his desk to use. Then Professor Decker took his place directly in front of me, leaning back against his desk and drumming his fingers against its surface.

"Are you okay, pro— Adrian? Is something on your mind?" I asked, remembering halfway through my sentence that I didn't have to be so formal with him. Something about his demeanor seemed off; his usual confident and suave behavior had changed to be more anxious than I thought him capable of being. The feeling didn't sit well with me, as I knew how badly anxiety could mess with one's mental state. He waved his hands dismissively.

"I'm fine, I just received some... not so great news just before you came by. Nothing you need to worry about, though," he answered with a smile that didn't quite reach his eyes. I didn't completely believe his words, but I did not push him for more information. "How are you doing, Georgie? I wanted to set up this meeting to check in and make sure everything was alright with you. I apologize that it's been so long since we've been able to chat like this."

"I'm alright. My classes are going the same way they have been," I answered.

"And your friends, is everything good alright with them?

Vincent told me that the two of you had a little argument the other day, but I'm sure it's probably blown over by now." I audibly swallowed upon hearing his words, my mouth suddenly dry.

"Did- did Vincent tell you what we were arguing about?" I asked hesitantly.

"No, he did not. Why, was it something that I should know?" At this point Professor Decker - Adrian - looked at me with such an intense gaze that I let out a nervous chuckle and turned my head to avoid making eye contact with him.

"Uh, no. It was nothing. Not anything of importance, anyway. I was just wondering how much he told you," I assured. The tension seemed to leave Professor Decker's body upon hearing my words and his face softened.

"Well if it's nothing of importance then I'm sure everything will be right as rain in no time." All I could do was nod my head. "How are things between you and my other teaching assistants? Are you still getting along with them?" he asked. There was a sense of trepidation in his words. I thought that maybe Damian had told him that I wanted to switch courses with him, but I was pretty sure that I was supposed to be the one to bring up the idea first.

"Yeah, everything is fine," I lied. Part of me wanted to tell him everything - about the threatening note that had been pinned to our front door with a knife and the suspicion we had of one of the teaching assistants being behind it - but at best that would worry the already stressed man and at worst it would end in my friends getting hurt. That thought was the deciding factor that kept me from spilling my guts.

"That's good, that's good." Professor Decker's eyes were on the door again. "Is there anything else on your mind? You know you can always talk to me."

I shook my head. "No, I don't really have anything going on right now," I lied again. I felt guilty for doing so. Professor Decker had made me feel like I could come to him about anything even from the first time we talked, but this was something beyond what he could help with.

"Are you absolutely sure? I am here if you need me," he insisted. His gaze felt like it was looking past my visage and into my soul, and I found myself hiding once more behind the curtain of my hair.

"I promise, professor. I know you're only an email away should I need you."

"Good," he responded, a smug note in his voice. "In that case I will see you in class tomorrow and rehearsal on Wednesday," he replied. "You make such a wonderful Eliza, I'm very glad that you wanted to be part of the production. I can't imagine anyone else in the role." He flashed a smile in my direction that seemed a little too forced, like he was trying to hide something.

"Yeah, I was surprised that I got the lead. I haven't had the greatest track record with theater stuff," I said, keeping my eyes on him though I wanted to look away in embarrassment. I explained what had happened when I was in high school, but he merely let out a chuckle, surprising me.

"Oh Georgie, those girls were just jealous of you for getting the part that they wanted. You have no need to doubt yourself and your place in the production. If you ever need a reminder of that, you let me know."

"Right. I... I'll keep that in mind." It had never occurred to me that anyone would harbor any jealousy towards me, but the professor's words made sense. They echoed my own thoughts of why someone would threaten me with a knife in my door, a motivation that still seemed outlandish to me even if it was the only one I could think of.

I quietly gathered my things and made my way to the door, but it did not open when I turned the knob. Professor Decker immediately rushed over and apologized for having it locked. He reached over my shoulder to turn the key in the deadbolt and I could feel the heat radiating off of his body from how close he was standing.

He paused there for a moment and did not move until I cleared my throat, at which point he backed off and let me through the door. I made my way down the hallway and looked back before turning the corner; the professor lingered in the doorway, wordlessly watching me. He gave a polite nod that I returned before rushing off towards the library where Ollie was waiting for my return.

Chapter Thirty-Five

I WAITED IN THE living room for River, nervously tapping my foot on the plush carpet. They had promised to come get me in order to walk me to my anthropology class, but I was almost running late and they still hadn't gotten back to Radcliffe House. I checked my phone for the dozenth time in the last five minutes and contemplated sending another message asking where they were, but decided against it.

The familiar creaking of a door sounded out in the otherwise silent room and my head shot up, but instead of it being the front door to the house, it was the one leading into the front end tower. Ailani came through first followed by Damian.

"Hey, Georgie, are you coming to class?" Ailani asked. She seemed more tired than usual.

"Oh, yeah. I was waiting for River for... something, but I

guess they're not going to make it back before I have to go," I answered. I checked my phone one final time, still no messages, before pushing myself off the couch to follow my classmates out the door. In my head I repeated to myself that it was okay to walk with Ailani and Damian to class as I wasn't alone with just one of them and we would be in a brightly lit public space.

I trailed behind the two of them, lingering a few feet back. They didn't say much to each other - I guess none of us were in a chatty mood. Then Damian surprised me for a moment by turning around; I paused, but only for a second because it seemed like he was waiting for me to catch up.

"So, how's your day been?" It was strange to hear the question coming out of his mouth so casually. Damian never seemed like the type for small talk.

I shrugged. "Fine, I guess. I haven't really done much." We took a few steps in silence before I realized I probably should return the question.

"I can't complain," he said, which seemed like an outright lie. If anyone could find something to complain about in any situation, it would be Damian. "So, I was wondering if you've talked to Decker lately."

"Yeah, we had a meeting a few days ago."

"Did you happen to mention what you and I had talked about last week?"

"About... switching classes to TA for?" I asked. He nodded,

and I was relieved that I had understood his intentions. "It was a really quick meeting, we didn't really have time to talk about much."

"That's fair, but there's always next time you talk, right? You have practice for your play soon, don't you?"

This time it was my turn to nod. "The next one is Friday."

"Great, so you can talk to him then and maybe this weekend the three of us can meet up to iron out the details?"

"Uh, sure." Damian smiled, and it was strange to see him without an ounce of anger in his face. I guess even he couldn't be upset all the time.

"Yo, Little, is that you?" a voice called from a window as we passed the last of the Lake Houses, the one that sat almost directly across the lake from Radcliffe House.

Damian and I, along with Ailani who was still a few steps ahead of us, stopped to look at who had called out, seeing a guy with reddish-brown skin and a shaved head leaning out of a window on the second floor of the house.

"Mark Medina, I had no idea you got into Westwood!" Damian called back to him.

"Yeah, after my gap year they let me in! But hey, let me come down there so I'm not shouting my business for everyone to hear."

Damian waved me on, clearly alright with being late for class in order to talk to an old friend, so I hustled to catch up with

Ailani who had made it a few yards further while I hesitated. My heart jumped when I realized I was alone with someone who very well could have been the person threatening my life, but it calmed down when I went back to mentally repeating to myself that nothing was going to happen to me while I was in a brightly lit public space.

"You're going to ask about switching classes with Damian so that he gets Travel Literature next semester?" Ailani's voice went up at the end like a question, but it was clear that she already knew the answer.

"Yeah, he brought up the idea to me the other day and it makes sense. He gets what he wants and I get to be on his good side," I explained.

"And what about Clara? She wanted that class too, why not tell Decker that you want her to have it?"

I thought for a moment; it hadn't even crossed my mind that that was an option. "She's not the one who came to me with the idea," I answered simply. I thought that was the end of the conversation, but when we were just down the hall from the classroom Ailani stopped me for a moment and pulled me over to a little alcove. She kept her hand on my arm as we talked.

"Why did you agree to take on the teaching assistant position?" she questioned.

"I don't... you said it yourself, it's a great opportunity, and who knows when I'd get offered something like this again," I replied, completely caught off guard by her actions.

"But do you really want it? Aside from what I told you, what do you get out of the deal?" She gripped my arm tighter and I wanted to pull out of her grasp but felt frozen to the spot as I was put under the pressure of her questioning.

"Did you not want me to say yes to the offer? You could have said it was a bad idea or whatever when we talked and I probably would have turned it down," I admitted, trying hard to keep the panic out of my voice.

"I'm not saying you should have said no. I can't make your decisions for you, I just want to know if you really are making those decisions or if you're doing what someone else wants you to."

I winced as her nails gripped harder into my upper arm; they probably wouldn't break the skin but would definitely leave a mark. Ailani then seemed to finally notice what she was doing and she pulled away with a muttered apology.

"I didn't mean to scare you Georgie, I just want to make sure you know what you're getting yourself into."

With that she turned and made her way to the anthropology classroom, myself following a few steps behind. I vaguely registered Damian coming into class about ten minutes late, but for the most part my mind was stuck on the cryptic things Ailani had said to me in the hallway. I hoped that Professor Rhodes wouldn't notice my lack of concentration in the class

- I didn't need another lecture from her or my brother whom she seemed to tell every little thing she could about me.

Chapter Thirty-Six

I WALKED HOME FROM class mostly alone despite the promise I had made to my friends about always having someone with me. River hadn't responded to any of the messages I sent earlier in the day and both Ahra and Ollie were in class, so I didn't have much of a choice. One of my classmates, Mickie, walked with me part of the way until we arrived at Beckford House where she called home, and for that I was grateful. The remaining trek to the far side of campus where Radcliffe House sat felt like every second was an hour, and with every step my heart pounded in my chest.

The house was empty when I got there; at least, there was no one who lived in the back tower - I wasn't sure about the other one. I hurried to the safety of my room. It was early evening yet, so after I worked a bit on a paper for Modern

British Literature, I killed some time by taking a long, relaxing shower with the water hot enough to melt away my worries, even if just for a little while. When I got out I was surprised to still be the only one home.

I sent quick messages to my housemates and only received a response from Ollie - he was at the library working on a group project with a couple of his fellow classmates from the photography discipline and was likely to be late getting home. Ahra and River didn't respond. Making myself a simple early dinner of pre-cooked chicken nuggets and frozen vegetables, I sat down in front of the television to watch whatever mindless reality show was currently airing. I purposefully chose the seat closest to the back tower door just in case I needed to make a quick escape for whatever reason.

I managed to get so engrossed in the petty drama and ridiculous problems that the people on screen were having that I didn't hear River and Ahra coming through the front door and only realized they were home when River let out a loud, wheezing laugh at something Ahra had said. Flinching slightly, I turned towards the sound and when the two of them noticed I was in the room the laughter quickly died down.

"Hey guys, what's up?" I asked. The two exchanged a glance before answering.

"Uh, nothing. Ahra just said something funny about this guy we saw when we were out and about today," River explained with a noncommittal shrug. They scratched at the back of their head and looked everywhere around the room except at me.

"Where did you guys go? Ollie said he was at the library but the two of you never responded to my texts."

"We just went to this event hosted by the theater department. It was so cool, I didn't even think to check my phone," Ahra responded.

"Yeah, it was awesome," River added.

"Oh, I wish you guys would have told me about it. I would have loved to go with you!" I said. River made a strange face but a sharp look from Ahra made them go back to a more neutral one.

"Well, to be honest Georgie, we kind of just wanted a night to ourselves. You know, like something we would have done back in the good old days where there wasn't a stressful investigation and a potential crazy man out there attacking people," Ahra said gently. She tilted her head ever so slightly and her eyebrows came together in a look of pity. "When River invited me out I brought up asking you, but with the stress of having to look out for you we were worried we just wouldn't have a good time, and then what would have been the point of going out?"

I took a deep breath as her words settled in my head. "I get that the threat was directed at me, but the investigation was your idea in the first place," I started, speaking slowly in an attempt to work out my confusion. "The two of you convinced me and Ollie to join you guys in looking into things. Neither of us really wanted to do it - hell, after what happened to Noemi I didn't even want to stay at this school until you guys convinced me to. Why would you purposefully leave me out if you wanted to forget about something you started?"

"Could you blame me for not wanting to see you when you've made it so clear that you don't care about my feelings, hanging out with those people behind my back?" River snapped, finally breaking their facade of calm.

"I'm not hanging out with anybody behind anyone else's back," I replied, getting louder than I meant to. "Besides you guys, the only people I hang out with are the other teaching assistants, and that's only when you're not around and because you guys convinced me that I could figure out who threatened me. Whatever's bothering you so much isn't my fault." River's eyes widened in shock at my outburst but Ahra spoke first.

"Hey, you guys both need to calm down, there is no need for things to get this heated right now," Ahra said, stepping between the two of us.

"You know what River? Don't worry about having my face ruin your day by reminding you that your boyfriend might be some psycho who wants me dead, I'll make sure I'm only around here when you're gone," I shouted.

With that I turned on my heel and headed straight up the stairs, ignoring Ahra's protests. I slammed my door behind me making sure that the two of them could hear it from two floors down and flopped face first onto my bed. My pillow muffled my enraged screaming, and I screamed until my throat felt hoarse. Luckily I had a glass of water on my bedside table from the night before; the room temperature liquid helped soothe my aching throat a bit.

Part of me wanted to leave the house and find something to do to help rid my body of the bitter energy coursing through me, but I couldn't bring myself to leave my room and risk passing River on the way out. Because of this I simply changed into my pajamas and got under the comforter to try and sleep despite it not being that late. Unfortunately, the angry thoughts running through my mind kept me up for a long while staring at the ceiling.

I didn't even realize that I had fallen asleep at all until I awoke several hours later in my darkened room with the sound of rain splattering against the window pane. I pulled my phone over to check the time and the bright screen read 10:57pm. The draft coming in through my not quite aligned window chilled me to my bones through my thin pajamas, so I put on the coziest sweater I owned and a pair of oversized sweatpants and made my way downstairs to warm my body with a mug of peppermint hot chocolate. To my surprise, my three housemates were seated at the dining room table in the middle of a heated discussion.

"What are you guys talking about?" I asked, directing my question to Ollie and refusing to look at the other two.

"We're discussing any progress that we've made in the investigation," he replied.

"Oh, I thought you wanted to forget about that for a little while?" I said snarkily. Ollie looked at me, clearly confused, while Ahra stared at her lap and River had the decency to look ashamed. "Well, have fun without me." I made my way over to the kitchen and felt all three of their sets of eyes lingering on me.

"You don't want to join the conversation?" Ollie called after me.

"Not right now. I'm... just not in the mood," I responded, keeping myself from snapping at him, as he was the only one in the room not upsetting me at the moment.

"Oh, well, I can fill you in on anything new," he offered.

"That sounds great, Ollie."

I made my hot chocolate as quickly as possible and moved back up to my room, keeping my eyes straight ahead of me so I wouldn't be able to see if my friends were looking at me. When I finally stopped moving I had a new message from Lourdes reminding me about the movie invitation, but I made some excuse about being too busy with a project and that I'd let her know when I was free. In reality I felt like I had nothing going on and no one to hold onto as my anger and anxiety about the situation I'd been thrown into spiraled once more.

Chapter Thirty-Seven

AFTER A HANDFUL OF dreamless nights, it seemed like the nightmares had come back in full force. When I had woken up in a cold sweat for the fourth time that night at 6:12am, I decided I might as well just start my day.

I crept quietly to the shower and back up to my room, careful not to wake anyone up, and got dressed in a cozy dark orange sweater and pair of grey thermal leggings to fight off the early morning windchill. The library opened at 7am every day except Sunday, so I made my way to the castle and hoped I'd be able to focus on something other than the mess my life had become. My heart raced at the thought of walking across campus alone with only the barest bit of the sunrise lighting my way, but I was still too hurt by River and Ahra's actions to ask any of my friends to walk with me.

The student worker at the circulation desk gave me a strange look as I entered; they probably weren't used to students coming in right when the library opened, at least not until finals season. That's how it worked at my last university - the later it got in the semester, the more students went to the library and the more time they spent there. I set myself up in one of the private study rooms and pulled out my copy of James Joyce's *Ulysses* with every intention of getting as far into it as I could. Professor Decker had only given us two weeks to read it and complete a four page response essay, so I wanted to give myself as much time as possible for writing the actual essay.

I managed to get through the first two episodes of the novel, though the character Deasy made me supremely uncomfortable with his antisemitic remarks. I knew that the main character, Bloom, was Jewish - or half Jewish like myself - and therefore was not surprised to find unsavory characters like Deasy. Still, despite feeling disconnected to my Jewish heritage due to my mother's passing and my father being raised Christian, the character's comments made me feel queasy and I opted to take a bit of a walk about the library stacks before reading more.

I lingered in the aisles, running my hands along the dusty shelves as I read the titles of dozens of books I knew I'd never read. Occasionally I'd come across one that seemed slightly interesting. In those cases I'd pull the book down and flip through the pages for a moment before adding them to the pile of books to go back on the shelves so the librarians knew how much traffic there had been through the aisles.

Three different books I kept with me to check out and peruse later on - one on the history of the literary vampire and two collections of poetry. I even made an effort to look for the book Ollie had recommended to me on the history of the conservatory, but it seemed all copies had been checked out. I made it to the end of one aisle and turned to go down the next but stopped short to keep from smacking into a man I was surprised to see was Professor Decker. I muttered an apology of sorts and tried to shuffle around him but he quickly stepped in my way and initiated a conversation.

"Georgie! What a coincidence, running into you. What are you doing here?" he asked. I shifted uncomfortably from one foot to the other while he stood strong, his confidence seemingly back in full force. There was no trace of the strange, paranoid man I had seen him start to become over the past couple of weeks.

"Oh, I just came to get work done. I thought I'd take a break and look for a couple of books I could read for fun," I answered, gesturing to the ones I held in the crook of my arm. Professor Decker stepped closer to the point that I could smell his deep, woodsy cologne as he glanced at the cover of the book on top of the stack.

"Ah, Christina Rossetti. A good choice," he said with a

wink. He didn't step away from me, so I took the opportunity to retreat back into the aisle a bit. "Are you going to be here long? Maybe we could get work done together, perhaps planning for next semester's Travel Literature class," he suggested. "It is a bit early in the semester, but better to start things early than late."

I meekly shook my head. While he was back to being the calm and confident man I had first known him to be, I had become the paranoid one barely able to hold a conversation.

"No, I was actually just leaving. I've been here all morning and could use some lunch." My stomach growled loudly as if on cue. Rather than look dejected like I expected, Professor Decker's face actually perked up a bit.

"Oh, well then I could walk you to the café, maybe buy you a coffee."

It bothered me how quickly he was able to adapt to the situation and change his plans, and my plans for that matter. Mentally chastising myself, I reminded myself that he just genuinely enjoyed my company and wanted to make sure I was alright. Still, I wasn't in the mood for even the professor's company.

I shook my head with slightly more vigor this time. "No, really, it's okay. I have plans with my housemates," I lied. "I should get going."

"I understand. Another time, then."

Before he could rope me into an actual commitment I nodded and turned on my heels to return to the private study room so I could gather my things. When I went to head downstairs and leave the library I saw that Professor Decker had set up his work at a table right near the main staircase. I hung back, not wanting him to notice me as he looked up from his work every now and again to give cursory glances about the space.

I decided to take the long way out, stopping only to check out my books at the circulation desk. Thankfully it was tucked in a corner away from where the professor sat. I walked through the castle to take the furthest exit from the library just to avoid being seen if Professor Decker so chose to look out of a window for me.

Chapter Thirty-Eight

Lourdes had finally worn me down and convinced me to go to the movies with her, and much to my surprise and relief two of her other friends came along as well - they introduced themselves as Devon and Alice, and they were the co-leaders of Westwood Conservatory's Transgender Network. The three of them were busy chatting most of the car ride over to the theater about last minute preparations for their Trans Day of Remembrance event and I was able to keep to myself.

It felt so strange to be leaving campus even if just for the evening; the only other time I had left the school's grounds was to attend Professor Decker's Halloween dinner party, and even that was barely off campus. I stared out the car window watching the mostly bare trees rush by as more and more buildings appeared in place of the woods, the space quickly becoming a proper town. I found myself ogling the strip of businesses that lined the street as if I had never been to a town before.

The movie was quite good, though the eeriness of it all made my skin crawl in a way that, while once a welcome reaction to good media, now only reminded me that I was living in my own horror plot. I immediately felt ridiculously stupid for going out and seeing a movie when I had much more important things to deal with, but at the same time if I was going to be stalked by someone who wanted me gone enough that they would attack my friend, why shouldn't I spend an evening doing something that I enjoy? Even if one of the people I spent the evening with might well possibly be the person who wanted me gone. Lourdes was still unlikely in terms of suspects, but she was a suspect nonetheless.

And just like that, we were back on campus and it was almost as if we had never left in the first place. Something about Westwood felt all-encompassing, like this little corner of Pennsylvania somehow made up the world in its entirety. The fog that had settled over the campus only served to strengthen that feeling, as I could barely make out the trees and buildings ahead.

"Georgie, I'm gonna head to the library to talk more stuff over with Devon and Alice, do you want to come with us?"

Lourdes asked once we exited the castle, drawing me from my thoughts.

I glanced past Lourdes at her friends and then focused back on her. "I think I just want to get back home. It is getting pretty late." I should have been thinking about safety in numbers, but something inside of me desperately wanted to be back in my bedroom as soon as possible. The movie must have gotten to me more than I realized.

"Are you sure you want to walk back by yourself with all the fog?" she questioned, cocking her head to the side.

"Um, yeah, I should be fine," I said hesitantly, not wanting to do that at all. Not for the first time, I found myself wishing that I lived in one of the closer Lakehouses and not Radcliffe House where it sat on the far northeastern border of the grounds.

Much to my surprise, Lourdes saw me off with a hug, but before I could even tense up at the unexpected contact it was over and she was making her way towards the library with her friends, calling over her shoulder that she expected a text from me once I got back to Radcliffe House. Taking only a moment to breathe, I steeled what little remained of my courage and plunged into the fog ahead, shivering involuntarily as the chilly moisture in the air caressed my skin.

Without being able to see the usual landmarks ahead of me, the path back home seemed to stretch forever onward into the fog. My phone had died halfway through the movie so I couldn't check what time it was or how long I had been walking. Though I could see various shapes looming in the distance, things only became clear when they were barely five feet from me. If I ever was to be attacked in the night like Noemi had been, this would be the night.

Focusing on the rhythm of my steps and the feeling of the hard earth beneath my thin shoes, I pushed aside my fears and powered onward in what I hoped was the direction of Radcliffe House, knowing that if I stopped for even a moment I would start to feel overwhelmed and panicked, and that feeling never brought me anywhere good.

A sharp pain shot through my hip. It took me a moment to register that I had run into a picnic table. Was I really near the Galleries already? Already, or finally? It felt like I had been walking for ten minutes and ten hours at the same time. I rubbed the aching spot that I was sure would have a mottled green and purple bruise in the morning and carefully inched my way around the rest of the tables.

The fog thinned slightly as I moved, letting me see further ahead of myself as I walked. Off further than I could see clearly was the shape of a person, forming more solidly with every nervous step I took closer. Oddly enough I found myself more and more sure that it was Ahra; her forearm crutches and large, poofy hair were unmistakable features. I slowed, unsure if I was ready to face her yet. Only a couple of days had passed since the argument between myself, her, and River, and the wound still felt fresh on my heart. I lingered for a moment near the last of the picnic tables before ultimately deciding that it would be safer for the two of us to walk together.

Then strange things began to happen. The figure in front of me sharpened into Ahra's outline for just a brief moment before dissipating completely, once more leaving me in complete solitude. A shiver ran up my spine, causing a chill I couldn't shake. Either Ahra managed to get far enough away that I could no longer see her or the figure hadn't been her at all, hadn't been anybody really. I shook off the terror that the latter thought threatened to bring.

The next thing I bumped into came from directly in front of me - I must have been paying too much attention to what was coming up that I hadn't looked down far enough. My knees banged into the wrought iron bars of the fence while the blunted tips dug into my stomach, knocking the wind out of me. I was at the cemetery, as far to the east of campus as I could have gone. I tried to tell myself that this was a good thing, that I just had to follow the fence north and that soon I'd end up at Radcliffe House, but with the mysterious figure still fresh in my mind I couldn't help but imagine what other ghosts and ghouls might have been lingering in the fog.

With every passing minute I found myself moving faster and

faster, not quite at a full run because I was scared of what might happen if I were to trip when I couldn't see what was around me, but fast enough that my breathing became as ragged as the harsh winds pushing through the dead branches of the trees around me.

When I finally made it to Radcliffe House - oh the relief of seeing its red brick and dark wood exterior come forth through the thinning fog - my lungs were burning with the effort of keeping up the punishing pace I had made for myself. I paused outside the door, leaning over with my hands on my knees, gasping in an attempt to get enough air back into my lungs. Then I flung myself back upright, the momentum pushing my damp hair out of my face.

Out of the corner of my eye I thought I saw something moving in one of the windows of the front tower, but when I turned to give it my full attention, nothing was there. I had had quite enough of mysterious figures and looming shapes for the night, so without any further pause I let myself into the building and made my way up to my room to decompress, making sure to close and lock all doors behind me.

Chapter Thirty-Nine

I STILL WASN'T ON speaking terms with River, partially by their choice and partially by mine, but at least they were polite enough to walk with me to our *Pygmalion* rehearsal. This was most likely the first step on the long road to an apology I would get once they had worked through whatever issues they had with me. I still had no idea what those issues could have been aside from the threat on my life interrupting theirs, but that was hardly something to get angry with me for. It also felt like the issues went deeper than that.

Rehearsal that day was dedicated to running through the third act of the play. My character Eliza was only in the middle portion of the act, so while the beginning and ending parts were being practiced I was able to sit in the audience and watch everything unfold. Lourdes joined me as the opening of the act began.

Clara was amazing to watch on stage, not only having all of her own lines already memorized but being able to supply the other actors with theirs when they faltered. Her character was funnily enough named Clara as well, a proper young lady from the upper class meant to act as a foil to Eliza.

Lourdes leaned over to whisper, "I'm so glad you made it back home alright, that fog was absolutely terrible. I could barely see ten feet ahead of me!"

I nodded and gave a small smile, unsure of how to respond. I didn't want to get sucked into a conversation and potentially miss the professors calling me on stage to work on my scenes. I also didn't want to think about my trek through the fog last night. The last of its tendrils had lingered into the morning and gave me the chills as I went through my day, though by noon they had finally dissipated.

"Did you see any ghosts? There's a legend that when the late autumn fog comes out, even the ghosts that are normally quiet and keep to the cemetery come out to wander across the grounds," Lourdes said with a chuckle. She must not have noticed the way I tensed up at the mention of ghosts as I thought back to the strange figure that I had thought was Ahra. Luckily I was saved from answering any questions she might have had by Professor Decker calling me to the stage.

I wasn't quite as good as Clara was with her lines, I still needed a handful of them prompted to me, but overall I was happy with the progress I had made on learning them. Clara seemed to roll her eyes every time I paused to think of what I was supposed to say next, but I chalked that up to her still being upset that I had been given the lead role instead of her. Part of me still thought it was a mistake, but with every rehearsal I felt more and more like my stage fright was being chipped away and that by the time the performance rolled around, I would be ready to get on stage in front of everyone.

By the time I was able to sit down again my throat was starting to ache and I was practically running for my water bottle. The line 'Walk? Not bloody likely!' was bound to be stuck in my head for the rest of the semester with how many times I had to say it tonight. Apparently it was one of the most famous lines of the play and I had to get my take on it just right for the performance.

As I chugged my water someone tapped on my shoulder. I turned around, fully expecting to see Lourdes, but instead came face to face with Professor Rhodes. I choked on my water from the surprise but recovered quickly, though my cheeks still flushed with embarrassment.

"Georgie, can we talk for a moment?" she asked. I nodded and let her lead me to a pair of seats in the front row where she could still keep an eye on what was happening on the stage. As we sat down, I couldn't keep myself from interrupting the professor as she was about to say something.

"Am I doing a good job?" The words were out of my mouth before I could even think about what I was asking. I felt so juvenile, like a fifth grader performing in the school talent show instead of an adult attending one of the most prestigious conservatories in the country.

Professor Rhodes gave me a kind smile. "You are doing wonderful, Georgie, just like I knew you would. You know, Professor Decker was surprised when I suggested we give you the lead role, but he quickly came around and agreed that you would do well and that it would help you gain more confidence."

I looked over at her quizzically. "You were the one who suggested that I be Eliza?" I asked.

"I was," the professor answered with a nod. "You're an exceedingly bright and talented young woman, you just need a little push now and then to get out of your comfort zone."

"That is a relief to hear," I said, not sure how to process what I had just been told.

"That's actually what I wanted to talk to you about. I wanted to make sure that you realized how well we all think you're doing. I know you struggle with anxiety, and thought that maybe some outside encouragement might help."

Before either of us could say anything more, Professor Decker was calling her back to the stage. Flashing another smile at me, Professor Rhodes excused herself. I remained where

I sat, mulling things over in my brain until there were more scenes for me to practice.

Rehearsal was over not long after that. I risked River leaving me behind to hurry over to Professor Decker.

"Ah, Georgie my dear, what can I do for you?" he questioned.

"Do you have some time to talk? I have a few questions for you," I said as I fiddled with the end of my skirt.

"Oh, actually I can't talk much right now," he said, glancing over to the side. I followed his eye line to see Clara packing her bag up. "But if you shoot me an email in the morning, I would be more than happy to set up a time to meet." I assured him that I would do so.

I caught eyes with Vincent across the stage and almost instinctively I gave a little wave. He didn't sneer at me or start yelling like I half expected, but he certainly didn't look pleased with me either. His mouth turned into a tight little frown and I looked away.

As I turned to leave, relieved that River was still waiting for me though they looked annoyed while doing so, I felt like I was being watched. Like someone was staring daggers into the back of my head. I tried to shake off the feeling by telling myself that everyone feels like they're being watched while in a theater, but it seemed to linger the entire walk back to Radcliffe House.

Chapter Forty

River was already in the kitchen when I made my way downstairs to make lunch before class. I waited for them to move back to the stove where they were making stir fry before pulling out my container of leftover chicken alfredo from the fridge and popping it in the microwave. As I waited for the timer to count down, River moved behind me to grab a plate from the cabinet to my left.

"Could you get out of the way?" they snapped. Shocked by their tone I stepped over, accidentally swinging my arm into their side in the process. They rolled their eyes at me and moved back to the stove.

"Are you... alright?" I asked hesitantly, knowing that the answer was obviously no and wondering why they were in such a bad mood.

"I'm fine, Georgie, just focus on yourself. You're the one being targeted by an attempted murderer who very well might be the guy I've been seeing, after all," they replied sarcastically.

"I... yeah. I can see why that would upset you," I said. This was something we had known for a while now, and though River had seemed annoyed with me before, this outright hostility was new. They turned to face me, waving the spatula dramatically through the air.

"Well that's good, at least you can see why that would upset me," they mocked.

"You don't have to take it out on me, you know. It's not like I asked for this."

"I know you didn't Georgie, that's not why I'm upset. I mean, of course I'm upset that you're being targeted by a psychopath and that said psychopath hurt Noemi, and of course I'm upset that the psychopath could end up being Vincent, but those aren't the reasons why I'm upset with *you*," they half shouted. I flinched and glanced at the door to the front tower, hoping none of its residents were home to hear River's outburst.

"Well then why are you upset with me? I'll do my best to fix it," I offered, leading River to let out a dramatic sigh.

"You don't get it, do you? There's nothing for you to fix. You can't un-befriend Vincent, although he doesn't seem to be your friend anymore anyway, and you can't un-befriend

Lourdes, and you can't keep Decker from wanting you to be one of his prized teaching assistants, just like I can't stop myself from being in love with Vincent," they snapped.

"I- wait, you're in love with Vincent? Like, really in love?" I asked incredulously. I knew they cared for each other, but love was a strong word, especially coming from one of the two of them. River turned away quickly, though not so quick that I couldn't see their face turn a shade of red that almost matched the peppers in their stir fry.

"That's not the point of what I was saying," they muttered, angrily stirring their food as it sizzled away in the pan.

"Alright, then what does Professor Decker even have to do with any of this?" I asked. "It's not like he made one of his teaching assistants act like this, if it really is one of them who's after me."

"He has everything to do with this!" River shouted.

They took a deep breath and paused for a moment before explaining themselves, but though they spoke more softly the anger in their words was evident.

"He's the reason why Lourdes and I stopped being friends. She abandoned me for the rest of the group when she got picked to be his TA and I didn't. She's got other friends, but they were never considered for the position. It's like when Decker decided I wasn't worthy, she saw the same thing in me. He's also the reason why Vincent isn't anything more than someone I can call to get dinner and make out with every now and then, because why would he actually want to date someone so intellectually inferior?"

River's outburst shocked me. I had absolutely no idea that they had been keeping all of this inside basically the whole time we had known each other.

"I'm sure that's not true. I mean, Vincent seems super into you, maybe even loves you too. Why else would he be so upset about you blowing him off?" I said weakly.

"Oh please, he only cares about his reputation. He's just embarrassed that someone like me would dare stand him up."

"Okay, well, did you want to be one of Decker's teaching assistants then?" I asked. I knew it was a stupid question but I wanted to keep River talking. Maybe if they got it all out now, we could work through things and be friends again.

River rolled their eyes again, hard enough that I was sure they'd fall out of their sockets the next time they tried to repeat the action. "Of course I wanted to be one of his assistants! I am a literature major, aren't I? All of us wanted the chance to work with him. It was a real kick in the teeth when my best friend and the guy I started to have feelings for got picked and I didn't. Then to top it all off, this year you show up out of nowhere and instantly get his attention! It just isn't fair!"

"I... I don't know what you want me to say, River. I didn't ask for any of this, and I certainly didn't do anything with any intention of hurting you."

"I know, Georgie. And that's the hardest part of this whole situation to deal with."

Just then the microwave beeped, so without another word I took my freshly reheated food and grabbed a fork from the cutlery drawer. I glanced back at River over my shoulder, but I didn't bother saying anything else partially because I didn't want to upset them further and partially because I hated that they were making me feel guilty for things beyond my control. Even if making me feel guilty wasn't their intention, it still hurt for me to hear them say those things.

I ate my lunch from the comfort of my bed, and a little while later when I went downstairs to leave for Modern British Literature, River was nowhere to be found. I figured they had left without me, and so I made my way to Winsford Hall alone. It was almost funny to me in an ironic way that things had changed so much over the course of just a couple of months. The semester had started off with three of us going to class together, then Noemi left after the incident, and now River was gone from my side. A shiver ran through me as I thought about the possibility that if whoever was threatening me succeeded in their plan, I'd be gone soon enough too.

To my surprise, River wasn't in the classroom when I made it there. Clara and Lourdes sat in their usual seats; luckily neither of them so much as looked up at me as I made my way to my own seat. I didn't know if I'd be able to keep from making a face while they were still on our suspect list for the investigation. More and more students filed in, but River was not one of them.

Eventually Professor Decker arrived and began the class. I looked at the two empty seats to my side and couldn't help but think about how River and Noemi should have been sitting in them. In a perfect world, things would have been just like they were during the first few weeks of the semester. Noemi would be safe and healthy, River wouldn't be angry with me for things beyond my control, and there wouldn't be a target on my back for reasons unknown.

My mind was filled with thoughts of how different things had become over the past month, which then expanded to how much my life had changed in the past year. It seemed anyone I had been close to either got hurt or abandoned me when I was the one hurting. I didn't hear a word Professor Decker said during the entire lesson, though I did catch him looking over at me a fair few times.

With my thoughts wandering as they were, class flew by in the blink of an eye. My chat with the professor after class started off with the usual 'how are yous' and 'I'm fines' before the topic was changed to what I had wanted to discuss after rehearsal the other day. I had wanted to talk about the fact that Professor Rhodes had been the one to suggest me for the lead role, but now I remembered something else of more pressing importance.

I almost called him 'professor' but caught myself at the last second, knowing that he preferred to be less formal with his teaching assistants. "Adrian, do you really think I'm well suited to be your TA for Travel Literature?"

His eyes lit up when he heard me call him by his first name. "Of course, Georgie. I wouldn't have offered it to you if I didn't think that was the case. Don't tell me you're second guessing yourself now," he replied.

"It's just that, well, it's one of your most intensive course loads in your lower level classes. Wouldn't it make more sense for someone who has more experience as a teaching assistant to help you out there? Maybe you could give it to, I don't know, Damian, and I could take over his course. It definitely seems much more suitable for a first time teaching assistant." I did my best to sound nonchalant about the whole thing. The embarrassment that would come with him knowing I'd practiced these lines before this conversation would have been too much.

"Is that so?" he mused, eyes narrowing slightly. "Did Damian put you up to this?"

"No," I answered a little too quickly.

"Well, I'd rather Mr. Little stay where he's at and you take Travel Literature. It makes more sense for there only to be one person learning the ropes rather than two. Damian knows his own class so well, and besides, I think you're perfectly capable of helping me with the more intensive course load, as you put it."

He patted my head as one would a child before excusing himself, saying he had an unavoidable faculty meeting to attend at Corbyn Hall, but that he'd love to meet up more often. Despite having some place to be, he still offered to walk me wherever I was going, almost seemed to insist on it, but I assured him that I was headed only to the library and needed no escort since it was barely a two minute walk from Winsford Hall.

Instead, once he was gone I made my way out of the building as quickly as possible and to the greenhouse. I spent the entire evening there and even though I had promised Ahra that I wouldn't wander around by myself after the sun had set, I stayed there for several hours tending to the different plants that I had grown accustomed to taking care of. It seemed like there were a handful of students who came to the greenhouse on a pretty regular rotation, Ollie being one of them, but plants could always use a little more love and I was ready to give that to them.

It felt like midnight by the time I left, though my phone said it was only 7:34 in the evening. As lovely as it was spending time with the plants, I regretted my late stay at the greenhouse.

My whole body felt on edge during the walk back to Radcliffe House, but I repeated to myself that if I could get through the fog then I could get through a normal walk. Still, the goosebumps covering my skin lingered long after I was safely back inside with the door locked behind me. Only once the curtains were drawn and my comforter was pulled up to my chin was I able to finally relax.

Chapter Forty-One

I HAD NO CLASS the following day and instead decided to make my way to the greenhouse. Despite the tension I'd have walking alone, I craved the calmness I knew awaited me inside the glass walls. Thankfully no one else was there, and after I ate a quick lunch comprised of a bag of chips and the sandwich I had quickly thrown together before leaving, I made my usual rounds of the plants. Everything seemed fine, which was unsurprising considering I had just stopped by less than twenty four hours earlier, until I reached the large pot of lilacs that sat in the far corner away from the entrance.

Everything in the pot was dead. The white and purple flower petals were wilted and shriveled up and the once green stems were all a dull and dying brown. I ran my fingers over the flaking leaves and felt my heart grow heavy in my chest. I sniffled to hold back the tears that already threatened to spill and the strong scent of weed killer invaded my nose.

That had to be the reason the plant had died - there was no way the lush and healthy flowers could have died so quickly of something natural. The realization begged the question, who would have poured that much weed killer on the lilac bush? Why spend the time and money to do such a thing, and only target this one plant out of everything in the greenhouse?

My mind flashed to the threat against me; I gripped the edge of the flower pot so tightly my fingers began to ache as I contemplated the possibility that this was related. Whoever wanted to hurt me had to have been watching me - the picture taken of Noemi and myself proved that. What if they had watched me come to the greenhouse and taken note of the fact that I was so fond of this plant? The notion seemed crazy to me, but then again, so did the idea that I could have unknowingly done something to someone that made them want to hurt me. I felt stupid for growing complacent in the days of hearing nothing new since the threat.

The entire situation became too much and my breath quickened at the instruction of my anxiety. It was getting hard to stand so I let my body fall to a sitting position on the ground with an unceremonious thump, twisting so I could support my back against the lilac's flower pot. I scrunched up my eyes and pressed the heels of my hands to them as hard as I could without causing myself too much pain and tried to will the panic attack away from my body. My body trembled with the effort and deep breaths were not helping as they normally did.

My brain was so focused on trying to control the physical reactions my body was having to the stress I was under that it took a moment for me to register when the sudden banging sound of the door closing joined the pounding of my heartbeat in my chest. From my spot on the floor in the back corner of the greenhouse I could not see the door or who was currently making their heavy footed way towards me, so I did my best to shrink back among the flower pots as well as I could.

The first thing I noticed when the figure stepped around the corner from behind the center rack of plants was a familiar pair of slightly beat up and dirty grey hiking boots. My eyes traced a path upward, taking in the black skinny jeans that were tucked into the boots, the long grey overcoat and tan sweater, before coming to rest on the familiar face of none other than Radcliffe House's own Ollie Byrd. His black camera bag was swung over his right shoulder and a knit beanie was pulled tight over his head.

"Georgie? What are you doing on the floor?" he asked. Relief flooded my system and I quickly wiped away the tears that were making their way down my face and stood up on shaking legs.

"I, uh… the lilac bush is dead," I responded, gesturing weakly to the pot next to me. Ollie stepped over to get a closer look and let out a sad sigh.

"Do you know what happened to it? I was here just a few days ago and it was fine," he stated. I was secretly grateful he hadn't questioned why a dead plant would make me cry.

"Yeah, I was here last night and it was perfectly healthy then. The only thing that I can think of that could kill a plant that quickly is a ton of weed killer." I sniffled and felt a bit better now that I was talking to someone and not just wallowing in my own anxiety.

"Are any of the other plants dead? Maybe there was a leak and it got into the water somehow," Ollie suggested. I feebly shook my head.

"This one's the only one." Ollie took a quick glance around at the nearby plants to confirm what I was telling him.

"That's... weird. Why would only this plant be dead?" he mused. It was probably a rhetorical question, but I gave him an answer anyway.

"I think it's because of me. I took care of that plant better than any other one in here, I really came to love seeing it grow, and now that's the only one in here that's been killed in such a short amount of time."

"Why would someone go out of their way to kill a plant just because you were fond of it?" Confusion dawned on Ollie's face as he asked me that.

"Why would someone go out of their way to attack Noemi and threaten to kill me?" I countered with a harsh, humorless laugh, my voice still broken from crying.

"You think this is connected to the threat?"

"Why wouldn't it be? We know whoever sent the threat has been watching me - how else would they have gotten that picture of me and Noemi? Who's to say they haven't been watching me all the time since then, completely unnoticed? Who's to say they aren't watching us have this conversation right now?" My voice grew louder and more frantic as I continued speaking.

Ollie reached over to place a hand on my shoulder but I shrugged it off. Scanning the room and the short distance I could see through the glass walls of the greenhouse revealed nothing to me but I wasn't surprised; anyone skilled enough to put Noemi through the hell she suffered without any of the rest of us hearing it must be a little bit proficient with staying out of sight.

"Georgie, I don't think that's the case. I think you might just be a little stressed by the whole situation, so you're trying to make connections where there aren't any." Ollie spoke to me the way one speaks to a child blaming their sibling for something that was obviously their own fault or to a senile person who thinks the world is conspiring against them. Hearing that tone of voice aimed at me set me on edge more than I already was.

"Of course I'm stressed! There's someone out there who wants me dead, someone we all know is capable of making that happen! That does not mean I'm crazy," I asserted.

Ollie tried once again to calm me down by placing his hand on my arm but this time I pushed him off of me. I didn't think that I had pushed him that hard, but he staggered a step backwards into the rack at the center of the greenhouse. He put his hand back to steady himself on a shelf and smashed through a small pot. From where I was standing it didn't look like the ceramic shards cut his skin, but the palm of his hand was definitely covered in dirt and crushed leaves.

"I didn't say you were crazy, Georgie, but honestly now you're kind of acting like you are," he said. His voice was surprisingly calm for the altercation that had just taken place. He took a hesitant step in my direction. In return I sidestepped so the distance between us would be maintained, but I would be closer to the door.

"You try being on the receiving end of a death threat that was pinned to your bedroom door with an actual knife and coming out the other side unaffected," I said through gritted teeth. All of the emotions I had been doing my best to suppress for weeks - anxiety, anger, confusion - bubbled just underneath my control.

I turned sharply on my heel and strode out the door, leaving

Ollie to deal with the aftermath of our argument. As I walked away I had that eerie feeling of being watched that I dreaded, but I couldn't tell if it was just Ollie watching me go or someone more sinister lurking in the woods somewhere plotting my demise.

Chapter Forty-Two

AFTER SPENDING TWO DAYS locked in my room to keep the rest of the world out, I knew I had to go somewhere – even just for a little bit. I had nowhere else I could think to go, so I showed up to stage combat class despite my original plan to skip it. I took my usual spot at the back of the room and hoped no one would try to strike up a conversation with me. I gave Lourdes a weak smile when she greeted me, but everything else became background static to my thoughts. Even when Professor Decker came in and started the lesson I continued to stare into space, grateful that after only a moment of talking he put on a short film about combat scenes in cinema for the class to watch.

The film took up the entire time allotted to class, so once it was over I quickly began to gather my things and made my way towards the door. Unfortunately, Professor Decker was faster than me and blocked my path of escape. He asked if I could stay for just a moment and I simply nodded in response. I waited off to the side while everyone else exited the room, giving a curt goodbye to Lourdes and ignoring the way I could feel Vincent and Clara's dislike of me radiating off of them.

After everyone had gone I stood my ground waiting for Professor Decker to break the silence himself. He gestured for me to take a seat on the ground, which I begrudgingly did; he sat down next to me.

"Georgie, what's wrong? You're not acting like your usual self," he said. "You missed rehearsal on Wednesday, and I appreciate you letting me know about that ahead of time, but Professor Rhodes told me that you skipped class yesterday with no warning."

I shrugged noncommittally. "I've just been feeling a little unwell, that's all. But I'm getting better." I refused to meet his eyes, though I could feel his gaze on me.

"This doesn't have anything to do with that argument you had with Vincent a little while ago, does it? I've noticed that you seem to be distancing yourself from the others."

"It's nothing to do with that. I just tend to keep to myself when I'm feeling ill. There's nothing bad going on between us." I knew I was terrible at lying but hoped he'd believe me anyway.

"I won't push you if you don't want to talk to me, but I don't think that's the truth. At least not the whole of it." He placed a hand on my shoulder and gave what I figured was supposed to be a reassuring squeeze. I wanted to shrug him off so he wasn't touching me, but the close proximity made that a hard move to make. Luckily he dropped his hand himself.

"You know you can always come to me, right?" His calm voice was betrayed by something darker lurking underneath. Was it possible that he knew what I was really going through? If he did, why would he bother asking what was wrong?

I shook slightly with sudden chills, causing him to tighten his grip on my shoulder. I forced my breathing to remain slow and even.

"I know, Adrian," I said, and really I did. He said that phrase often enough for it to repeat in his voice in the back of my mind any time I felt like my life was starting to spiral out of control, which as of late seemed to be all of the time. I forced a smile onto my face that I hoped he thought was sincere. "I think I just need to go home and take it easy today, then I'll be right as rain tomorrow."

I finally looked up from my lap and found him to be leaning even closer to me than I had expected. I fought the urge to jump back in surprise, managing to not flinch. He stood up first, offering me a hand to help me get up. Then before I could get out of his arms' reach he pulled me into a surprise hug. This was not the first embrace we had shared, but it certainly didn't feel the same as the last. The first had been calm and comforting whereas this one felt slightly more aggressive and possessive. I carefully peeled myself out of his grasp and stepped back.

"I'll be sure to tell you when I need you," I called out, making my way to the exit. I hurried out of there as fast as I could, craving nothing more than the solitude I had surrounded myself with lately.

Part Four

December

I heard a bird sing
In the dark of December.
A magical thing
And sweet to remember.
"We are nearer to Spring
Than we were in September,"
I heard a bird sing
In the dark of December.

—— Oliver Herford, "I Heard A Bird Sing"

Chapter Forty-Three

I SAT ON MY bed, perusing my reading options. The sensible decision would be to start reading the collection of poems by Siegfried Sassoon for Modern British Literature as it was the last piece of literature for the course, but I had recently acquired a few *Sherlock Holmes* novels from the library that I was itching to break into. Part of me wondered if it was because of the seemingly unsolvable investigation in my own life that I wanted to see mysteries figured out so easily. Before I could decide, a knock sounded at my door.

I hesitantly pulled it open, revealing Ahra already in her pajamas despite it only being 8pm. It was as dark as midnight outside, though, so it didn't seem too strange. She looked up from gazing at the floor, her eyes puffy and tinged red from crying.

"Georgie? Can we please talk?" I nodded and stepped to the side to let her into the room. She took a seat at the foot of my bed and waited for me to join her before talking again. "I'm so sorry about... well, everything. I've been a terrible friend," she said, and her voice betrayed that she was on the verge of bursting into tears again.

"It's okay, Ahra, I forgive you." I was surprised to find that I meant it. All of the anger and resentment I had been holding towards her and Ollie and River seemed to dissipate in that moment; maybe I just needed a friend more than ever. I reached out to rub comforting circles into her back and it was like her body melted into my own.

"I know you've been so stressed and I've just been ignoring you! I was just thinking about myself and how all this was such a huge bother in my life, but it can only be infinitely worse for you," she admitted. "Ollie finally talked some sense into me, though, and I just feel awful."

"Shh, it's okay. I'm sorry you have to deal with this because of me," I replied. Ahra sat up and looked me in the eyes, a pout creasing her face.

"Georgie, you don't have to apologize for that. It's not like you asked for someone to threaten you like this, and besides, we're friends. Friends help and support each other, and I'm going to be a good friend again," she insisted.

I responded with a nod and did my best not to start crying

myself. Ahra brought up the investigation and how determined she was to figure things out, and I let her know about how weird Professor Decker had been acting lately. A look of horror dawned on her face.

"You don't think he could be behind all of this, do you?" I paused for a moment and considered the possibility before shaking my head.

"No, it wouldn't make sense. I mean, he likes me. Why would he want me dead? And we've had ample time alone together where he could have hurt me. On top of that, he only started acting weird recently. The timeline just doesn't add up," I explained, blurting out every excuse I could think of. I refused to believe that someone who seemed to want the best for me could be behind such misery.

"You said that he brought up that argument we all had with Vincent again recently. Could it be that Vincent finally came clean and told him about the investigation? That might explain why he would start acting strange," Ahra suggested.

"I... I really don't know what I think anymore. I know if I ask Professor Decker about it again, he'll just say Vincent never told him any details."

"Why don't we ask Vincent then?"

"Do you think he will want to talk to us at all, let alone be honest with us?"

"No, but maybe if we ask him as nicely as we can he'll talk to us anyway."

I sighed, not completely convinced. Suddenly Ahra stood up, pulling me with her as our arms were still wrapped around each other, and pushed me gently towards the door. "Come on, we're going now. If he's home, we're gonna confront Vincent about this." I froze in my tracks.

"Uh, are you sure that's a good idea? What if he's the one behind the threats and attacks us?" I asked. I was positive Ahra could hold her own in a normal fight even with her disability; she would probably use her walking aids as weapons. Despite his own disability though, if Vincent was able to harm someone the way Noemi was harmed, I wasn't so sure that would be enough. As for myself, I'd probably just burst into tears or throw up from the anxiety of it all before he could even get a single hit in.

"We'll bring Ollie along. I don't think he would try anything when we're in a bigger group like that no matter how mad he was," she answered without missing a beat.

Begrudgingly I went along with her plan. I understood why she would suggest bringing Ollie but not River. I doubted that they would want to see their paramour whom they were not currently speaking to just to ask about the investigation where said paramour was a suspect in the first place.

We had to knock twice before someone answered the door to the front tower. That someone was Damian Little, his signature scowl gracing his face mere moments after registering who was bothering him.

"What do you want?" he demanded. He glared at me and I wondered if Professor Decker had mentioned the rejected idea of us trading classes to him. I tried to take a step back, not wanting to be near the frightening man, but Ollie's body blocked me from going anywhere.

"We need to talk to Vincent, is he home?" Ahra asked, apparently unaffected by Damian's rough demeanor. Damian rolled his eyes and called out for Vincent to come to the door and meet his company. Vincent wheeled his way into view and scoffed at us, but invited us into his room anyway.

Clara was sitting on his bed and rolled her eyes when she saw us coming in. "I guess we'll pick this project back up later." She made a show of packing up her things before stomping out of the room and up the stairs after Damian.

"So, what is it that you guys are here for?" Vincent asked deadpan.

"Georgie has a question for you," Ahra said, putting me on the spot. I struggled to speak for a moment as Vincent looked at me expectantly.

"Yeah, uh, I just... I was just wondering what it is you told Professor Decker the other week, you know, when you mentioned that we had a... disagreement," I stuttered quietly, not wanting to risk talking too loud and having the others hear me.

Vincent squinted in confusion before responding. "He asked me why I seemed so on edge and I told him that I got into a fight with some friends. After a bit of prodding I told him you were one of them. I didn't go into any details though, if that's what you're asking. I know I threatened to, but you really seemed adamant that I shouldn't, and I'm not that mean," he explained. I felt the slightest bit of tension lift from my shoulders. "Why do you ask? Has he brought your stupid investigation up to you or something?"

I shook my head. "No, he's just been acting strange around me lately. Kind of paranoid." I decided to leave out any details about Professor Decker's recent possessive behavior. I wasn't even comfortable thinking about it, so I knew I would not enjoy talking about it with a group of people, even if they were my friends. Vincent nodded in understanding.

"I noticed that he was acting a little odd, too. More fidgety than usual, like he's got a lot on his mind and no time to sort it all out. I hate to break it to you, but if someone told him about the investigation, it has to have been someone else, because it sure as hell wasn't me."

"Thanks for clearing that up, Vincent," I said quietly.

"Well if that's all you wanted…"

"Right, of course." The three of us left without another word. We waited until we were back in the safety of our own tower before we spoke to each other.

"So, what now?" I asked. It felt like we were no closer to figuring out who was after me than we had been for weeks.

"We get back to the investigation, I guess. I know you haven't been fully in on the investigation so far, Georgie, but why don't you come with me the day after tomorrow to check out the woods one last time?" Ahra answered.

"It's been two months, do you really think you'll be able to find anything?" Ollie questioned.

"No, but it's worth a shot. Those records didn't tell us anything new, but I can't just sit around doing nothing. What do you say, Georgie?" My friends turned to look at me and I shrugged.

"Sure, maybe we'll find something that'll crack the case wide open," I said with a forced smile. I knew that if we weren't planning on going to the police, I should have been in this investigation wholeheartedly since I received the threat on my door. What kind of friend had I been that I just let my friends worry about me and try to solve my problem while I just sat around trying to pretend nothing was wrong.

"That's the right attitude," Ahra said with genuine positivity. "Hell, maybe we'll be able to figure this all out and get it squared away so quickly that we'll be able to enjoy the Winter Festival without this shadow looming over us."

"If we don't figure it out by then, I think we should go to the police," Ollie admitted. "It's been two months since Noemi was attacked and one month since Georgie was threatened. We have to have a back up plan for if we don't figure it out."

Ahra and I nodded. The Winter Festival took place right before final exams, which were a little over two weeks away. One way or another, this would all be over soon.

Chapter Forty-Four

"Okay so we already looked at the ground all around where we found Noemi, so I thought that maybe we could look on the opposite side of the amphitheater, just to cover our bases," Ahra explained as she and I trudged through the trees back to the site of that fateful event on my birthday.

Goosebumps rose across my arms and the back of my neck at my anxiety from being here. I rubbed my arms to spread warmth over them, telling myself that I was just cold and there was nothing to be scared of.

"Over here is where I found that scrap of fabric," Ahra explained, pointing to a thorny bush. The scrap of fabric she was referring to was more like a handful of white threads she had shown everyone a few weeks after the incident occurred, now more than a month ago. "It wasn't much to go off of, but the fact that we found something is encouraging, right?"

"I guess, but it's been two months. There's no way we'll find anything from that night that hasn't been tampered with," I argued.

"Just because it's not likely doesn't mean it's not possible," she countered. "We know that anything we find might be from another time, but it is just as likely to be from that night as any other, so we have to keep looking. People don't come out here nearly as often as you might imagine."

Ahra continued to chatter about anything and everything she could think of, and today that happened to be ghosts exacting their revenge on the living as she had watched some horror movie the other night and had made it almost her entire personality. I did my best to tune her out; I knew her stories would do nothing but freak me out even more than I already was and I did not want to deal with the possibility of a panic attack so early in the day.

At one point Ahra suggested we split up and look in separate places, so she went off one way and I went the opposite direction, making sure to keep each other in our peripheries. I kept my eyes locked on the ground, partially to see if I actually found anything of interest but mostly to keep myself from tripping over my own feet. The morning sunlight dappled through the canopy of trees and that coupled with the uneven ground made it impossible to walk, especially since I seemed to have a habit of wearing the wrong shoes to every occasion; my heavy boots were not agreeing with the soft dirt.

Ahra was still talking, but even though she made a conscious effort to speak louder the further she walked away from me, I continued to actively tune her out. My ears focused on the whistle of the wind through the trees and the crunch of the underbrush beneath my boots. Ahra's words became an indistinct melody in the back of my mind.

We wandered through the woods like that for the better part of an hour with no success at finding things to help with our investigation. I stooped to admire a few purple flowers growing at the base of one of the trees and while I was down there, something metallic glinting in the sparse sunlight caught my eye. I pulled the tiny object out of the dirt and wiped it off, revealing a gold butterfly shaped charm with four small blue gems embedded in the wings and a broken loop at the top.

"Shit! I'm going to be late for class, we have to go!" Ahra yelled, loud enough that three birds in a nearby tree cawed and took flight. I stumbled after her - for someone who used mobility aids, she moved surprisingly fast over the tree roots, mud patches, and piles of leaves.

I tried looking at the charm as we went, but there wasn't much to see on it. The only identifying mark was something that might have been a serial number, a string of five numbers printed in a neat, tiny font on the back of one of the wings. I put the charm in one of the interior pockets of my bag, one that zippered shut so that I knew I wouldn't lose it before I could show Ahra and the others.

Chapter Forty-Five

THE FOUR OF US sat on the floor in Ollie's bedroom because he had the most open space for us and we didn't dare use the dining table to meet, not since Vincent surprised us that one day. His room seemed just as sparsely decorated as mine, but something about it was cozy and made me feel comfortable and safe. River still refused to look at me, staring instead at any other point in the room. Since neither of our friends seemed like they were going to confront them about this rift building between us, I decided to ignore it as well.

"There wasn't really anything interesting on the other side of the amphitheater. There were patches of footprints, but there was no way to tell how old they were or even what type of shoe they came from," Ahra started explaining.

"I found something," I said, and suddenly all three pairs of eyes shot to look at me. Then River remembered themself and looked away. "This charm was wedged in the dirt at the base of a tree." I pulled out the little metal and gem butterfly and handed it off to Ahra, who then passed it to Ollie, who then gave it to River. A sudden look of recognition donned River's face as they paled in realization of what they were holding.

"I know where this came from... it's part of a bracelet that belongs to Lourdes," they admitted. They sounded skeptical, not in the way that they didn't believe what they were saying but in the way that they didn't want this to be true.

"How would you know that, River?" Ollie asked. River continued turning the charm over in their hands a few more times before responding.

"I bought her that bracelet. It was a Christmas present during our first year here, back when we were still friends. She loves butterflies, so when I saw the bracelet at a garage sale I instantly thought of her."

"Are you absolutely certain? That could implement her," Ahra said, her voice solid as stone and just as serious. River shot her a look that was equal parts pain and anger.

"Yes I'm sure, you think I don't know what that means about her?" they replied.

"But I thought we had basically ruled her out of this, or at least put her as the least likely suspect of the five," I interjected. "We walked home together that night with no one else there, so why would she have waited until I was safe in my room to threaten me instead of just hurting me when she had the chance?"

"You were all drinking. Maybe she didn't realize she had missed her opportunity until she sobered up a bit, and that's what prompted her to leave the threat," Ahra suggested, shifting uncomfortably where she sat.

"I still don't think she's involved," River insisted.

"I did find the charm on the back side of the amphitheater, far away from where we found Noemi. It probably ended up there from something completely unrelated." I could see that I was not doing a good job of reassuring them.

"We were stupid to have ruled her out in the first place. It could be any one of them," Ahra said.

A tense silence filled the room as none of us knew what to say. Our eyes were all locked on the butterfly charm as River turned it over in their hand.

"So... what next?" they asked after a few moments.

"We have to go to the police now. We're never going to figure this out," Ollie said. It hurt to see Ollie, ever the optimist, giving up like that. Though of course we all should have known from the start that this investigation was doomed.

Ahra pouted. "Give us some more time, my friend says he can get the police records this week."

"You have a friend who's breaking into police records for us?

Ahra, that's so dangerous!" I exclaimed.

She turned to look at me, a hard expression in her eyes. "What's dangerous is someone out there having the capability to hurt Noemi the way they did and then turning around and terrorizing you for weeks. I won't let them get you." Then, to Ollie, "We agreed that we'd go to the police after the Winter Festival. Those records have to reveal something."

Ollie assented with only the slightest hesitation.

"At this point would the police even believe us?" River asked, eyes still fixated on the butterfly charm. "I mean, it's been so long at this point."

"They'd understand once we showed them the note that said not to go to the police," Ollie insisted.

"And what if they just think it's a prank? That was the conclusion Vincent came to, so it's not unreasonable to think that other people would see it that way, too."

"We'll deal with that if we get there. There's no use stressing ourselves out over things that might be the case when we already have enough to deal with," Ahra insisted.

Ahra took my hand in her own and I gripped it harder than I meant to. The Winter Festival was coming up fast and yet felt so far away. If we didn't figure out who was after me by then and stop them, I hoped that the police would be quick enough to keep my friends safe, even if it meant I would be put in more danger.

Chapter Forty-Six

I chafed under my many layers of clothing as Ollie and I walked to Castle Blackscar, braving the twenty degree weather. Professor Decker had sent out a mass email to all of his teaching assistants asking to meet with us and though I had originally wanted to feign illness and skip out on it, I knew that I had to go. Ollie offered to walk with me because my stomach churned at the thought of not having a friend to ground me amidst my anxiety.

The professor's office door was already open when Ollie and I got there; I was the last to arrive, so six pairs of eyes turned to watch me as I said a quiet goodbye to my friend and stepped into the room.

"So nice of you to finally join us," Damian muttered under his breath at me.

I don't know what came over me, but almost without thinking I glanced at my watch and replied, "It's still six minutes until nine, there's no need to snark at me when I'm not late." My face burned with embarrassment as Damian looked at me as if he couldn't believe what I had said, but luckily my cheeks were already red from the cold wind that had whipped at my face on the walk over.

"Well, why don't we get started with the meeting," Professor Decker said, his words cutting through the tension like a knife.

He held himself stiffly as if there were something on his mind, but his presence in the room was like a lifeline to me despite how strangely he had been acting recently. Still, he stood tall and commanded attention like he did in any room he entered. The six of us all looked to him and waited for what he would say next.

"This semester is nearly at its end and we need to get things squared away before the next one starts. Obviously for those of you staying on campus through winter break we can continue to meet when needed and for those of you leaving there's always email, but I wanted to touch base with everyone to know where we all stand."

"Did we really all have to be here? Or could this not have just been a meeting with her?" Vincent asked, his eyes darting to me with the last word.

As much as I didn't like it, I found myself agreeing with him.

Professor Decker had been working with the others for several years and there was no doubt that they all knew how to make things run smoothly. I was the outsider here who needed to learn, and aside from Ailani I didn't see a need for any of the rest of them to be there.

"I wanted you all here because though you help me out with different classes, you are all one group. Georgie is now part of that no matter what you may think. I have heard about some plans some of you have had regarding her involvement with me."

My heart caught in my throat at these words. Decker's eyes flicked from my face, which must have resembled a deer looking at the oncoming headlights of a truck, past Clara and landed on Damian.

"Mr. Little, did you really think I wouldn't see that you were the one behind the idea of Georgie taking over your class so that you could have Travel Literature next semester?" he asked. I breathed a sigh of relief that the professor still didn't seem to know about the threat that had been left on my door.

"What?" Clara exclaimed. "Why would she switch with you and not me?"

"She's not switching with anyone," Professor Decker asserted.

"And why not? Give her a class, fine, whatever, but why does it have to be that one? It feels like you just want us to be angry,"

Damian spat.

"Guys, can you just calm down for once?" Lourdes cut in.

"Yet another reason why we shouldn't have had this meeting with all of us, because it's not like we didn't see this happening," Vincent muttered. Ailani nodded in his direction, seemingly too tired to even speak.

There was too much noise happening with everyone talking over each other, so I shrank back against a bookcase in a poor attempt to get away from it. Something, the corner of a book sticking out at an odd angle most likely, dug into my spine, but I didn't move. The jab of pain helped ground my thoughts and kept me from spiraling into an anxiety attack.

"Enough!" the professor shouted. I flinched at the noise, though I couldn't go very far. I bit my lip to keep from crying out as the book dug further into me. "It seems you were right, Mr. Alexander. I thought you could all behave like rational adults here, but I guess I was wrong. Georgie, Ailani, if the two of you would please stay here. I'll contact the rest of you when I'm ready to meet with you."

Both Clara and Damian looked like they were going to protest, but Lourdes stepped up and physically herded them out of the room. She flashed me an apologetic smile as she passed, and I hoped the one I returned didn't seem too forced. Once the three of them and Vincent were gone, tension seemed to drop from the professor as he dropped into his chair with a sigh.

"They haven't always been like this, have they?" he asked Ailani as she cleared off the two other seats for us to sit in.

"It's never been this bad," she admitted. She didn't look at me as she spoke, but I could tell there was a silent second part to that sentence, that they were never this bad until I was invited into the group. I looked at my lap, too ashamed to face either of them.

"It's not your fault, Georgie," Professor Decker assured as if he could read my mind. "The things they say and the way they act is their decision, and they have no right to try and pin the blame on someone else."

His words helped cool my shame and anxiety ever so slightly, though I still blamed myself a bit. My mind flashed back to when I was younger and my brother would get upset that he couldn't play with me the way he wanted to because I was too little thanks to the age gap between us. My father would always assure me that my brother's anger had nothing to do with me and though I didn't always believe him, it would make me feel better.

I felt like I was on autopilot for the rest of the meeting, but the fact that both Ailani and the professor seemed to not want to be there either made me feel less guilty about my lack of conversational contribution. Most of it was stuff that Ailani and I had gone through before anyway - the basic format of

Travel Literature, the general syllabus that Professor Decker and I would finalize later, expectations I would have to fill as the teaching assistant.

After what felt like ages - I hadn't checked my watch at all for fear of the professor thinking I was being rude - we were all satisfied with everything that had been discussed and Decker released Ailani and I to go about the rest of our day. I let Ailani leave first and to avoid being alone with her in the halls, I hesitated in the doorway.

"Is there something else you wanted to talk about, Georgie?"

I turned to look at the professor. He looked much more tired than usual, slouching at his desk, as if dealing with his unruly teaching assistants and whatever else was on his plate weighed on him physically as well as mentally.

"Thank you," I said quietly. "For always defending me to the others. Sometimes it's hard to feel like I deserve all that I've been given, and their words don't help that. So, thank you for being on my side, Adrian."

"Of course. You're a special young lady, Georgie. You deserve all of the great things you get, and I want to help you see that."

For the first time in several weeks it seemed like the professor's smile was a genuine one, and not forced or full of tension. I held onto that moment for just a second longer, and then my phone buzzed to let me know my meeting with Professor Rhodes was supposed to happen in just ten minutes. I had hoped that Ollie and I could get some lunch together between the meetings, but it seemed like that would not be the case. I shot him a quick text as I hurried to the other wing of the castle in order to make it to Professor Rhodes's office on time.

Chapter Forty-Seven

I STILL HADN'T SHAKEN my stupor by the time I made it to Professor Rhodes's office and she immediately noticed that something was off. Well, something more than usual.

"Is there anything in particular I can help you with, Georgie?" she asked, her tone like the one you would use when talking to a child.

I shook my head and kept my mouth shut.

"This is our last meeting of the semester and I just want to make sure everything is squared away. How do you feel about your finals coming up?"

"I have your exam on Tuesday and my final presentation for Stage Combat on Wednesday, and I don't see why I wouldn't do fine on both of them. I've already finished the translation piece I had to do for my Hebrew class and my partner and I are putting the final touches on the paper for Modern British Literature." In truth I had been partnered with my classmate Liam, who was very controlling about schoolwork. He had me pick out the topic of the paper and then said he would do the actual writing. I tried to protest this, but he assured me that I could just put my name on it at the end. It felt wrong, but at least it was one less thing to worry about.

"I'm glad to hear you've got everything all under control. It seems you've done an excellent job settling into your life here at Westwood despite the... issues you've had to deal with."

I suppressed a dry, humorless laugh. She knew about Noemi, but that was only the tip of the iceberg when it came to my 'issues', though it was on purpose that she didn't know about anything else.

"Are we going to have these meetings next semester?" I asked. She watched me for a moment before answering and I tried my best not to squirm in my seat under her intense gaze.

"Do you think we need to keep meeting?" she replied back.

I shook my head. "I don't think that'll be necessary." I was trying to be as polite as possible, hoping that would convince her.

She spoke after a pause. "I don't think so either. A lot of people were worried about how you'd adjust when you transferred in so late in the system - your brother and several members of administration mostly - but it looks like you've adjusted as well as can be expected. I'd like to meet with you a couple more times next semester because I am still your academic advisor, maybe once a month at most, but anything beyond that seems like excess."

I was shocked that the professor was agreeing with me, but I wasn't about to bring that up and potentially change her mind. After a bit more small talk I was out the door and heading towards the library, where I was due to meet Ollie at our usual meeting place. Despite the stressful things that still remained, I felt relieved that there was at least one less thing to deal with, even if my meetings with Professor Rhodes were the smallest thing on my plate.

Chapter Forty-Eight

THE AIR WAS CRISP and the sun was bright with only a few clouds floating high in the sky. Birds chirped in the tree that grew beside Radcliffe House and I could see from my bedroom window that it was a family of sparrows. I focused on the birds and the sunshine and the cool December air as I got dressed, not wanting to ruin such a lovely day so early in the morning with my usual negative thoughts.

It was a special day and for that reason I pulled on my mother's black sweater and my most comfortable pair of blue jeans. Looking in the mirror I felt a little plain, so I grabbed my pink corduroy jacket to bring a bit of color into the outfit. I finished getting ready by pulling on my black boots and grabbing a small crossbody purse to hold my phone, wallet, and chapstick. I must have taken the least amount of time to get ready out of all my housemates because when I made my way downstairs, I found the common area still empty.

My stomach grumbled and I contemplated grabbing something to eat, maybe a cup of yogurt or a granola bar, just something small, but we had agreed last night that the first order of Winter Festival business for us would be breakfast at the café in order to try all of special dishes they brought out just for this weekend. I rubbed my stomach in an attempt to appease my hunger and relaxed on the couch to wait for my friends to get ready, nervously looking at the door to the front tower and hoping no one would come out of there. Ollie was the first to join me in the common area, dressed in his usual neutral tones with his camera bag in its regular place hanging over his shoulder.

"Good morning, Georgie. Are you excited for your first Winter Festival?" he asked, taking a seat on the opposite side of the couch.

"Very," I responded with a smile. "I just hope those two slowpokes don't keep us waiting for too much longer, I'm starving!" I joked. Ollie laughed as the door to our tower burst open once more. Ahra stood in the doorway fixing her hair into two large puffs.

"I'm coming, I'm coming. Don't get your panties in a twist," she playfully nagged through the bobby pins she held between her teeth.

"River! Are you coming down any time soon?" Ollie called in the direction of the upstairs. A noncommittal yell came back in response, and a moment later River bounced their way into the room.

"I don't need you rushing me - you know it takes time to look this good!" they beamed, showing off the outfit they had put together for the occasion.

They wore an almond colored button down shirt tucked into brown slacks, though half of the buttons were undone to reveal an off white t-shirt beneath it. Their belt and shoes were the same dark brown leather and matched the bag they had slung over one shoulder. They held a simple tan jacket in one hand and as they turned, the overhead light glinted on a gold necklace they were wearing. To complement the slightly disheveled yet still put together look they had going on, River's wavy sand colored hair had been styled neatly, but it looked like they had run their hands through it a few times to mess it up ever so slightly.

"You look marvelous, now can we get going?" Ahra asked as she pulled her bag onto her shoulder. She was wearing a simple plaid dress over a white collared shirt, black leggings, and a warm pair of boots. "I don't want to get to the café so late that they don't have any seating. Last year we had to wait forty minutes just to get a table," she groaned. River grumbled about how she had just finished getting ready as well, and the three of us followed her lead out the door and made the short walk over to the café.

Luckily we managed to grab the last open table before a line started forming. It was wedged into the corner and we didn't have quite as much space as the other tables would have afforded us, but it beat having to stand outside waiting for other people to finish their meals. The crowded café was louder than I expected and the noise seemed to take a toll on Ollie, who put in their earbuds in an attempt to block out some of it. I put my hand on his shoulder and flashed what I hoped was a reassuring smile and he seemed to relax a little bit. A moment later our waitress came to take our drink orders and I was pleased to see it was my classmate Mickie.

"I got this, guys," River said, presumably taking the lead because they were seated closest to where our waitress was standing. "Ahra over here will want an iced pumpkin spice latte, for Ollie a hot apple cider, and a peppermint hot chocolate for Georgie. Oh, and just a black coffee for me, please."

"Okay, I will get that out to you shortly and take your food order then," Mickie said with a smile before weaving back through the crowded café.

"How did you know I'd want a peppermint hot chocolate?" I questioned. River shrugged in response.

"I've seen you make it at home a couple of times, so I figured that's what you'd want. Did I get it wrong?" They seemed almost saddened by that last thought.

"No, not at all. I just didn't expect you to notice something like that." I replied.

"Well, you're my friend. I like remembering things about my friends," they said tentatively, as if they weren't quite sure they could use the friend for me. We smiled at each other, and I felt the rift between us begin to heal. Things weren't completely mended, it would take more than a hot chocolate to do that, but it was a start.

Before too long Mickie returned with our drinks and then a little while later with our food. Ollie ordered a belgian waffle topped with whipped cream and cranberries, River had cinnamon pancakes that they drizzled a generous amount of honey over, and Ahra and I both decided on caramel french toast. That turned out to be a wonderful decision as the sweetness of the warm caramel balanced out with the breadiness of the french toast itself. It was a perfect start to a lovely day.

After finishing our meal it was just approaching midday and the festivities seemed to be getting into full swing. The first thing we did was stop by a face painting booth run by three first year students from the art discipline that Ahra knew from the mentoring program she participated in. Ahra convinced me to get a cute snowflake painted on my cheek to match her and Ollie insisted he get a couple of pictures.

We posed by a tree that still had a surprising number of orange and red leaves clinging to its branches despite the late season. The pictures started off normal enough with wide smiles and peace signs, but eventually they devolved into tongues sticking out and the two of us clinging to each other to keep from falling over with laughter.

We moved on to a row of booths all hosting games and spent entirely too much time and money trying to win prizes. Ollie managed to snag a snowman plush by landing his hula hoop tosses around three small fake trees, but the rest of us only managed to get a handful of game operators telling us 'better luck next time'.

"We have to do the donut on a string! It's a Winter Festival must!" Ahra insisted, leading our gang over to a booth. Strung in three rows of four were donuts covered in powdered sugar. There were a few people attempting to eat the donuts as they swung wildly around.

"So... we pay money to get powdered sugar all over our faces while we make fools of ourselves?" I questioned. Ahra nodded enthusiastically.

"Ahra, you know they use apple cider donuts, and I'm allergic to apples," River protested.

"Yeah, but Ollie and Georgie aren't," she rebutted. She then turned to face me. "You're not allergic to apples, are you?" she asked, lowering her voice. I laughed and assured her that I was not. She paid for the three of us to enter the competition - one dollar each - and we were set up in a row with the fourth spot being taken by a young man who clearly had too much to drink already given what time of day it was.

"Ready, set, go!" the operator called, and the four of us jumped at our donuts. Since they were all on the same string, whenever one of us nudged one donut the rest of them went wild.

I let out a surprise squeak as mine hit me in the face and was grateful I hadn't put on any makeup for the day. The powdered sugar was doing a good enough job acting as a ghastly foundation.

"And we have our winner!" cried the operator just a few moments later. I groaned, sad that I had barely gotten through a third of my donut, but then cheered when I saw it was Ahra who had one. Her prize was a small bag of caramel popcorn. We thanked the operator and accepted the moist towelettes given to us to clean our faces before making our way back over to where River waited for us.

"Are you alright?" I asked Ahra, who was shivering fiercely. "Here, take my jacket." At first she tried to refuse but I wasn't taking no for an answer. She thanked me as she shrugged the pink garment on.

"See, you didn't even need Georgie or Ollie to help you out. You know you win every time," River playfully jabbed.

"Yeah, I know," Ahra bragged. "But it is more fun when

we're all doing it together."

We walked along the paths some more, stopping at a food stall to get grilled cheese sandwiches as part of a late lunch and then buying cotton candy from the stall next to that one. Though it was only around 5pm, the sky had gotten pretty dark already and people in charge of the Winter Festival began to turn on the strings of lanterns and fairy lights that were strung up between the booths and the surrounding trees. The golden glow cast on the scene gave everything a magical aura and I gasped at the beauty of it all.

Ollie crowded Ahra, River, and me in front of a painted backdrop of a snowy landscape and snapped a few pictures. Someone he seemed to recognize came by a moment later and offered to take pictures so that Ollie could be in them as well. We spent the better part of half an hour doing that, wanting to make the most of dying sunlight. Everyone agreed that the best pictures were ones where River stood in front of a snowman decoration made out of stacked tires sprayed white and mimicked its pose, followed by the one taken immediately after where River, terrified, realized the crow on its arm was not part of the decoration after it cawed at them.

"Alright, it's getting to be about that time, what do you guys say we get some spiked eggnog?" they suggested, trying to recover their ego from that embarrassing moment.

"That sounds like a wonderful plan," Ollie said as he

thanked his friend and took his camera back. He snapped one more candid picture of us before putting it carefully back in its bag. River led us to the booth that handled the alcoholic drinks and introduced us to their friend René who was the one running it at that moment.

"René, can you get us four eggnogs please? And can you put extra cinnamon on top?" they asked. René got the drinks back to us much quicker than I expected, and that first sip was like nothing I had ever tried before.

The creamy liquid was thicker than expected, reminding me of melted ice cream though it was much warmer than that would have been. The cinnamon gave it a little spice and there was definitely a bit of a kick from whatever alcohol they had put in it. René said it was rum, and I made a mental note to try recreating this back at home. Wishing René a good night, we made our way back out to the festival proper.

I nearly knocked Ahra over as I bumped into her, not noticing that she had stopped walking. I looked up to see what the hold up was and made direct eye contact with none other than Damian Little. He stood mere feet away, Vincent to the left and Clara to the right of him. Lourdes and Ailani stood a bit behind the three others. Their group stood facing ours in a beat of silence that felt like hours in a single moment.

There was a strange tension in the air, a mix of the different relationships and feelings that lingered between the individuals, muddying the interaction of the groups as a whole. Each of them seemed somewhat okay when I had to face them one or two at a time, but the five of them together made a much more imposing sight, especially without Professor Decker there to reassure me that everything was fine. I managed to not think of the threat on my life all day, but seeing our potential suspects here in front of me, my mind and heart started racing and I clung to Ahra's arm.

Chapter Forty-Nine

"Are you going to apologize for running into me or what?" Damian asked, cocking his head to the side. He accepted a napkin from Lourdes and began dabbing at whatever liquid ran down the front of his shirt.

"I wasn't... I didn't—" Ollie stuttered, eyes focused on the ground. He gripped his half empty cup tightly and his face began to twitch, signs that he was beginning to feel overwhelmed. I moved to step over to him, but River beat me to it.

"You're the one who ran into Ollie," they insisted, taking a firm stance in front of their friend. "Maybe next time you should look before barreling around a corner like an elephant."

"What did you just call me?" Damian moved as if to surge forward, but stopped as Vincent put a hand on his elbow.

"Oh calm down, you know nothing they say should carry

any weight."

"Excuse me?" This time it was River who looked like they were seeing red.

"We should all calm down, there's no reason to get all worked up over this," Lourdes said, trying and failing to stop the altercation. She flashed me an apologetic look. "Seriously, it's probably just the alcohol talking."

"I wouldn't be surprised if they all planned this out. River's always been jealous of us, and Georgie seems to be very good at getting into things where she doesn't belong. Maybe they thought they'd take the opportunity to make us look foolish," Clara said, jumping into the conversation. I choked on my spit, surprised at being dragged into it.

"Maybe we should leave..." Ailani mumbled.

"No, maybe they should. No one wants them around anyway," Damian insisted.

"I, um... I'm gonna go find someone. A professor," Ollie murmured to my left. Without another word he turned and started walking quickly into the crowd of people.

"Well at least that's one of them out of the way, now the rest of you can move," Damian said. A few people had noticed our little quarrel going on and moved to skirt around us. With Ollie gone there was no need for the rest of us to move; the path was certainly wide enough for even Vincent in his wheelchair to make his way past. Now it seemed everyone was just arguing for the sake of arguing.

Insults were thrown by both sides and returned with vigor, the argument devolving from the current issue to encompass all of the petty squabbles between everyone. I stayed to the back, not wanting to get into the middle of things, though Damian and Clara did both direct their anger in my direction. Luckily Ahra stood her ground and defended me.

Vincent and River yelled about their latest relationship troubles. Ailani seemed to be in a similar position to me - hanging back to avoid confrontation. Lourdes was the one rational thinker, trying to get everyone to stop shouting so much, to no avail. Some people stopped to stare and watch the drama unfold, but most moved past us with only a roll of their eyes or a comment about being annoyed.

Just a few minutes passed before Ollie came back with none other than Professor Decker, but those few minutes of shouting were enough to bring my anxiety bubbling to the surface. Ahra did her best to shield me, and her protection was the only thing keeping me from being pulled fully into things, which probably would have brought me to tears from the stress.

To his credit Professor Decker broke up the fight pretty quickly, managing to stop the yelling with only a bit of his own. He gave Ahra and River a stern scolding before turning to reprimand Clara, Damian, and Vincent. While that happened Ollie pulled the three of us away from things and tried to talk us into visiting a few more of the booths. I lingered, not sure why I felt the urge to stay near Decker, but then moved on.

We headed back into the crowd, but things just did not feel the same as they had merely half an hour before.

While waiting in line for caramel apples I had that all too familiar feeling that I was being watched, but when I turned around I didn't see anyone looking in my direction. I tried to shake the feeling but it persisted.

River returned with their cotton candy just as Ahra, Ollie, and I received our apples. The sweet sugary goodness wasn't enough to get me back into the festive mood like I had hoped it would. Still, I followed my friends from attraction to attraction until they stopped at another cluster of games.

While they were distracted by trying to knock over tin cans with little pumpkin shaped balls, I wandered away through the crowd to find a trash can for my now empty cup and the stick my caramel apple had come on. Despite how late it was and how dark the sky had turned, the festival was just as crowded as it had been all day. I glimpsed a trash can about fifty feet away as two girls stepped past me so I walked over. As I went to throw my items in the can I felt a hand on my shoulder. Fearing the worst I spun around, coming face to face with a concerned looking Professor Decker standing only inches away. I instinctively tried to step back but the trash can kept me from moving very far.

"Professor Decker - um, Adrian - you scared me. I didn't realize you were there," I said, pressing my hand down on my chest in an attempt to calm down my heart rate.

"I'm sorry about that, Georgie. I just wanted to make sure you were okay after that little... altercation, shall we call it? You seemed bothered by it so after I finished talking to the others I wandered back this way to try and find you. Are you feeling alright?" he explained.

"Yeah, I'm fine. Things just got a little heated, probably because of the alcohol. I'm just not a fan of huge crowds or loud noises or fighting or anything like that," I rambled.

"I can't imagine anyone would be," he said, flashing me what I assumed he thought would be a reassuring smile. To me it was just unnerving, showing a little too much teeth and pulling the skin around his lips a little too tight. I attempted again to maneuver around the trash can so I could put a little bit of space between the two of us but I just ended up stumbling again, this time over a rock I hadn't noticed.

Professor Decker reached out to grab me by my left shoulder and right wrist to steady me, his grip almost painfully tight. I felt the stained part of my sleeve stick to me uncomfortably.

"Here, why don't we get you on more stable ground?" he suggested, pulling me a dozen feet further from the main festivities so we were standing under a tree that was hidden behind one of the now vacated festival booths. This one had less lighting than the others in the area, and I noticed one of the strings of fairy lights had burnt out.

"I should be heading back to my friends," I said, trying unsuccessfully to break the grip he still held on my wrist. "They're probably wondering where I am right now."

"You shouldn't have wandered away from them in the first place," he replied. "Especially not with the person who threatened you out there. You're lucky I found you - I'll keep you safe." He pulled me closer to him until I could smell the cinnamon and apple tinged alcohol on his breath. The hand that was not holding onto my wrist slid its way around my waist and held me in place. No matter how much I wriggled and writhed, he had me trapped.

"Really, Professor—"

"Adrian," he asserted.

"Adrian. I just stepped away for a moment to throw out my garbage. I only planned to be away from my friends for a quick second, and then I'd be back in the safety of numbers—" I pleaded, stopping myself short. It dawned on me that he mentioned the threat against me, something he shouldn't have known about. Not unless he had something to do with it. I wanted to scream for help, not knowing what was going on or what would happen next, but my voice caught in my throat.

"Shh, it's okay, it's okay," Decker murmured, his breath hot against my ear. "You're safe with me."

His lips brushed mine in the barest sense, but before things could go further a sharp pain in the back of my skull as my hair was yanked pulled me out of his grasp. I fell against a much smaller but just as solid figure. Arms wrapped around me from behind as one hand clasped around my throat and another held a wet rag solidly over my nose and mouth. As a sickly sweet smell akin to the lemon disinfectant I had smelled when visiting my father in the hospital invaded my senses, a look of horror and anger crossed Professor Decker's face.

I willed my body to fight back against the figure holding me, but my arms and legs felt like they were filling up with lead and refused to listen to my brain. The professor rushed forward to try and pry me out of the person's arms, and the last things I registered before falling unconscious were the sting of nails digging into my throat and the metallic tang of blood as I bit harshly into my own tongue.

Chapter Fifty

AT FIRST I WASN'T sure if I had actually opened my eyes or not because the room was that dark. I groggily sat up, the dull ache in the back of my head reminding me of what happened. For a split second I thought that was the worst of what my body was feeling before the nausea kicked in and I promptly leaned over to avoid vomiting on myself. My head swam and I barely managed to shift myself so that I wouldn't land in the vomit as my shivering, aching body lost the ability to sit up on its own.

I laid there for what felt like an eternity, my body convulsing in part from the cold and in part from my insides trying to process whatever was in my system that made me feel so wretched. My stomach churned and it felt like a blacksmith had made a home in my head as a rhythmic pounding throbbed behind my eyes. Even though I was laying on solid ground, the dizziness made it feel like I was on an airplane with turbulence issues and I was sure that I was experiencing what it felt like to be dying.

An unknowable amount of time later I awoke, unaware that I had even fallen asleep. In the state I had been in I thought it impossible, sure that if I were to fall asleep it would have been for good. I stayed on the ground for a long time, letting the dull ache in my head and the minor nausea I was still feeling subside before I gingerly propped myself up with first one arm and then the other, finally achieving a sitting position.

Without the distraction of my body in major distress my eyes were finally able to adjust to the darkness in the room and I could begin to make out what few features there were. As I took in details almost clinically I knew that there must still be something wrong with my brain - I should have been panicking, but somehow I couldn't bring myself to feel anything other than numbness. A side effect from whatever had been used to knock me out, I guessed.

Above me were two windows at the top of the stone wall. Their location against the ceiling made me think I was in a basement, otherwise they wouldn't have been placed so high up. The dim light shining through let me know that it was night.

On the wall directly across from me was a door. I crawled

over on my hands and knees, not quite trusting my head to stay on straight if I were to fully stand up, and was careful to avoid the mostly dried patch of vomit on the floor. When I first placed my hand on the ground I was surprised to feel a piece of rough fabric instead of the cold stone floor. It was a tattered and dirty blanket; I lined it up in one of the back corners of the room away from the vomit and continued my slow and painful journey to the door.

Once there, I rose painfully to my knees, the stones beneath me biting at the joints through the thin fabric of my jeans. Unsurprisingly, the doorknob did not yield to me when I tried to turn it - it was locked. I let out a disappointed sigh and wearily made the trek back to the blanket in the corner.

A sharp pain erupted in the palm of my left hand as I placed it down on the ground. When I pulled it closer to my face to look at it a metallic clang rang out as something small hit the ground in front of me. After wiping the blood off of my palm and making sure that the cut hadn't gone too deep, I carefully rubbed the ground in front of me to find the source of my new pain. What I found was a small, rusty nail. I threw it to the far side of the room where it couldn't get in my way again and made a mental note to get a tetanus shot once I made it out of here. If I made it out of here, I amended. I crawled my way back to the corner more carefully and sat on the blanket.

My ears became so accustomed to the silence in the bare

room that I began to pick up sounds I wouldn't normally have noticed. My stomach was making a constant gurgling noise and I could hear the faintest thumping of my heart in my chest. I hugged my now dirt-covered sweater closer to my body, wishing I had chosen something less sentimental to wear. A single cricket played his nighttime symphony for me from outside one of the windows and his rhythmic melody lulled me not quite into sleep, but rather into a semi conscious state that allowed my still aching body to rest while I remained aware of my minimal surroundings.

Chapter Fifty-One

THE SOUND OF A lock clicking open shocked me out of my exhausted trance and my eyes shot up to watch the door to the room swing open. The hallway beyond was just as dark and I could only just make out the familiar figure of one Clara Marie Williams.

She stood in the doorway staring back at me with an intensity equaling my own, and I was surprised to take in her disheveled appearance. Her normally stick straight, confident posture had become slouched, nervous almost as she shifted her weight every now and then from one foot to the other. Her hair was pulled back into its usual high ponytail but chunks of it were pulled out and hanging limply around her face. Dirt coated her clothing and smudged her hands and face, as if she had fallen outside and not bothered to clean herself off before coming here.

It clicked while I was staring at Clara that if she was the one standing there, then she must have been the one who had pulled me away from Professor Decker and knocked me unconscious. She was most likely also the one who had attacked Noemi and left the threatening note on my bedroom door. We stared at each other and I hoped she couldn't tell how paralyzed with fear I was becoming. I was completely at her mercy. At least with that revelation I could feel the emotional numbness wearing away; I only hoped the inevitable panic coming for me would energize me enough that I could figure out a way to escape.

After moments of agony passed with our eyes locked on each other she slowly reached over to her bag. I resisted the urge to flinch back further into the corner, terrified of what she could be pulling out. It was a nondescript plastic bag that she slowly bent over to place on the ground, never once breaking eye contact with me. She then stepped back into the hallway and pulled the door closed after her. The lock clicked back into place almost immediately, but I still waited several long, tense minutes before crawling my way over to see what she had left behind.

Inside the bag was a soft apple wrapped in a piece of paper towel. My stomach growled angrily at the sight of food however meager it was and I couldn't help but tear into it.

All too soon it was gone. My stomach almost seemed to ache more than it had before; now that it had received the slight bit of nourishment the apple had provided, it just wanted more. I wiped the juice off my face and the little bit of dried blood off my hand with the napkin and left it next to the door with the core of the apple and the plastic bag. I contemplated feeling around the room a little more just in case I had missed something, but I knew deep down all there was to find was the rusty nail, cobwebs and dust, and my own dried vomit.

I returned to the corner of the room with the blanket and curled up in the fetal position to try and get whatever rest I could manage. My sweater was the only thing keeping me somewhat warm in the freezing room I was locked in, and I silently thanked my mother for it. The worn out blanket would not have provided much extra warmth to my body, so instead I used it as a weak excuse for a buffer between myself and the rough stone that made up every surface in the room except the door. Eventually I found myself falling into a restless sleep.

Chapter Fifty-Two

IN AN ATTEMPT TO keep my mind from becoming overwhelmed with the terror that came from realizing Clara could do anything she wanted to me at any point, I busied my waking hours with taking stock of various aches and pains in my body. Focusing on my physical issues kept the mental ones at bay.

There was the constant pang of hunger in the pit of my stomach as well as a soreness I could feel in each and every one of my joints thanks to the rough floor. At one point I tried to rake my fingers through the rat's nest that my hair had become, but I gave up on that endeavor after an accidentally too sharp tug revealed that my scalp still hadn't recovered from where Clara had pulled to get me out of Professor Decker's grasp. At the very least that pain revealed that too much time couldn't have passed since then.

After a while had passed I thought myself ready to face the situation Clara had placed me in, and as I picked at the scab on the palm of my left hand I tried to formulate a plan of escape. Nothing came to mind. Nothing that I thought would work, anyway.

My only options for leaving the room were through the door or through one of the windows. The door was locked from the outside and even if I wasn't tired, starving, and in pain, I didn't think it would be possible for me to break through it. The windows were both too high for me to reach even if I stood on my toes, and also too narrow for me to squeeze my body through.

I resigned myself to accepting the truth: I was well and truly trapped in this room. I slouched in on myself, gripping the hem of my sweater for comfort as I waited for the panic to set in.

Suddenly the sounds of distant voices made their way to my ears and I paused to listen. They were coming closer to the room and I quickly rolled over onto my side so that my back was facing the door. I sucked in sharply as my kneecap slammed the floor and caused pins and needles to course down my leg, but as the lock on the door clicked open I made sure to steady my breathing so that whoever was entering the room would hopefully think I was asleep.

"Look, see? I told you she's fine. You have no reason to

worry," Clara said as the door creaked open.

"I'm not sure being held captive in a dark and dirty room can constitute being fine," replied a flat voice I recognized as Professor Decker's. I barely managed to keep myself from flinching as I remembered the feel of his arms around my waist and his breath on my face. "You need to let her out of here. We can't have another Noemi situation."

"You're the one who gave me the idea to get rid of my competition," Clara barked in response. "Why don't you just go to the police if you want her out of here? You've known about what I did to Noemi for weeks and had all that time to go report me and yet you didn't." My heart pounded harder in my chest. He had known about what really happened to Noemi this whole time?

Professor Decker let out a deep sigh that hung in the air for a moment before he spoke again. "Everything I've done has been to protect you, Clara," he said, his voice quiet and calm. "You know this. You are my first priority. You and the others."

"If that were true you never would have tried to bring anyone else into the fold. This is all your fault. You're such a greedy man, you already had the five of us. You said that we're your favorite group out of every set of teaching assistants you've ever had, so why would you need anyone else?" Clara sneered.

"I thought Georgie was special, too. I thought she would blend seamlessly into our little family. Never in a million years did I think that any of you would have taken it upon yourselves to 'get rid of the competition' as you said, you least of all. What could I have said to you that made you think I wanted you to do all of this?"

His voice started out mild enough, but by the end of his piece Professor Decker had begun to sound like an exasperated parent scolding a young child who would not learn their lesson no matter how many times they messed up. I imagined Clara defiantly staring him down, refusing to admit to her mistakes. The gentle embarrassment inflected in her voice when she replied, however, made me change my mental image to instead feature her looking at her feet, too ashamed to make even the slightest eye contact with the man she disappointed.

"You told me I needed to work harder to show I was worthy of the position I wanted, and I thought that maybe if I could prove that I could handle the extra workload you would see that I deserved Ailani's class. You know how hard I've been trying. You always knew it," she said with a whimper.

Professor Decker immediately began making comforting shushing noises and I heard muffled sobbing. I pictured the professor holding the distraught Clara in his arms as he pet her hair comfortingly, horrified by what she had done but still more than willing to help her out of it. All at once I felt sick to my stomach thinking about the way this man had brainwashed her into relying so much on him for a sense of self worth. I struggled to stay in my position, still pretending to sleep.

"I'm sorry I said that to you, my dear. I know you work so hard and I didn't mean to hurt you with my careless words. You know you'll always be my favorite," Professor Decker assured. Clara must have pulled back from his embrace because her next statements came out of her mouth clear as day.

"I know that's not true. You may have yourself convinced, but I saw the way you looked at her. We all did. We already figured you were getting tired of us. It hurt us to think about it. It hurt me."

The silence that had settled uncomfortably over the room following Clara's words was fractured by the sound of a loud thump followed by a crinkling sound. It took all of my willpower to keep from flinching at the sudden noise, knowing that if I did then Professor Decker and Clara would realize that I had been faking being asleep.

"Let's just... get out of here. I'm not letting her go right now. I can't," Clara said, sounding defeated. Professor Decker let out another sigh, this one more resigned than disappointed.

"We'll figure it out together. I told you I'd always be there for you and I meant it. I still mean it."

They spoke no more after that. After hearing the door close and lock once again I listened intently to the sounds of their footsteps fading down the hallway. I remained in my semi fetal position for a further few minutes to be sure they wouldn't return. Cautiously I rolled over, feeling the grind of my vertebrae against the rough stones of the floor through the fabrics of the worn out blanket and my quickly deteriorating sweater. With how old and well loved it was I wasn't surprised that the sweater started to come apart, but it still saddened me to accept that.

Next to the old bag, dirty napkin, and rotting apple core was another plastic bag. I slowly made my way over to it and peeking inside I found another apple, two slices of plain bread, and a small plastic water bottle.

I tore into the water bottle first, taking two gulps to lubricate my aching throat. I hadn't realized how dry it had become until that moment. Somehow I managed to stop myself from drinking it all in one go and put the now half empty bottle down at my side. I then ate the two slices of bread in small bites. It was slightly stale, as if it were still in date but the bag hadn't been sealed properly so it had sat in the open air. The apple was soft and mushy again, but I had no room to be picky. Besides, even if I had wanted to complain about the quality of food I was receiving, there was no one around to listen.

Clara and Professor Decker's conversation replayed in my head as I ate. Clara must have come clean about Noemi's attack and her plan to do the same for me; that was the only explanation I could come up with that explained why Decker suddenly became so paranoid when Vincent swore that he hadn't told him about the investigation. It was clear the professor didn't want me to get hurt. At the same time, he was now willing to let Clara do whatever she wanted to me despite his protests and was helping her get away with it. I wondered about the sort of relationship they would have for that level of commitment to be involved.

I recalled the moment at Decker's Halloween dinner where I saw two people holding each other in the kitchen when they hadn't realized I could see them. It very well could have been the professor with one of the students. I then thought about how he had followed Clara upstairs after her outburst and my mind raced with the thoughts of what they could have been up to. I balked at the realization that Professor Decker had fully intended on having that same sort of relationship with me, one that could never see us as equals because of the authority he had over me.

Though I didn't have proof I was sure that the other teaching assistants had the same kind of relationship with him. And all of the students he had taken under his wing in the past - Clara had said this round of teaching assistants were his favorites, but they were far from his first. I put the apple down half unfinished because I couldn't bear to stomach these thoughts.

Lourdes's explanation of Clara's homelife echoed in my mind and I realized why she had latched onto Professor Decker so tightly. I wondered if the others - Lourdes, Ailani, Damian, Vincent, everyone who had come before them - had similar traumas and insecurities that made him target them. I knew I certainly fit his type; with the recent death of my father and my general loss of direction I must have seemed like the perfect candidate for Professor Decker's grooming. I hated myself for falling for it.

I returned to my corner, Pulling my sweater up so that the neckline was covering up my mouth and nose. I laid back down and pretended that the sweater smelled of my mother's perfume. It had always reminded me of the ocean and a warm breeze and I willed myself to focus on that image as a form of escape from this room.

I wished desperately that my friends were on the other side of things trying to get me out of whatever circumstances they imagined had befallen me. Unlike with Noemi, there was no body left behind for them to discover, so I hoped they didn't just assume the worst and think I was already dead. Still, I knew I could not rely on their help and that I had to get myself out of this.

I realized that I would have to find my way out of here sooner rather than later, or else I would be forced to accept whatever Clara had decided my fate would be. I returned to the few options I had come up with earlier, feeling hopeless but determined to not just passively let things happen to me.

Not now that I had learned more of the truth. It wasn't just about me anymore - it was about every one of the professor's victims.

Chapter Fifty-Three

THE NEXT TIME I heard footsteps coming down the hallway, I scrambled into a crouched position with my knees pulled to my chest instead of pretending to be asleep or hiding in the corner like I had done previously. The door opened to reveal a solitary figure, Clara, which is exactly what I had been hoping for.

She entered just a few steps into the room and stared at me with her usual disdain. She was much more cleaned up than she had been the last time I saw her. Clearly she had showered and this angered me more as I felt the grime on my skin and remembered the poor state my hair was currently in.

Before she could do anything, I knew I had to act, so I took a deep breath to steady my thundering heart and sprang up onto my toes to launch myself at her. I barely registered the look of shock that crossed her face as I slammed into her, trying to put as much power behind my slim and weakened frame as I could.

Clara fell backwards into the half open door, the hinges creaking as it was pushed up against the wall. The loud slam echoed through the tiny chamber and hurt my ears. I had hoped I would just be able to knock Clara out of the way so that I could dart out of the room, but as I felt her arms lock around my midsection and her nails dig into the skin of my back I knew I was not so lucky.

We grappled like this for a few moments, neither of us able to gain any leverage on the other. I let up my assault for a second and Clara nearly gained the upper hand, but then I swung my head at her face with as much force as I could muster and felt the sickening crunch of her nose give way beneath my forehead. She let out a savage scream as I felt her blood begin to trickle down my face and I used her momentary distraction to repeat my action.

This time my head hit lower than expected and I felt her front teeth jab sharply into the fragile skin above my right eye. I pushed forward with more force and felt the skin break, but I ignored the pain. Clara howled as her teeth shifted under my effort and I finally pulled back.

Her face was a bloody mess made worse by the visual of her eyes screwed shut and her mouth agape in pain. I saw my opening and wrestled myself out of her weakened grip before grabbing her face and slamming her head into the wood surface of the door behind her. I repeated the assault again, and a third time, and a fourth as her arms flailed wildly in a panic.

After the final hit her eyes fluttered weakly and she dropped to the ground slumped onto her side. I hoped she might have been knocked unconscious but didn't stick around to find out. At the very least she was in enough of a daze that I had my opportunity to run, barely managing to close the door behind me. I wished I could lock it to prevent Clara from being able to run after me, but this had to be enough. I ran as fast as my legs would carry me, paying no mind to where I was going as long as it was away from Clara.

Chapter Fifty-Four

Every glimpse of the stone walls I ran by looked the same as the last. I passed dozens of identical doors, taking turns at random and becoming more convinced by the second that I had somehow been locked in an inescapable maze of stone and wood. The thought of checking the doors occurred to me, but still being in the basement made me decide to just press on until I found a door that was more likely to lead me outside.

My blood coursed through my veins like magma beneath the surface of the earth waiting for its time to burst through and my lungs ached like I hadn't had a breath of fresh air in decades. The bleeding above my eye where Clara's teeth cut me hindered my sight, but I pressed the heel of my hand to the wound as hard as I could to try and keep most of the blood out of my eye. Of course that didn't help my tears from blurring my vision, but it did something.

I pushed my body as far as I thought it could go and then kept going until I came down on my left ankle wrong and crashed down. As I lay there, chest heaving and muscles burning, I was surprised to feel worn but soft carpet against my face rather than the rough stone that had started out under my feet.

The carpet was a dark red that went wall to wall with a simple line of gold stitched in about an inch from the edges. I recognized it as the same design as the carpet used in the upper floors of Castle Blackscar. If I was in the castle, it was not an area that I had been to before. Still, this gave me the hope I needed to push on.

I slowly rose to my feet and limped forward, keeping my right hand pressed above my eye still and my left hand on the wall beside me in order to bear some of the weight that my now swelling ankle couldn't handle. I rounded a corner further up the way and came face to face with a set of stairs that seemed to extend forever onward. I cursed out loud. The word felt strange in my mouth and it dawned on me that that was the first word I had uttered since talking to Professor Decker at the Winter Festival.

Deciding that my arms had more strength than my legs did, I sat on one of the lowest steps. I then used my arms to prop my body up and hop it onto the next one. I did this again and again until the only thought on my mind was making it up just one more stair. I did not dare think about the journey beyond that, knowing if I did I would lose all hope of escape and give up. It was better to take things inch by inch, stair by stair, even though this felt like the longest staircase in existence.

Arriving at the top, my arms aching with overuse, I pulled myself to my feet and came face to face with two paintings that I recognized framing the stairs. Kame hime on the left and osakabe hime on the right, two figures from Japanese mythology that I had spent a whole day researching after the first time I saw the paintings.

Seeing the two portraits was like a jolt to my foggy brain; I knew exactly where I was. This was the wing where some professors had their offices. I would have to pass by several to make my way out, Professor Rhodes and Professor Decker's included.

I contemplated heading back down the stairs to find another way out, but after peering down into the darkness I decided that taking the way I knew was the better of the two options. I told myself that I wouldn't run into anyone as I walked, seeing as it was the middle of the night, but even so I crouched slightly and took slow, careful steps to keep quiet and aware. The floor still creaked and groaned under my weight, but with the carpet there the sound was muffled enough that the only way someone would hear it would be if they were a few feet away from me, at which point they would already have seen me so the creeping around would have been pointless.

I slowed to the slightest of crawls as I neared the corner that would take me into the hallway that housed Professor Decker's office. Peeking around the corner, I let out a quiet sigh as I saw that his door was closed. Before I could bring my body around the corner there was a sudden pressure on the back of my head not unlike when Clara yanked my hair. I was pulled backwards and engulfed completely by someone much larger than myself.

Smelling his woodsy scented cologne before I saw his salt and pepper colored beard as my face came close to his own, I fought as hard as I could against Professor Decker. Things would not end well if I let him get the better of me. Unfortunately in my weakened state I was no match for his strength and I was dragged down the hall toward his office. Even though I didn't expect anyone to be around to help me I tried shouting, but my voice came out as a rough croak from my dry throat. It burned terribly, but I kept trying until Professor Decker grabbed the lower half of my face and gripped my jaw painfully tight in his dry, calloused hand.

As it turned out, his office door was not closed, but open just enough that he was able to push the two of us through without having to struggle with the doorknob. Once in the room, he quickly shoved me away and I went flying, landing in a heap of books in the corner. I felt their hard corners jabbing into my ribs and chest, but I was too sore and tired to move off of them. Instead I laid there, breaths heaving, watching Professor Decker as he closed the door behind him, made a show of locking it, and turned to face me with an emotion on his face that I couldn't quite read.

He took one menacing step towards me and then another and another until he became a looming figure stretched out above me, my perspective making him seem ten feet tall. He leaned close to me and as I felt his breath tickling my cheek I flinched, fearing that he would try and take advantage of me while I was in this vulnerable state. Any screams I had left in me died in my aching throat as he began to talk.

"You really thought you could get away from all of this, didn't you? I did my best to advocate for you despite Clara's thoughts and feelings and then you went ahead and attacked her. Seeing what you did to her... now I'm not so sure you deserve to be let loose, though I still don't think you should die." His voice was quiet but there was a venom to it that made my heart race in fear.

Clara wasn't here in the office and I wondered what he had done with her once he found her bloody and disoriented where I left her. Defiantly, I managed to push myself into an almost sitting position and was surprised when Professor Decker leaned back to give me the space to do so.

"She... she attacked me first," I croaked out. "And Noemi." Compared to the sure confidence that Professor Decker's words exuded, my own seemed weak and full of doubt. He narrowed his eyes in anger.

"Clara only did what she thought she had to do. She saw you as a threat to her relationship with me and so she came up with a plan to eliminate you. Aside from the obvious misunderstanding that you were a threat in the first place, and her mistaking Noemi for you, I see no faults on her side of things."

"You're sick," I managed to mutter. To this he let out a short, humorless laugh.

"You know nothing about me, Georgie. You could have, if things had turned out differently, though I feel now that you might not have gone along with my plan even if Clara hadn't done what she did. I would have given you everything if you let me."

"You mean your plan to groom and coerce me into doing whatever you wanted, just like you did to Clara and the other teaching assistants?" I spat.

"Grooming? Coercion? You have it all wrong. I merely saw children in need of guidance and authority and gave them what they needed. All I asked in return was that they love me and listen to me, which they all do unconditionally." He flashed his devilish grin in my direction, clearly proud of the empire of abuse he'd built. At this point he walked over to stare out of the window a moment.

"They didn't need you." I had thought my assertion would

get under his skin, but he acted as if he hadn't even heard me say anything.

Decker didn't turn to face me as he spoke, listing off everyone's traumas as if they were puzzles to be solved. "Clara's parents have always been hard on her and held her to such high standards due to her sister's success, so I have been gentle, encouraging, and loving.

"Damian had to deal with the divorce and new marriages of his parents at such a young age and never quite got over feeling replaced when his half siblings were born, so I have been trying to show him that he doesn't have to shout to have his voice heard. He's still a work in progress.

"Lourdes fell to the background as a child, not completely removed from her family but certainly ostracized to a certain extent due to the nature of her gender and sexuality. For her I have been nothing but accepting of who she is so that she could learn confidence. Of course Clara being so outspoken certainly makes that difficult, but we have been making headway.

"Vincent has issues forming attachments which I assume has to do with being in the foster care system for so long before finally being adopted, so the going has been slow with him but he certainly sees me as a caring figure who will never leave him.

"And Ailani is certainly the most well adjusted and independent of the group, but like Clara she is under immense pressure to succeed and she puts herself under so much unnecessary stress that she needs someone like me to tell her to take a break every once in a while."

With his hands clasped behind his back he turned to face me again, looking as composed as ever. His face showed how he pitied me, not in a 'let me help you' sort of way, but like he was saying it was a shame what I had been through and a shame of what I'd have to go through next.

"You see, Georgie? You would have been perfect - I could have made you perfect. I knew from the first time I saw you peeking in at me through that door right there that you were a lost soul. You fell under my guidance so quickly, dropping that math class and joining my stage combat course after just talking with me once. Then I learned about the deaths of your parents and after what happened with Noemi, well, I should have had you then but I wasn't careful. You were like clay for me to mold however I wanted you to be. You would have—"

"No," I said, causing Professor Decker to stop speaking mid sentence. He looked almost amused by my defiance, as if I were a child telling their parent what to do.

"No? You don't agree?" he questioned.

I struggled for a minute to shift onto my feet before rising unsteadily to a standing position. Leaning on the bookshelf for support I took one wobbly step closer to him. I was sure that it was pure spite and rage keeping me upright rather than any strength or energy I had left in my body.

"No. I may have been lonely and a little lost, but that does not mean you could have or should have taken advantage of that just to stroke your own gross ego."

I took another step, a sharp pain shooting through my left ankle as I put weight on it. I winced and then did my best to ignore it.

"Clara deserved a better mentor, one that helped her through her issues without damaging her so severely that she'd resort to kidnapping and attempted murder."

Another step.

"You ruined her, and all of your other teaching assistants, and who knows how many other children throughout the years."

Another step. At this point I was coming close enough that Professor Decker's smug look turned startled.

"And to think, River was actually jealous of me for getting to work with you," I finished with a dry chuckle.

Before Professor Decker could respond, I pushed myself off of the bookshelf and flung myself at him, hoping the momentum behind my weight would make up for the fact that I barely had any strength left in me. He managed to get his hands out to catch me and we struggled for a few minutes, thrashing about the space behind his desk. As the new wave of adrenaline surged through me I felt all of my aches and pains begin to subside and I was able to focus on just the man in front of me.

Decker slipped on a sheet of paper we had knocked onto the floor in our struggle and I took advantage of his being off balance by pushing him as hard as I could. I had meant to knock him against the wall, but we were further over than I had realized and instead he slammed into the large glass window, shattering it. I instantly let go of him and backed up the second I felt his weight shift away from me.

His hands clutched desperately at my clothing but my all but destroyed sweater ripped as it took the full weight of his body and I was able to maintain my footing. I could only think of my mother protecting me one last time.

We locked eyes, a look of shock and horror on his face that I'm sure resembled my own - eyes bulging and mouth open wide. A moment later he was gone from view and a silence settled in the air for just a second before it was broken by a distant thud. Cautiously, I peered out of the now open space where the window had been, but it was too dark and the ground was too far away for me to see anything. It was like the whole world, Professor Decker included, had been swallowed by an abyss and I had been left all alone.

Chapter Fifty-Five

IF NOT FOR THE sturdy walls of Castle Blackscar I would have fallen many times on my way out of its stony interior. As it was, I already had to stop every few dozen feet to catch my breath and give my pained legs a rest; falling would have just made the journey that much harder. The nearest exit was near the interior entrance to the library and as I limped my way through the wide corridor I was surprised to run into people leaving the library this late at night - none other than Ailani, Lourdes, Damian, and Vincent.

They stopped short, sentences ending mid thought, as they took in my disheveled appearance. I wanted to shrink back against the wall but instead I stood tall, or as tall as I could, daring any of them to try something. I didn't think that they had anything to do with Clara's plan, but they were still part of Professor Decker's special group and I didn't know if they were capable of the sort of nefarious deeds Clara had been up to. Lourdes was the first to speak.

"Georgie, what happened? Are you okay?" She let go of Ailani's hand and stepped over to me, reaching out for my face. I flinched, instinct telling me that she was going to hit me, but she just used the sleeve of her sweater to wipe some of the grime off of my cheek. "When you didn't show up to the *Pygmalion* performance earlier we were all so worried! Adrian told us that you had gone to him earlier in the day not feeling well, so you were resting at his place. Akasha had to take your place as Eliza."

"I, um, wasn't sick. I got into a fight. Well, two fights," I said tentatively, swallowing hard. I eyed the group cautiously as Ailani walked over to help Lourdes clean me up. She pulled a couple of wet wipes out of her bag and I let the two of them gently wipe my face and hands. The other two just stared at me in confusion.

"They must have been some bad fights," Vincent said. "Who were you fighting with, the Hulk?" I pulled away from the girls, unsure of how I wanted to go about answering that question. Then I took a deep breath and replied.

"Clara, actually. And... Professor Decker." Looking at each of the four of them in turn, they all had these looks on their faces that were varying degrees of shock and horror and concern; I knew that none of them could have been in on Clara's plan and so I recounted the entire story from talking to Professor Decker towards the end of the Winter Festival on Friday all the way to the present moment.

"No," Damian said, his voice gentler than I ever expected to hear it. I stepped back instinctually, but he didn't move. "He wouldn't want to hurt anybody. He loves us."

"Damian, you knew this moment was coming," Ailani said, speaking quietly as she turned to face him. "He knew exactly what to say to get each of us wrapped around his finger, and we were just too blinded to see the manipulation."

"That's why the three of you have been distancing yourselves from him, isn't it? He asked about that sometimes, wondering if he'd done something wrong to upset you, but I assured him everything was fine," Damian said. The hurt in his voice reminded me of the whimpers of a wounded animal.

"I realized over the summer that what he was doing was wrong. He wasn't helping us because he loved us, he just wanted to control us. I convinced Lourdes and Vincent to see the truth, but we thought…"

"You thought Clara and I were too stupid to realize?" At this point Damian looked about ready to cry, a look I'd never expected to see on his face.

"Too absorbed in his manipulations, and too stubborn to think that you could have been wrong about him all this time.

That everyone's been wrong about who he is. We wanted you two to come to the realization gently and in your own time," Ailani assured him.

"Is that why you wanted to steer me away from accepting the teaching assistant position?" I asked, interrupting the tender moment. "I know you didn't say anything outright, but I could tell that you didn't really want me to join your group." Ailani nodded. "I should have taken the hint."

"So, we should call the police now, right?" Lourdes suggested. Vincent took the task upon himself and also sent River a text so that my friends would know that I was safe.

"I think I need some fresh air, I'm going to go for a walk," Damian said. Before he could get very far Ailani grabbed his arm, saying that while we could go outside, all of us were staying together until the police and paramedics arrived.

Once outside we found a bench to sit on and Lourdes continued to chatter kind and reassuring words to me. I suspected it was just as much for her benefit as it was for mine; knowing what type of relationship they had all had with Professor Decker made me realize it couldn't have been easy for them to hear what he had let happen to me. I understood if they didn't want to fully face that just yet. Ailani stayed near Damian, probably afraid that he might bolt at any minute. Vincent came out moments later, and the only sounds to be heard were Lourdes's reassuring words and the rustle of wind through the dry tree branches. The first snow of the season coated the ground, painting a picture that was still and serene.

River, Ahra, and Ollie arrived in mere minutes, none of them looking like they had slept recently. Ahra explained that when I never came back from throwing out my trash, Professor Decker told them I wasn't feeling well and had gone back to Radcliffe House. They hadn't realized he was lying until the morning after because they had gotten back late and gone right to bed. River apologized profusely, saying that if they hadn't been drinking they'd have realized something was wrong much sooner. While Ahra and Ollie tried to figure out what had happened, River had gone ahead with the *Pygmalion* production in order to snoop around Decker and the teaching assistants.

I shivered in the cool night air, clutching the front of my ripped sweater and trying to pull it tighter around me. Before anyone else could react, Damian shrugged off his coat and held it out in my direction. I hesitated and looked up at his face, but when he gave me a soft nod I accepted his offering with a quiet 'thank you' and enveloped myself in the warm material that was much too large for my body.

My friends surrounded me, all seven of them counted because I knew even Damian was in this with us now, and I let myself relax in their presence. Lourdes continued to mother me, checking me over for any major wounds and doing her best to clean me off. Ahra had thought to bring me a water bottle and a container full of leftover pasta, which I wolfed down as soon as it was placed in my hands. Vincent and River conversed in hushed voices too quiet for me to hear but stayed near enough that I could call out to them if needed. Ollie stood in the doorway of the castle so he could direct the police and paramedics to me when they came from off campus. Damian stood watch over us all, observing like a silent guardian. For the first time in days, I felt safe.

Chapter Fifty-Six

THE POLICE AND PARAMEDICS and even the one and only James Hansen arrived just as the first golden rays of the rising sun began to shatter the indigo night. I couldn't help but let out a short laugh as I realized I had lived through something that the conservatory deemed bad enough to let the police on campus.

One woman with a medical bag slung over her shoulder and a name tag pinned to her shirt that read 'Cindy' tried to pull me away from my friends to do a preliminary check on me, but Lourdes and Ahra insisted that they stay by my side the entire time. River and Vincent were the first to talk to both the police and Mr. Hansen to give them background knowledge on the situation before they spoke to me.

Cindy was artificially cheerful, presumably a side effect of the job she had. She smiled widely and assured me that everything was going to be fine. I was too tired to protest the fact that I was being treated like a child by yet another person. Her assessment of my heart rate, blood pressure, and other basic health statistics proved to be fine, but when she began examining my head the troubles began. At first she began prodding lightly on different areas of my face, which felt uncomfortable but not outright painful until she got to my nose.

I shouted out in surprise, startling everyone into looking at me. I looked down at my lap, sheepish from the sudden attention, which seemed absurd given what I had just gone through.

"Yeah, that is definitely broken. I'm going to have to set it for you when I bring you to the ambulance. The last thing on my list is to check for a concussion. Can you stand up for me and walk a few feet and back?" As I did just that the paramedic asked me a few more questions. "Are you experiencing any dizziness, headache, mental fog, or problems with vision?"

"A headache yes, maybe a little dizziness, no mental fog, my vision seems fine but maybe a little sensitive? I've been in the dark for so long that the sunlight seems really bright." My throat was still sore from disuse and then overuse and saying so many words in a row hurt, but I pushed through. As I said this I turned to walk back towards Cindy and slipped a little bit. I don't think I would have fallen, but River still rushed to my side to make sure I stayed upright. It vaguely registered that they had to drop Vincent's hand in order to do so, but before I could think about the implications of that Cindy called out for my attention again.

"Okay, so you'll definitely have to get tested for a concussion. I think you're going to have to spend the day at the hospital, maybe even overnight as well just to get a full evaluation. The police can just get your statement from you there, alright?" I nodded and let River lead me back to the bench.

A second police officer came outside and whispered briefly with the one that had already been outside with us. He then left again and the one that remained cleared his throat before speaking up.

"I would just like to let you all know that Clara Williams has been found. She has been arrested and is currently on the way to the hospital to deal with the injuries she has sustained from this whole ordeal," he started.

For some reason I felt guilty about hurting her. She had attacked my friend thinking it was me, threatened my life, verbally accosted me on several occasions, drugged me, and kept me imprisoned in the basement of the castle with plans to do who knew what else to me, and yet I knew she was a victim too. That idea certainly didn't excuse her behavior, but I couldn't help feeling sorry for all of the things that she had gone through that led to her making the choices she did.

The police officer continued talking, saying, "Adrian Decker has not yet been located but our force is working tirelessly to track him down. I would advise you all to remain on alert until he is found. We will have officers escort those of you not coming to the hospital back to your housing just to be on the safe side."

My heart beat harder in my chest upon hearing those words and I clutched onto River's arm. They murmured in my ear that everything was going to be okay as they gently lowered me back onto the bench. This time I was on the end as Ailani had slid over to sit next to Lourdes.

"I can ride in the ambulance with you if you'd like, Georgie. I know you probably don't want to be alone right now," Ahra offered, taking a step towards me.

"I'll be right there too. I can drive anyone else who wants to come down to the hospital," Ollie added. Several of my friends echoed their agreement that they would be there for me, but I was already shaking my head.

"It's okay guys, I can handle being on my own for a little while. It's been a long weekend for you too, and I want you all to get some rest now that you know I'm safe. You can all come visit me later on," I responded, much to everyone's shock.

"Are you sure?" Ahra asked, and I nodded.

"I'm sure. Can you just give my brother a call to let him know what happened and that I'm safe? His name is Eli, and his contact information is in the front section of my planner. You'll probably have to get someone to let you in my room, though. I don't know what Clara did with my bag."

"I can take care of that," Mr. Hansen said, stepping away as he pulled his phone out of his pocket, presumably to update some of his higher ups on everything.

Ahra and I watched him go for a moment. "Okay, just make sure you let us know if you need anything else."

"I will." I slowly stood up, making sure to steady myself with a hand on the back of the bench. I moved to pull off Damian's coat, wincing as the muscles in my shoulders strained, but he shook his head and told me he'd get it back later. Ahra, Ollie, and River each gave me a quick hug before letting Cindy wrap her arm around me to support my weight as we walked back to the castle entrance.

I stopped in the doorway to turn and face my friends. I looked at each one in turn - Vincent and River now holding hands again, Ahra and Ollie standing near them, Ailani and Lourdes on the bench, and Damian standing solitary and stoic as ever, though the expression on his face looked softer than I had ever seen it before. It almost could have been a smile, albeit a sad one. I turned and left them behind as I was willingly enveloped once more by the great stone enormity of Castle Blackscar, knowing I'd come out on the other side just as sure as the sun rose above us after the long night.

Acknowledgments

THERE ARE SO MANY people I have to thank because without them, this book would not have been possible.

The first is Marta, who has read every draft since the start. The feedback and support she gave me each step of the way has been invaluable. Of course the other Chaos Queens, Crystal and Violet, are due thanks as well for their feedback and for listening to me ramble on about my story at all hours of the day.

Thank you to Anne for showing me the ins and outs of all of the things that go into publishing other than writing the actual book. I genuinely couldn't have put this book out without her help.

I'd also like to thank all of my other amazing writer friends that I've made in the past few years, of whom there are too many to name unless I want this acknowledgements section to go on for ten pages. I love exchanging snippets of writing and story ideas with each and every one of you. Your excitement for my projects only encourages me to work harder on them.

Thanks are also in order for my Ko-fi members, whose support gives me a little extra wiggle room in my day to work on my books.

Finally I'd like to thank everyone I knew at Arcadia University and really the campus itself for inspiring me to write this dark academia tale. They say to write what you know, and after spending four years on campus with amazing professors, wonderful classmates, and a literal castle, I'd say I know that setting pretty well. Without that experience, this story wouldn't have been able to come to life the way it has.

About the Author

MG ELLISON IS A writer from the American Mid-Atlantic who studied creative writing at Arcadia University. They run the YouTube channel somberhoney books, where they post content about reading, writing, and other shenanigans. When they're not devouring books 100 pages at a time or working on their countless story ideas, they're usually playing D&D, watching anime, or snuggling their cats, Gremlin and Chloe. *Revelry in the Dark* is their first novel.

youtube.com/@somberhoney
instagram.com/mgellison.shb
ko-fi.com/somberhoney

Printed in Great Britain
by Amazon